Three for the

ALSO BY D.B. BORTON

THE CAT CALIBAN MYSTERIES
Book 1: One Deadly Take
Book 2: Two Points for Murder
Book 3: Three for the Kill

THE CAT CALIBAN MYSTERIES

Three For The Kill

D.B. BORTON

JOFFE BOOKS

Revised edition 2025
Joffe Books, London
www.joffebooks.com

First published in the USA in 1994 as
Three is a Crowd and as *Three-Ring Circus* in 2020

This paperback edition was first published
in Great Britain in 2025

Cover art by Dee Dee Book Covers

ISBN: 978-1-83526-961-9

A NOTE TO THE READER

Please note these books are from the 1990s, a time before DNA testing and CCTV, when social attitudes were very different.

To my partners in crime—
Andrea, John, and Lynn—
antiwar at Antioch, 1967-72, and beyond

CHAPTER 1

The outside light was off. I fumbled for my keys and found the keyhole with my fingertips. The key turned easily. The door was unlocked. I pushed the door open and crossed into the deeper blackness of the hallway. I felt a breath of air on the back of my neck as the door swung shut behind me. I smelled bourbon, cigarette smoke, and sweat.

A hand clamped over my mouth and a body pressed against mine. A voice rasped in my ear.

I leaned forward, raising one foot, and brought it down hard on his instep. I spun around, swinging my purse, and clobbered him with it. I heard a gratifying howl.

It was over in an instant. So fast, in fact, that I hadn't had time to register what the voice had said.

"Don't say nothin', Cat. It's me."

Now there was another voice speaking.

"Aw, man, what you want to pull this shit for? I *told* you not to pull this shit on Cat. Who you think you are, man, the Boston strangler? You scarin' Cat. Plus, she a trained *detective*, man. You can't go jumping out at her and expect not to get your ass beat."

Actually, I was a detective in training, which wasn't quite the same thing. But if my adversaries wanted to think I was the Bruce Lee of geriatric gumshoes, it was okay by me.

The lights flashed on. I blinked.

"Here, lemme see where you hit."

A middle-aged, medium-height, gray-haired Black man was bending over a white man whose face I couldn't see but who was wearing a camouflage jacket. It was Curtis, unofficial leader among the street people of my acquaintance, and one of his pals, a Vietnam vet named Steel. If they had other names, I had never heard them.

I should have been pissed. To tell you the truth, though, I kind of appreciated the opportunity to practice my self-defense skills. And if somebody's going to break into your apartment building and sneak up on you in the dark, you'd like it to be a friend. I couldn't wait to tell Mel that her training had paid off. Who says your reflexes slow down when you get older?

"Aw, man, whadja hit me with, Cat? I feel like I've been hit in the head with a fuckin' grenade, man."

"Oh, lighten up," I said. "It was just a purse." I held up a bag the size of Mount Rushmore. For two hellish years during my career as a mother, I'd been suckered into service as a goddamn Girl Scout troop leader, and now I was being rewarded for having to cross-stitch that stupid motto on a mangled doily: "Be prepared."

"This was his idea, Cat," Curtis assured me. "I didn't have nothin' to do with this part of it. You got some ice?"

I nodded, unlocked the door to my apartment, and headed for the kitchen. Three cats came racing down the stairs to follow me in.

"What are you, on break or something?" I said to Sidney, my little black watchcat. "You couldn't tell me they were there?" He purred loudly and circled my ankles, pleased with all the commotion. He knew the difference between friends and enemies, even if they both tended to break in and act weird afterward. In my first case, he had captured a burglar, but that poor sucker had probably made the mistake of failing to scratch Sidney behind the ears.

I wrapped some ice cubes in a towel, dropped some crunchies in the cats' bowls, and went back to the living room. "What've you got in that bag, Cat? A block of concrete?" Steel took the ice from me and stretched out on the couch.

"Law books," I said. "I've been reading law over at the UC library, and Al lets me check stuff out on her card."

I figured the law books prepared my mind for detective work, and toting them around prepared my body. Already I could feel a twinge in my shoulder and a throb in my ankle. If I'd thought about it, I wouldn't have used the foot attached to the ankle I'd sprained in February. My reflexes were young, but my joints and muscles were fading fast.

"Listen, man," Steel was mumbling to Curtis, "if I don't make it — like, if I get a brain hemorrhage or something — you can have my medals. Sell 'em to that guy on 10th. Don't go to that bastard on Vine, man, he'll rip you off."

"Say, you guys sure do know how to make yourselves welcome," I observed. I wasn't worried about Steel. Anybody who could survive winter on the streets of Cincinnati wasn't going to kick the bucket over a little thing like a cracked skull. "How'd you get in?"

"Credit card." Steel wasn't too far gone to miss an opportunity to impress me.

I stared at him. "Where the hell did *you* get a credit card?"

Curtis intervened. "Now, Cat, don't ask; you don't want to know. It wasn't yours, I promise."

"What the hell were you doing here in the dark, anyway?"

"It was his idea, Cat," Curtis reiterated. "'Bout turnin' out them lights. I told him to come see you, but I didn't never say nothin' 'bout turnin' out no lights and sneakin' up on folks in the dark."

"Yeah, well, you ain't no fugitive from justice, neither, are you? If the cops was after *you*, you'd be turning out lights, all right." Steel tried to rise up to emphasize his point, but a look of pain crossed his face and he collapsed again. "Fuckin' pigs."

"Now, Steel, don't you start. Fair is fair. Maybe you disremember them shoes and glasses you got from the FOP back in December, but I don't."

"I didn't *need* no glasses! I can see clear as anything!"

"Pardon me," I said, "but I'd like to go back to the part where you are a fugitive from justice."

"Now he don't know that, Cat. It's just this thing he got in his head."

"I *know*, man, 'cause I know how them pigs think. They got a stiff with his throat cut in a parking lot, they going to round up every goddamn Nam vet they can find on the street. That way, they don't have to do no thinkin' or work too hard."

"Could we maybe start from the beginning?" I asked. "What stiff? What parking lot?"

"Fountain Square," Curtis said, designating himself the spokesperson. "See, me and Steel was over there today, workin' the rally."

"What rally?"

"It's some big antiwar rally. Ain't you heard nothin' about it?"

Like most people, I had assumed we weren't at war with anybody in 1985, but my daughter, the professional protester, had disabused me of that notion by explaining how the CIA was supporting the right-wing contras against the socialist government in Nicaragua. Happily for both of us, she was living in another state, so my war bulletins were few and far between.

"It was a rally protesting the government support for the fucking contras in Nicaragua," Steel said. "Goddamn government wants to send millions to some goddamn CIA-trained, anti-commie commandos in Central America someplace, and all we get's secondhand shoes and glasses we don't need."

"Yeah, okay, so they was holding this rally. And me and Steel went over there, 'cause them young white liberal types is the best they is if you lookin' for handouts. Okay, so we split up and work the crowd. They was makin' speeches and chantin' and singin', like they do, you know."

"How many people?"

"Oh, I don't know, Cat. Pretty good turnout, I'd say — the biggest this year, maybe in a couple years. The square was full, and it was pretty tight-packed. And then finally, you know, by and by, they sang 'We Shall Overcome,' like they do when they windin' up. And that's when you really get hoppin', 'cause when folks is leavin', they ain't lookin' at the podium no more, you got a chance to get they attention.

"So, 'bout this time, I done work my way over to the garage entrance on the Vine Street side and I hear this commotion down the steps. Seem like it wasn't even a minute 'fore I hear sirens. I seen a cop on the steps turnin' folks back, and everybody was crowdin' around, talkin' and tryin' to figure out what was goin' on. And the cop cars pull up on Vine, and about that time the rumor starts goin' 'round that it's been a man killed in the parking lot. And somebody asked did he get run over, but somebody else say they don't think so.

"And then I feel somebody grab my arm, and it's Steel, tryin' to hustle me away. I want to know what's goin' on, I say. And he say, I'll tell you what's goin' on, they got a stiff with his throat cut and if they get holt of me, them bastards will send me to the chair, sure. Well, I figure he overreactin', way he do, but I let him drag me off. He got this idea in his head that the cops is goin' to go lookin' for a vet, and I can't talk him out of it, and he won't go nowhere or see nobody. So I told him to come tell you about it, so you can find the murderer and get the right person arrested, and he can stop actin' crazy and I can get on with my business."

"You know what your problem is, man?" Steel interrupted. "For a Black dude, you ain't got no imagination. If it was a white woman, and she'd been raped, cops'd be lookin' for you, man. Well, I *seen* this stiff — throat cut ear to ear just like they taught us in basic. And I'm tellin' you this whole fuckin' town's gonna be out lookin' for some 'crazed Vietnam vet,' like they gonna say in the papers. And I'm gonna be their number one suspect, 'cause my ass was near the scene of the crime."

"Yeah, that's the part I want to hear about," I put in. I didn't want to tell Steel that I basically agreed with his analysis. He wasn't exactly crazed, in my view, but he wasn't laid back, either, and you wouldn't exactly invite him for Sunday dinner and introduce him to your minister. So if he was anywhere near the scene of the crime, as he claimed, he could be headed for a rendezvous with the boys and girls in blue.

"Okay, it's like Curtis said. We were working the rally, see? Curtis on one side, me on the other. But after a while the speeches were goin' on and nobody was paying me much attention except the kids, and I had to take a leak, see? So I head down the steps toward the garage, to that men's room on the landing. I figure I got plenty of time, but then I hear singing, see? And I think, shit, they're breakin' up, so I hurry, but when I open the door again, I realize it's not that civil rights song, but something else, which means I'm okay on time. But before I start up the steps I hear somebody yell from down below, where the garage is. I don't know what he said, but I ran down there and there's some people kind of gathered in a corner, not too far off, and they're all lookin' at something on the ground. And when I got closer I seen what they's lookin' at was this dead man with his throat cut.

"Well, it shook me up some, but not much, 'cause I seen that kind of thing before, in Nam. But it didn't take me long to figure out that I better get my ass out of there, and I split. I found Curtis, and since then, I've been layin' low. Soon's somebody mentions they seen a guy in a camouflage jacket hangin' around, my ass is grass."

I didn't know what that meant, but I got the general idea, and, like I said, I agreed with him.

"Did you recognize this guy?"

"What guy?" A flicker. Too defensive. Was he buying time?

"The dead man."

"Shit, no, why would I recognize him?"

"I don't know. Did you see him earlier at the rally?"

"No, man, the place was packed, like Curtis said. I mean, maybe I saw him, but I didn't notice him."

"You didn't speak to him?"

"No."

"Are you sure?"

"Well, I'da noticed him if I spoke to him, right?"

I sighed and checked my watch: seven o'clock. I never knew what time the news came on on Sundays, but I flicked on the TV and started channel hopping. I landed on Norma Rashid and cranked up the sound.

The top story was still the Ohio Savings and Loan crisis. Cincinnati-based Home State Savings had gone belly up a little over a week before, and many S&Ls were shutting their doors to avert a run on their assets. The story gave me an idea, but I figured if the murdered man had been Home State CEO Marvin Warner, we would already have heard. Maybe he looked like Marvin Warner. You didn't need to go walking the streets to find bitter, angry, desperate people in Cincinnati right now.

Now Norma was talking about the murder, calling the guy an "unidentified murder victim," and they flashed his picture on the screen, from the chin up. Norma said that robbery was a possible motive, but police were still investigating and anyone who could give any information about the crime might receive a cash reward of up to $1000 from Crimestoppers.

"There you go, Steel." Curtis nudged him. "Turn yourself in, they give you a G."

Norma went on to talk about the rally, which meant that the rally had been as big as I'd heard and that today had been a slow news day. They even interviewed one of the organizers on camera. As they scanned the crowd, Curtis's face suddenly popped up in front.

"Damn!" he said, all smiles. "They used my picture!"

I was scanning the crowd for anybody who looked like the dead man, but I didn't see him. Of course, the dead man in the picture probably didn't look much like he had before he got croaked.

Norma moved on to cover a tap dancing contest for three-year-olds out at Florence Mall and I turned off the set.

"So far, so good," I said. "Maybe you don't have anything to worry about. After all—" And here I gave Steel one of the piercing looks I used to give the kids when they told me they didn't feel well enough to go to school. "—If you don't even know who he is—"

CHAPTER 2

The door swung open.

"Surprise!"

It was my youngest, Franny, surrounded by a suspiciously large number of bags, one suitcase, and one guitar case.

Damn, I was going to have to stop opening doors. Every time I opened one, something bad happened. Just once I wanted to open a door and find that guy with a dozen roses, the prize patrol van, and the check as big as a billboard.

Before I continue, let me say that I love my children, and Franny happens to be my favorite. She is also the one who shows the least interest in growing up, or in deciding what she wants to be when she does, despite her thirty years of working at it. Mostly, she attends college — Penn State for pre-med, Syracuse for social work, Stanford for psychology, Washington State for women's studies, Berkeley for biology. I probably got them all mixed up, but you get the general idea. The majors weren't all that important anyway, as far as I could tell, since she seemed to spend more time out of class than in — abortion rights at Albion, homeless rights at Hobart, porpoise rights at Pepperdine, refugee rights at Rider. When she was in transition, as she so frequently was, she came home.

On a scale of surprises, Franny's reappearance ranked right up there with Reagan's re-election. The biggest surprise she'd ever handed me was the news that I was pregnant.

Nevertheless, part of me was always glad to see her, so I gave her a big hug, while the retired mother part of me peeked over her shoulder and eyed her equipage with alarm.

The strains of "Teach Your Children" drifted down the stairs from Al and Mel's apartment. They'd been on a Crosby, Stills, and Nash kick lately, and I figured any day now the whole Catatonia Arms was going to break out the bell-bottoms and tie-dyes. Franny's appearance would only accelerate the event, since her sartorial style favored the late 60s.

"We wanted to make it for the rally last Sunday," Franny was explaining, "but we had car trouble in Albuquerque, so we stayed at this, like, religious commune that gives asylum to Central American refugees. Garf was really bummed to miss the rally, but anyway, we're here now, and I'm sure there'll be lots we can do. I can't believe you're really living in Northside, Mom. That's so cool!"

"'We'?" Garf?

"Oh, me and Garf. Jon Garfield is his name, but everybody calls him Garf. Oh, don't worry, Mom. He's not staying here. He has a friend at UC, so he'll stay in Clifton. I told him you didn't have much room in your new place." She looked around with obvious curiosity.

"That's right, Fran. This place is pretty small. I'll probably have to give you and your guitar separate rooms." Not to mention your luggage, I added silently.

"Oh, that's okay, Mom. I don't mind cramped quarters." She beamed at me. Franny loved a challenge, especially the kind that gave her a chance to share the experiences of the oppressed. If Cambodian refugees could live five to a room, we could live two to an apartment. Unfortunately, I thought the Cambodians were better prepared for the situation in the way they trained children to respect their elders. After two weeks with Franny, I was willing to bet that if I so much as adjusted the volume on her boombox, she'd be demanding that the INS send me back to where I came from.

I predicted a short visit that would seem like a winter at Valley Forge.

"Mrs. C, I hate to be the one to complain — you know I'm not that kind of tenant—" Kevin was sticking his inquisitive nose in the open door, which was the kind of tenant he was. He was apparently oblivious to Sidney, who was clawing his way up the back of Kevin's leg, little feline acrobat that he was. "But did you know that someone has dumped a bunch of bags in the hallway? Oh—" He smiled at Franny, giving her the full benefit of his Irish charm and good looks. "I didn't know you had company." And I didn't know who the next Republican nominee was going to be.

"My daughter Franny. Kevin O'Neill."

Sidney gained a shoulder and wobbled there.

Kevin sparkled. "Oh, so this is Franny. We've heard so much about you. It's a real pleasure."

Maybe I should clarify here that Kevin's expansiveness was familial, not sexual. His only designs on my daughter involved satisfying his insatiable curiosity about my life up to the point when we met. He'd always had trouble imagining me as a suburban housewife and mother. To tell you the truth, I have trouble imagining it myself.

I had found Kevin in residence when I bought what was once the Patagonia Arms, and he had soon become an enthusiastic devotee of my plan to launch Caliban Investigations, a private inquiry agency. I would launch it, that is, as soon as I could persuade the powers that be to consider thirty-nine years of motherhood the equivalent of two years of experience in detection for licensing purposes. Apparently, none of the powers that be was a mother. Kevin, despite his lack of experience in either detective work or motherhood, had turned out to be a natural detective, and his pointed inquiries had driven away several prospective tenants before he had condescended to welcome two women whose credentials he found potentially useful to my new enterprise: Alice Rosenberg, an attorney with Legal Aid, and Melanie Carter, an artist with considerable expertise in the martial arts. I always assumed it was the martial arts experience that had recommended Mel to Kevin, though he is a staunch supporter of the other arts as well. When a retired police officer named Moses Fogg had shown up to look at the one remaining apartment, Kevin had plied him with banana bread and witty repartee. Kevin would make a good talent scout — or gossip columnist.

Now, however, he was sitting on my sofa, chatting up my daughter Franny like a long-lost brother I'd given up for adoption. He'd get Franny's life story out of her before the night was out, but if he hoped to get my life story out of her, he was whistling Dixie. Most kids don't know much about their parents' lives, as you may have noticed; they are too absorbed with their own. Kevin's listening skills had been honed on a well-established career as a bartender, so he was extraordinarily attentive for someone his age.

Now he was volunteering to make dinner.

I never turn him down when he makes this offer. If Pierre Franey showed up on your doorstep with a well-seasoned skillet in hand, would you thank him politely and explain that you'd just as soon run down to the Big Boy?

There was a knock at the door and Al stuck her head in.

"Say, Cat, need anything from the food co-op? We're just getting ready to order." Her eyes slid to the sofa.

"My daughter Franny. Alice Rosenberg."

"Franny!" Al cried, a picture of delight. "Great! We've heard so much about you!" She advanced on the sofa.

"I saw her first," Kevin muttered.

"And so you're cooking dinner, I hear," Al said to him, betraying her own tendencies to snoop. "What time?"

Moses was next, with Winnie at his heels.

"Say, Cat, I damn near broke my neck on this here guitar case somebody left laying in the hall. You planning a musical career?"

"And give up basketball?" Kevin quipped. "Never." They had put up a basketball net out back during my last case. It had resulted in the previously mentioned ankle injury.

"My daughter Franny. Moses Fogg."

"Well, I'll be. So this is Franny. I didn't know your daughter was coming, Cat. Why don't you tell us when your family's visiting?" He assumed an avuncular air and a seat in the chair kitty corner from the sofa. Winnie availed herself of full beagle privileges and climbed into Franny's lap. Sophie and Sadie were looking on in amusement from the Olympian heights of a nearby bookcase, paws and tails draped over the edge like Dali clocks. "You cookin' tonight, Kevin?"

Mel appeared in the doorway. As usual, she was more direct.

"Whose bags? What's going on around here?"

"My daughter Franny. Melanie Carter."

She stared at Franny. "This is your daughter? She doesn't look like you. Is Kevin cooking dinner?"

Mel had already met my older daughter Sharon, who didn't look much like me, either. I was waiting for someone to accuse me of fabricating my whole past as a suburban supermom and hiring myself a bogus family. Believe me, if I could write the script, Sharon would be living in Connecticut; my son, Jason, would be blissfully sharing parenthood with an adoring wife instead of whining about child support; and Franny would not be moving into my living room, lock, stock, and guitar.

Kevin cooked while we stowed Franny's bags, or rather Mel stowed Franny's bags, traipsing around behind me as I wandered the apartment, looking for any extra space I might've missed before. The guitar wound up in the small room I optimistically think of as my office, and the suitcase in the basement.

The general moratorium on revealing our true natures was thankfully short-lived and minor skirmishes had broken out before the raspberry vinegar hit the arugula. These escalated into open conflict by the time Kevin was whipping the cream. I'd seen his face when Franny turned down his beef stroganoff, saying she was vegetarian, and I knew he was getting testy.

"No, really, Kevin," said Mel, who was vegetarian herself, "this tofu cheesecake that Gina made tasted just like the real thing."

"Mel, *real* cheesecake is made with cream cheese, not tofu, so tofu cheesecake cannot, by definition, 'taste just like the real thing.' You'd better get your taste buds checked." He plied his wire whip with vigor.

"No, but there's this soft tofu, Kevin. It's got a similar consistency. Ask Al. She had some and she told Gina it was great, didn't you, hon?"

Al clearly wanted to change the subject but couldn't think of a new one on short notice.

"Yeah, that's right," she said.

Kevin narrowed his eyes at her. "So are you saying it was 'just like' real cheesecake?"

"Well, no," she said uneasily, not looking at Mel. "I didn't say that. I mean, it was great, for tofu cheesecake."

"You told me it was just like the real thing!"

"No, I didn't, Mel. *You* said that, and I kind of nodded. I mean, if it tastes like that to you—"

"Hold on, y'all," Moses interrupted. "Time out. Any of y'all plannin' on makin' this cheesecake and servin' it around here?"

"Nobody makes cheesecake around here but Kevin," Mel said.

"Right. And, the Lord willing, Kevin ain't never gonna serve no tofu cheesecake, so we ain't never going to know what it's like. I say we take Mel's word for it that it's good, thank the Lord for whatever fat, cholesterol, and calories He chooses to send our way out of Kevin's kitchen, and be done with it."

Maybe it was all that time he spent working Juvie, but when Moses laid down the law, we all subsided like we'd been sent to our rooms.

Franny broke the silence. "So what do you guys think of Mom's new career?" she said brightly.

"Which one?" Kevin asked. "Her real estate empire or her Philip Marlowe imitation?"

"Her career as a detective. I mean, don't you think it's cool? Lots of women her age just, like, move to Florida and play bridge and vegetate. That's why I think she'll be great. Nobody will ever expect her to be, like, this ace detective."

A backhanded compliment if I ever heard one.

"You got a point there," Moses said. "You young people think us senior citizens is all creaky and senile. You always surprised to discover how smart we are."

"Yeah, and as long as Cat stays off the basketball court, she's in pretty good shape, too," Mel put in.

"Yeah, she's been doing all that weight training at the law library," Al observed.

"And just last week she overpowered an assailant, right here at the old Catatonia Arms," Kevin told Franny.

"*Really*?" Franny was impressed. "What happened, Mom?"

"Oh, it was nothing," I said modestly.

"She mugged a street person," Kevin confided.

Franny looked at me in confused alarm. "*Mother*! You didn't!"

"It was okay," I said, glaring at Kevin. "He was a friend."

"And a potential client," Mel murmured.

"Yeah, well, he should've known better than to jump out at me in the goddamn dark and grab me. I haven't been asking you about self-defense techniques for nothing, you know."

I could tell Franny was thrilled, and I began to get a sinking feeling that she was reassessing her visit with me. With any warning, I would have bribed my cohort to paint my life as dull, colorless, and painfully predictable.

"So did you take the case, Mom?"

"There was no case, Franny. He just had a bee in his bonnet, is all. The least little thing happens, some people rush off to see their lawyers. Some people, my friends among them, rush off to see their detectives. They really just need someone to talk to, to convince them that everything's going to be okay. So that's what I did."

"After she flattened him," Kevin said.

"It took his mind off his troubles," I countered.

"That your phone, Cat?"

I listened. "The machine can answer it."

"But Mrs. C," Kevin insisted, "it might be one of your clients."

Kevin knows damn well that I don't have any clients and would get arrested if I had any of the paying variety anyway. He was playing to an appreciative audience in Franny.

"Maybe it's an emergency." Al was horning in on the act.

"I'll get it," Mel said, and sprinted for the door.

If they don't cool it, I thought, Franny will be attending the University of Cincinnati in the fall, and I'll be in a state of advanced alcoholism.

"Cat, it's Curtis." Mel stood at the doorway with an anxious frown on her face. "The police picked Steel up for questioning in the Fountain Square Garage murder."

So much for predictability.

CHAPTER 3

Franny wailed about bombers and butterflies, strumming away on her guitar and making no impact on her tin ear. I told you this music thing was catching — like the way women who work or live together have the same menstrual cycles. Once somebody starts playing something, everybody else plays it, too.

Things got pretty hectic after Mel's announcement. Al changed clothes and charged down to the Investigations Bureau to represent Steel while he was being questioned. I wrote him a note by way of a personal affidavit that she was not a police plant, federal spy, or representative of Army Intelligence, but a bona fide lawyer of the pro bono variety. Moses went upstairs to call around and see what he could find out from his old pals on the force. Mel and I turned on the television but didn't expect any news until eleven, so we turned the sound down and scanned the Sunday paper for any information on the case. Kevin washed dishes, his mouth going ninety miles a minute as usual. And Franny serenaded us to get our minds off our troubles. Apart from its atonality, since Franny's repertoire ran to songs of the downtrodden, it didn't do much to perk us up. Oh, and did I mention that

Winnie was helping her sing? It was like quadraphonic sound in a commune of the terminally tuneless located next to an SPCA.

According to the paper, the dead man had been identified as a Stephen Sanders of Rochester, New York, but the article didn't give any information about Sanders or how he'd been identified. In fact, to read the paper, you'd think the police weren't making any progress on the case. That was bad news for Steel, to my way of thinking. It might be just like he said: the cops wouldn't be able to find any legitimate suspects, so they'd fall back on the old standbys. And a homeless Vietnam vet of uncertain temperament happened to have been standing by in the wrong place at the wrong time.

Moses was gone so long I was beginning to think he was sneaking in a little postprandial nap. When he was in a grumpy mood, he'd tell me that he couldn't always be calling up his friends and former co-workers to pump them for information on my cases. When I was in a grumpy mood, I'd tell him that if his pals wanted to let cases go unsolved and arrest the wrong people, it was okay by me and I'd see them in court eventually. So far, I was two for two in my career as a detective — three for three if you counted a missing kitten named Blackie I'd found — and I was getting pretty damn cocky, if you want to know the truth. But an inside source was nothing to sneeze at.

Moses, who had had a large percentage of his life savings on deposit at Home State, was in a grumpy mood pretty often these days and it was hard to predict when the grumpiness would hit him, but he returned with a page of notes, sat down on Kevin's sofa, and fumbled for his bifocals.

Sanders had been identified the day before by a former college friend, but up until then, nobody had known who he was. The police had found no wallet or other identification on him, so they'd concluded that the murder could have resulted from a robbery. He had been wearing one of the anti-contra buttons that had been passed out at the rally, which led the police to believe he had attended at least part of it. He had been unremarkable, dressed in blue jeans and a flannel shirt, but he had been wearing a baseball cap and carrying a pair of dark sunglasses tucked into his shirt pocket. Since the day had been relatively cloudy, the police were speculating that the sunglasses and cap might have been intended to conceal his identity, but why and from whom they didn't have a clue. He had not been a particularly distinctive man, taller than average, thin, with curly blonde hair thinning at the temples, green eyes, and a full beard. The full beard had gone a long way toward covering a scar across one cheek and eyebrow — another reason the investigating officer believed that Sanders had not wanted to be recognized.

"But he *was* recognized," I observed, "by an old college friend, you said. How come it took his pal so long to contact the police?"

"Well, here's where it gets interesting," Moses said. "This friend, Tom Matthias, went out of town Sunday night and came back Thursday. Says he saw the picture on television, but he didn't think anything of it, didn't recognize the guy. Says he hadn't seen Sanders for fifteen years. Then Friday, he sees it again someplace, and it reminds him of Sanders, but when he asks his wife, she doesn't think so."

"Even with the scar?"

"Well, that's what *he* said, but she said lots of people have scars, and the guy just wasn't that distinctive-looking, so it takes him till yesterday to talk himself into calling the Bureau.

"Seems he and his wife and Sanders all went to Ohio State in the late 60s. They met up when they got involved in the antiwar movement — which gave him another reason for thinking that the victim was Sanders, because of the contra thing. He says Sanders was married to another OSU girl, but they'd been separated for a while and he doesn't know where the wife is. Says Sanders's mother lived in Shaker Heights outside Cleveland, last he heard. Says he hasn't seen Sanders since Sanders graduated in '70 and moved to Rochester. He'd talked to him on the phone a few times, but wasn't even sure what Sanders was doing for a living, and didn't know why the guy was in Cincinnati. According to Matthias, he and Sanders were once good friends and he still thinks of him as one of the leaders of the antiwar movement at OSU in the late sixties. Claims Sanders would have had plenty of enemies then, from the FBI on down, but doesn't know anything about his current enemies."

"So the cops are picking a Vietnam vet as a prime suspect for bumping off a Vietnam-era antiwar activist?"

Moses frowned. "Now, Cat, you know they ain't about to railroad Steel just because he's a vet."

"No, I don't know that," I said. "But I wish you'd convince me."

"It was my case, I reckon I'd have to talk to Steel. It's like he said, man's throat was cut the way they teach you to do it in basic training."

"How about police training? Or other kinds of training?"

"Now, Cat, you know we're trained to restrain people, mostly, not kill 'em. We for damn sure ain't trained to cut nobody's throat. We supposed to serve and protect, not slice and dice."

"Okay," I conceded. "I only wanted you to think about other people who might get that kind of training."

"Ain't nobody else, Cat, 'cept right-wing paramilitary yoyos, and they mostly out in Idaho somewhere."

"I don't think that's right, Moses," Franny ventured. She was still in awe of him. "I read that there were these bases all over the South, Florida and Georgia and Louisiana, where they, like, train contras and American mercenaries who want to go down there and fight the socialist Sandinistas in Nicaragua."

"She's right, Moses," Kevin said. "I read that, too."

"So what we've got here is a veteran antiwar campaigner who gets offed at an antiwar rally," I pointed out, "in a manner not inconsistent with the training of guys who are fighting the war he's protesting."

"You know, Mom, you should really find out if there were, like, counterdemonstrators at the rally, you know? I mean, most rallies, there are. There could have been contra agents, you know? Even infiltrators. Like, some of these guys are part of this huge international network of ultra-ultra right-wing organizations, like some of these anti-Castro Cubans in Miami? I don't mean all of them, of course, but some of them are. It's like the Mafia or something, you know? And these guys, they call up Miami if they want to hit somebody in the U.S., and then they either get paid off, or the other guy, like, returns the favor and bumps off somebody in *their* country."

I was staring at my daughter. "You've been watching too much prime-time television."

She rolled her eyes at me. "Mo-om! I never watch television, except the news!"

"So how do you know all this stuff? Peter Jennings never let *me* in on it."

"Jeez, Mom, you can't expect the mainstream media to tell you this kind of stuff. You've got to read the alternative press to really find out what's going on in the world."

Which alternative press? I thought. The *National Enquirer*? But I was damned if I was going to betray my ignorance. The thing about my daughter is she might sound like an airhead, but she is pretty goddamn smart. They wouldn't have let her into all those colleges if she wasn't.

"You know, she's right, Cat," Mel was saying. "This rally was pretty widely advertised. The contras could have sent a representative to see what was going on—"

"Or the CIA," Kevin said. "They're the ones who are up to their conservative neckties in contra training, and the Reagan administration is actively lobbying Congress right now to restore millions in contra aid."

"Look, I like this scenario. I do. But why would either of these groups send somebody down to kill a has-been activist that nobody even recognizes?"

"Or nobody admits to recognizing," Mel put in.

"Okay, but wouldn't it make more sense to kill one of the local organizers? And if everybody recognized him, and nobody wanted to admit it last Sunday, why does somebody want to admit it now?"

"Maybe this Sanders guy was an organizer," Kevin suggested. "Maybe he was the brains behind the scenes. Maybe he travels around in disguise, secretly helping local groups stage mass rallies and protests, and his job is so dangerous that he has to keep it all secret." I can always count on Kevin to come up with the most far-fetched possibility imaginable.

"Or wait—" He had an even better one? "Maybe the plan was to demoralize and destroy the anti-contra movement by kidnapping some famous activist from the sixties — somebody Ohio activists would remember and idolize. Only the kidnapping went wrong somehow and they had to kill him."

"Yeah, and I'm secretly running the Defense Department," I said. "First of all, nobody did remember him, so unless they've got morons in their research department, which is entirely possible, I admit, Stephen Sanders made a lousy choice for a kidnapped idol. Second, unless he is the secret superstar of the peace movement — say, the equivalent of whoever took a brain-dead former actor and sold him to the American people as president — unless he's that good, what's the point of killing him? Somebody else can always take his place."

"Okay, how about this: he graduated from college, went to work for General Motors, and sold out, and now he works for the CIA, only somebody found out, and—"

"Being the peace-loving, nonviolent types that they are, they tried to talk sense into him, only the knife slipped."

"Well—"

"Any of y'all interested in the rest of my information?" Moses asked. "'Cause if not—"

"I'm interested," I said. "Kevin sees too many movies."

"All right, then, ain't nobody asked me if Sanders had a record."

"He couldn't have a record, could he?" I frowned. "If he had a record, his fingerprints would have been filed in the computer, and the Cincinnati PD would have known who he was in a day or so."

"Okay. You right. He didn't have a record. Now ask me who did."

"Tom Matthias?" I said hopefully.

"Right on. He was arrested in a draft board bombing case in Columbus, Ohio, in 1970. But the charges were dropped."

"You mean, the charges were dropped and you guys still have a record of his arrest?" Franny was appalled.

"The plot thickens," Kevin intoned.

"So, wait," I said. "You're telling me that they got a guy on the scene who'd been previously charged with a violent crime and they want to question a homeless Vietnam vet?"

"I didn't say he was on the scene."

"Okay, in the vicinity. Do we know he wasn't on the scene?"

"He says he was at his office Sunday morning, getting some things together to take out of town."

"Any witnesses?"

"They're still checking."

"So we still got a guy charged with a violent crime, who knew the victim, and could have been on the scene."

"He wasn't charged with the bombing itself. He was charged with conspiracy. They didn't think he was in on the bombing."

"And the charges could have been dropped for any reason — lack of evidence, say."

"Right. Especially with a charge as vague as conspiracy."

"Okay, so who did he conspire with? Don't tell me; let me guess. A group of Ohio State antiwar activists."

"Aw, you no fun, Cat." Moses grinned. "You read this script already."

CHAPTER 4

When I started my training for detective work, I'd already realized that I had a free pass to the best educational institution around: the public library. Some detectives you read about don't even seem to possess a library card, much less carry it around with their driver's license, their PI license, their MasterCard, and their .38. I don't see how they get by; I really don't. And the truth is, they'd get by a lot better if they checked out their public library. How many times have you read a scene where somebody's trying to figure out something that a reference librarian could tell them before they could say *Encyclopedia Britannica*?

Me, I'm on a first-name basis with certain librarians down at the Public Library of Cincinnati and Hamilton County. Also with the cashier. I like to think they built the new drive-in window on their profits from my overdue library books.

The newspaper section isn't my scene, what with all the high-tech, high-maintenance machinery, half of it out of order at any given time, films and fiches and reels rewound backward, fifty untranslatable cut options for the size of your photocopy — none of them the size you need. But sometimes, like today, there was no avoiding it. Some information can only be gotten out of newspapers and I don't mean the ones that are crumpled in somebody's wastebasket with ship arrivals circled in red ink or letters cut out of them.

Trouble is, if you're looking up some specific event to read the press coverage and you don't know the date when the event occurred, you're out of luck unless you're using the *New York Times*, which publishes an index. If you're dealing with a local paper, you just have to hunt, page by page, reel by reel. This is about as much fun as a root canal and a hell of a lot more boring. Which is probably why most detectives don't do it, or don't tell you if they do. When they say "action-packed," they don't mean cranking a goddamn microform reader.

So I checked the *New York Times* index, just in case I might get lucky and spot some coverage of Matthias's arrest, but no soap. From what I remembered of the time period, I guess draft board bombings were as common as cow manure and didn't warrant national coverage.

We didn't own back issues of the *Columbus Dispatch* on microfilm, for reasons which escape me but which might have something to do with a rivalry between the two cities that dated back before Johnny Appleseed's brother Buck took to planting the state in buckeyes. Don't ask me why anybody feels this way; personally, I think Columbus is an okay city and certainly an appropriate one to house our state government. After all, some city has to do it, and better them than us. Anyway, without the *Dispatch* I had to hope that the arrest or trial had been covered in the *Enquirer* or *Post.* I was hopeful; Cincinnati papers were especially attentive to scandal attached to Columbus, and god knows the Columbus paper was having a field day with the Cincinnati Savings and Loan crisis.

I thought I'd stick to the front page on the first round. I knew myself well enough to know just how long I could tolerate staring at a blurry screen without any rewards, so I struck a deal with myself: first pages only, and if I reached August 1970 without a single hit, I'd give up and try to get the information another way. Speaking of rewards, I also knew myself well enough to bring along a bag of M&M's, and help myself to a little incentive every time I finished a month.

I had gained five pounds by the time I found what I wanted: a brief story on July 15th, 1970, under the headline "Four Arrested in Columbus Bombing." That was newspaper shorthand, since it turned out the bomb had never exploded but had been found and deactivated. The four people arrested were Matthias and his wife, Linda Genovese Matthias, a Michael Joseph McCafferty, and a Phyllis Jeanette Silverman. No mention of Stephen Sanders. No pictures. I made a photocopy and kept cranking.

I didn't find anything else until October 23rd, when an equally brief story reported the conviction of Michael Joseph McCafferty on a group of charges related to the attempted bombing in July. Charges against the Matthiases had been unaccountably dropped. And the fourth suspect, Phyllis Jeanette Silverman, had disappeared.

Disappeared? I thought. Hmm.

According to the paper, the police considered Silverman armed and dangerous. I wondered if they thought she was carrying around a bomb or just a screwdriver and a set of instructions. They were offering a one-thousand-dollar reward for information leading to her arrest. Allowing for inflation, that seemed like a respectable amount. Of course, these days, nobody with principles would rat out their worst enemy for a grand, although they might point vaguely in her general direction.

But there was still no mention of Sanders, so maybe he wasn't connected. He could have been peripheral to the bombing — say, a member of another antiwar group — while still knowledgeable about Matthias and his cohort. Could he have spotted someone at the rally he knew — somebody who had been running from the cops for fifteen years? Had he been killed to shut him up?

Alternatively, he could have been a member of this organization, even its leader. He could have masterminded the bombing and let his friends take the rap. That could explain the sunglasses and baseball cap — what the police had identified as a disguise. Maybe he'd attended the anti-contra rally incognito and had been recognized by somebody with a long-standing grudge against him. It would probably be McCafferty or Silverman, but I didn't have any information to suggest that they were anywhere within miles of the state of Ohio, much less the anti-contra rally in question. Matthias, on the other hand, had been in the vicinity, and even though the charges had been dropped, he might still bear a grudge, either on his own behalf or on behalf of his friends.

Obviously, I needed more information. I didn't wish I lived in Columbus, but I damn sure wished that somebody in Cincinnati owned back issues of the *Dispatch*. The University of Cincinnati library was no help; they, too, considered the *Dispatch* beneath their notice.

I was going to have to take a more direct approach. Maybe I could sell bail insurance to the Matthiases.

I headed home to hand over the beige bomber to my daughter, who wanted to cruise her old neighborhood. There had been a time when she wouldn't have been caught dead in a middle-aged Pinto, but that was before she took up identifying with the oppressed. This was only Day One of her visit, and already she was cramping my style. I had liked it better when I was the only person in the household with a driver's license. I suspected that as soon as Sidney could see over the dashboard, he would start lobbying for Driver's Ed, but it would be a while before I had to cross that bridge. In the meantime, my daughter had reverted to her teenage habit of regarding my car as community property.

In fact, you might say it was Franny's fault that I didn't know more about the antiwar movement of the sixties than I did. Also her fault that I knew as much as I did, if you follow me. In 1970, Franny had been fifteen, and I was wrapped up in family turbulence and self-pity. What was I being punished for that I was being forced to live through a third teenager?

And Franny was precocious; she had started early, practicing teenage behavior at the age of nine. Maybe that was why she had never grown past adolescence: she'd been a teenager so long she didn't know how to be anything else.

By the age of twelve, Franny had been marching, picketing, and sitting in. By fourteen, she knew what teargas was all about. If I'd stopped and analyzed the situation, I probably would have conceded that she was right and supported her. At least, that's how I feel about the whole Vietnam thing now. But we were locked in that eternal struggle between mother and daughter that she'd described to me when she was a psych major and revised when she started taking women's studies. She was busy individuating and I was busy having a breakdown.

Sometimes, when people ask me what I remember about the sixties, I say I don't remember anything; I was on the phone. And I conjure up in my mind's eye what seemed like one interminable conversation with Louise Schottenstein, mother of Franny's best friend and co-conspirator Janice.

"I don't care where they're sitting in," I'd grouse in a sympathetic ear. "If that kid misses her orthodontist's appointment again, I will personally escort her there and sit in at Dr. Jackson's office till he wires her jaw shut!"

Fred had been no help; he'd been more hysterical than I was. But then, Fred had been a law-and-order man and a veteran. On a couple of beers he'd give us his rendition of a my-country-right-or-wrong speech. Me, I couldn't see past the potential for injury. I had also thought that an arrest record would ruin her life forever, and that she'd end up an alcoholic on welfare — or worse, an alcoholic living off of Fred and me. Now that I'm older, of course, I see things differently. Some of my best friends have arrest records and I've flirted with one myself. And whatever had prevented Franny from growing up, it hadn't been her arrest record.

So, like I say, at the time the antiwar movement was going on, I couldn't see the forest for the tree that was standing in front of me, rolling its eyes at me and making plans to charge into another situation that would certainly be illegal if not downright life-threatening. As far as I was concerned, I knew more about the movement than I'd wanted to know in the first place. But now that I needed the information, I was beginning to realize just how much I didn't know.

Of course, appearances could be deceiving. The proximity of the murder to the rally could be coincidental. Sanders could have been the victim of a robbery gone bad. He could have been anything, really. The victim of a business partner who wanted to collect insurance. The victim of a lover or ex-lover who'd been insulted by him one too many times. Somebody who knew too much about some shady financial deal. An enemy of the mob. A drug kingpin.

And I am the ghost of Janis Joplin.

CHAPTER 5

For some folks in Cincinnati, the St. Francis Soup Kitchen was the closest thing they had to a permanent address — closer even than the Salvation Army Emergency Home down on Clay. After all, a person needed to eat, rain or shine, summer or winter, but shelter was optional for part of the year. My client and Al's had been released Sunday night after two hours of questioning, and my best opportunity to find him was at dinner time Monday night at St. Francis.

I had wrested the car keys from Franny before she could disappear for the evening. I figured it was Garf's turn to share.

I was a little early; my regulars hadn't yet put in an appearance. Some of them were probably still out panhandling at the Metro stops, hitting up the rush-hour crowds with approaches ranging from poignant to belligerent. I sincerely hoped my client wasn't in the latter category. Please don't let him be out making new enemies, I thought. Most of all, don't let him threaten anybody.

I stopped in the kitchen to see Sister Mary Jeanne, who was radiant in pink polyester, standing on tiptoes before an institutional stove twice as big as she was, her flushed face enveloped in a cloud of steam. She was upending a suspiciously shaped bottle of dark red liquid over a stew pot.

"Sister!" I exclaimed, shocked. "Is that wine?"

"Oh, my, Catherine, you startled me." She looked a little sheepish. "Well, yes, it *is* wine — just for flavoring, you know. I've been watching that French chef on television and trying to expand my culinary horizons, so to speak. Well, goodness, there is no reason why my guests can't be served haute cuisine, within the limits of our budget, of course. Now, I know Father Dalby expressed some concern about the alcohol content, particularly with our clientele. But you know something, Catherine? I prayed on it. And the very next day, why, Julia just happened to explain about how the alcohol gets cooked off some way — I don't remember exactly how she said. But if Julia said it, why, that's good enough for me. And that's what I told Father Dalby.

"Anyway, it doesn't cost us a penny. That nice Mrs. Prescott — you know, Betty's daughter? — she sends us a case of wine every now and then. I just wish Betty could be here to see it — and Lucille, too."

Betty "Bags" Grumbacher, a.k.a. Leda Marrs, had been my first unofficial client. She had shown up dead on the floor of one of my vacant apartments and had led me to my circle of acquaintances at the St. Francis Soup Kitchen.

"Well, it sure smells heavenly, Sister."

"Oh, I'm so glad you think so. I do feel our clients have been rather more grateful to God since I began spiking the stew." She flashed me an impish grin that took me by surprise. "Are you here on a case again?" She asked hopefully. I gathered that St. Francis had profited nicely from my last one.

"'Fraid so," I said. "I'm working on the Fountain Square murder."

"Oh, wasn't that awful!" she exclaimed, splitting a tomato with one chop of the knife. "And now the police keep bothering Steel about it — just because he was there at the time. Now, I know people think nuns are obligated to think the best of everybody, but that doesn't mean I don't know wicked when I see it, and poor Steel wouldn't hurt a fly, for all his tough talk. I spoke to Father Dalby about the church's obligation to provide sanctuary, and I didn't see why, if this dining hall is part of the church, we should let the police come in here and take somebody away. But he said he didn't think we should set ourselves up against the law, especially in a murder investigation." She split another tomato with a forceful whack, and leaning toward me, lowered her voice conspiratorially. "All I can say, Catherine, is things would be mighty different around here if I was in charge."

I smiled and nodded. I just bet they would be, I thought.

I wandered out to the dining hall, where guests were beginning to arrive. I spotted Curtis across the room, standing with two women I also knew.

"Hey, Cat," said the livelier of the two, a skinny white woman with long, stringy brown hair. Her grin showed chipped and discolored teeth. "You come for dinner? I'm telling you, girl, this here restaurant's getting better all the time."

"Yeah," Curtis said, "Trish right. Any day now they gonna slap five stars on it and write it up in the gourmet section, and ain't gonna be no room for folks like us — be full up with rich folks."

"Hell, Curtis, they can't get rid of us," Trish protested. "We're part of the am-bi-ants."

"The police already been here," said Zona, a tall, frail-looking woman who looked permanently drugged. "Maybe they're going to come take us away, one by one. Like those aliens do, in their spaceships."

"Would you quit with them aliens, girl?" Trish said impatiently. "You got aliens on the brain. The police can't take us away just for minding our own business. And they better not try to arrest Steel for murder, or Cat will give 'em hell. Right, Cat?"

"I'll do my best," I promised. "Speaking of Steel, where is my client? I need to talk to him."

They went all silent and secretive, which made me nervous. That is, Curtis and Trish did; Zona never changes her demeanor. Curtis took me by the elbow and steered me off into a corner.

"See, Cat, Steel — he don't want to come here no more. He think the police going to get him if he here."

"So where is he? And what's he eating?"

"Well, I 'spect he gone 'round to the kitchen door to get somethin' from Sister. But I got to warn you, Cat. He gone pretty near crazy 'bout all this here. Not crazy violent, least I don't think so. But he got his face all blacked up, like they done on night patrol when they was in Vietnam, so the cops won't spot him."

"Okay, thanks for the warning, Curtis. Now let me ask you this. You know I'm on his side. But do you think he's holding back? What I mean is, do you think he knows more about this murder than he's telling?"

"I don't know, Cat, truly I don't." Curtis shook his head. "Sometime I think he do, then again, sometime I think he jus' got this Vietnam shit to work out, and this here thing done shook him up and brought it all back somehow. I told him take a bus up to Northside to the VA and talk to somebody there, but he won't do it. He don't trust nobody right now, 'cept us and you."

"Okay. But keep me posted, Curtis. If you find out anything more, I mean. I can't help him if I've only got half a story. And I don't think he killed this guy, either, but I think there's something funny going on, and it doesn't help at all for him to go off the deep end and start going on night patrol around downtown Cincinnati, creeping around like he expects landmines and booby-traps on Race Street."

I walked back through the kitchen and waylaid Sister Mary Jeanne, who was crossing the room with a heavy paper plate full of food in her hand. I took it from her.

"He out back?" I asked.

She sighed and nodded.

I opened the door on the hazy darkness of a back alley. I didn't see anybody.

"Come on out, Steel," I said in a low voice. "It's me, Cat, and I've got your dinner."

He materialized in the shadows from behind a row of trash cans so silently that I almost didn't notice.

He took the plate from me. "This way," he whispered.

He crept back behind the trash cans and disappeared. I followed. When my eyes adjusted, I saw that he was sitting on the edge of a rectangular window well outside a basement window. The stench of garbage nearly overpowered me, but Steel had already started to eat with apparent gusto.

"Christ, Cat, get down, will you?" He waved a piece of bread at me.

I stepped down gingerly into the well, wondering what I was stepping on. I fished a handkerchief out of my pocket and applied it to my nose as inconspicuously as possible.

"We have to talk, Steel. I need to know everything you know about this Sanders guy." I had unconsciously lowered my voice to a whisper.

"I told you. I don't know the dude."

"I don't believe it."

"Christ, you sound like the cops."

"I may sound like the cops, but I'm on your side. So don't bullshit me on this, Steel. I need to know."

He chewed a little longer. "Okay. I recognized the dude, okay? I saw him once at an antiwar rally at Ohio State in the late sixties. I heard him speak. So when I saw him laying there in the garage, I knew who he was. I mean, I knew he was the same dude, even though he looked different. I didn't know his name or anything."

"What were you doing at an antiwar rally in the late sixties? I thought you were in Vietnam."

"I just got out of basic. I was home on leave before I shipped out. I heard about this rally, and what the hell. I was curious. Me and some buddies, we went down there to check it out, watch the hippies getting all steamed up and cuss out the government. Some of my buddies got into it with a couple of protesters, but I got them out of there before anything happened. That was it. I saw this guy Sanders speak, but I didn't pay any attention to his name." He was mopping up the sauce with his bread.

"So is that where you're from? Columbus?"

"Yeah. So what?"

His belligerence tipped me off that I was asking the right questions. But why? Sanders was from Cleveland.

"You know this guy Tom Matthias?"

"No."

"You didn't see him at the Ohio State rally?"

"Christ, I don't know if I saw him or not. I saw a lot of people. That don't mean I know who they were and what their names were."

"Did the police show you a picture of Matthias?"

"No."

"And you didn't tell them about this rally where you saw Sanders?"

"No."

"Okay. On the day of the anti-contra rally, had you seen Sanders at the rally before you saw him dead?"

"No."

His arm shot out, and I flinched. He gripped my elbow. He thrust his face at mine, one finger to his lips, signaling silence.

I hadn't heard anything, but a few seconds later came the scraping sound of a door being opened and the alley lightened. We crouched lower as a beam of light played on the brick wall over our heads.

"Well, if he *was* here, I guess he's gone by now," a masculine voice said. "You're sure he didn't come by here tonight, asking for food?"

"I told you." Sister Mary Jeanne's voice was indignant. "He hasn't asked here for food tonight."

I winced, wondering how much penance she would have to do for that little lie. We heard the scrape of the door closing and the alley was dark again.

"Fuckin' cops!" Steel whispered. "And I didn't ask for food. I didn't have to."

"I believe you were telling me that you hadn't seen Sanders the day of the rally," I said, rubbing my elbow.

"That's right."

"So you come out of the men's room, and what happens next?"

"I told you, man, I heard the screaming. And so I walk down to the bottom of the steps to see what's going on and I see this group of people — well, maybe three people — crowded around this guy who's laying on the floor in the corner. And then I split."

"Wait. You're standing at the bottom of the steps and then you split?"

"Fuckin' A. I wasn't gonna be hanging around when the cops showed up."

"How far away was the body?"

"Man, I don't know. Maybe from here to that sidewalk, where the alley starts."

"You were standing that far away from him and you recognized him?"

"Yeah." I reached over, felt for the pocket of his camouflage jacket, and extracted what I found.

"Hey!"

"Hey, yourself! This is me, Cat. Remember, Steel? The person you came to to get you out of this mess? Your old pal? The one who knows about the glasses that the FOP gave you at Christmastime, but which you refuse to wear because you don't think there's anything wrong with your eyesight because you're such a stubborn bastard?" I waved the glasses at him. "You are just fucking with me, pal, and I don't like it. I got better things to do with my time than picnic behind a garbage dump and I am going off to do them. So the next time your ass lands in the hot seat downtown, don't call me, okay?"

My exit was spoiled by the stiffness in my joints when I got up, which made it hard for me to climb out of the hole I was standing in. I finally clambered over the side, scraping an elbow in the process, and kind of rolled to my feet. I bumped up against a garbage can and knocked the lid to the ground with a clamor to rival a full brass band. I hoped the cops were gone.

"Okay, Cat, okay! Okay!" He stumbled in an effort to grab my arm and steadied me before I brought the whole damn alley down. "I'll tell you some more, but you ain't gonna like it."

"Good. Now can we please find a hiding place that is not in close proximity to a pile of garbage?"

"What time is it?"

I checked. "Seven."

"The cops are probably watching this place. You got a car?"

"Yeah."

"Why don't you go get it, drive past the alley with the door open, and I'll jump in?"

"Why do I think I've seen this before on *Rockford Files*?" But I went.

"Make sure you aren't followed!" he hissed behind me.

CHAPTER 6

So I did it like he said, and he climbed in the back and lay on the floor. I drove around for a while to lose any tails I might have picked up, but I didn't spot anything, so I headed down to the railroad yards under the expressway and parked. He slunk into the front seat and lit a cigarette.

After a minute of silence, he spoke. "Me and Sanders were in high school together."

"I thought he came from Cleveland."

Steel shook his head. "His mother remarried and moved there. He grew up in my neighborhood in Columbus."

"So how well did you know him?"

"Not well at all. We ran in different crowds. Still do." He smiled. "Or did. He was an ambitious bastard, football player, president of all kinds of shit, honors student. Me, I wasn't too interested in school."

"So was he a popular kid?"

"I guess so." Steel frowned into the darkness, his eyes unfocused. "Not really a Mr. Congeniality type exactly, but he kind of overwhelmed the other kids with his energy and ambition."

"Was he interested in the antiwar movement in high school?"

"No, I wouldn't have figured him as a protester type, but maybe that's where all the action was at OSU and he saw a chance to take over."

"You didn't like him much."

"Man, he was too clean for me. High school was just made for him, you know what I mean? All those positions and honors and awards to collect, all those cliques and in-groups and out-groups. Dating and popularity contests and who's taking who to the dance. Who's got more money than who and who's wearing what to school and whose old man's got a drinking problem. Some kids are just made for that shit."

"I know what you mean."

"Maybe I was jealous of him, I don't know. Me and my friends, the guys I hung out with, we just laughed at Steve and his friends and acted like we wouldn't serve on the student council if Jesus Christ himself came up and asked us. But maybe we were just covering up for the fact that nobody would ever ask us, much less Jesus."

"So Steve went to OSU after he graduated and you went into the Army?"

"Not right away. I worked a few years first, at the brewery. I didn't have money for college, even if I wanted to go. But I knew that if I went in the Army, I'd get the G.I. Bill, and I could get me some vocational training when I got out."

"And that's why you enlisted?"

"Hell, no. Shit, I was twenty years old, what the fuck did I know? I wanted to fight commies for my country. Maybe I wanted to die for my country and prove to assholes like Sanders that I was somebody."

"And meanwhile Sanders had become involved with the antiwar movement at OSU."

"I guess so. Seems like I'd heard something about it around the neighborhood." He finished his cigarette, rolled down the window, and flicked the butt into the darkness. He lit another.

"And when you came home from basic, you decided to attend this rally. Had you seen Sanders while you'd been home?"

"Nah, he was busy up at OSU, playing the BMOC. You didn't see him hanging around the neighborhood, especially since his mother had moved to Cleveland. Yeah, so me and my buddies, we thought we'd go check out this rally, just for laughs. Mostly we stood around on the sidelines, cracking jokes. But some of the guys started yelling at the demonstrators and then they got in a shouting match, and it was about to turn into a shoving match when me and another guy got them out of there. But Steve was up on the podium speaking that day, so I saw him there. Hell, that was the last time I saw him before I saw him lying in Fountain Square Garage with his throat cut."

"You're sure?"

"Sure, I'm sure. What is it with you, Cat? I told you I'd tell you, so I'm fucking telling you."

"Maybe it's the skepticism bred of habit, seeing as how you've told me twice before that you were telling me. Do you know who Sanders hung out with at Ohio State?"

"No, I wouldn't know that. Like I said, I didn't know him that well. I heard he got married, but that was afterward."

Now there was an interesting angle I hadn't even considered. I'd forgotten about Mrs. Sanders.

"Did you hear what he was doing for a living?"

"No."

"Okay, now let's hear about the anti-contra rally again, only this time with all the details in place."

"Well, it all happened like I said, except for, like you said, I got closer to him than I said before."

"How close?"

"I think my foot brushed against his foot."

"So what happened next?"

"Well, the girl, she kind of calmed down and started to cry, and that's when I did a double take on the body and seen that it was Sanders. Well, I got a kind of warning bell that goes off — you don't survive in country unless you develop this instinctive sense of danger. So I'm backing away before I even realize why. I mean, I just *know* my ass is in deep water before I even think about why. So I walk back up the steps, careful not to run, see, so I won't look guilty, and I find Curtis and we split. And that's all I know."

"How do you feel about the antiwar movement now, Steel? I mean, you told me how you felt before you went to Vietnam, but did you feel the same way afterward?"

His eyes narrowed as he exhaled a thin stream of smoke.

"It's like I told the cops, before I went to Nam I was fuckin' green. Wanting to do my goddamn duty and all that shit. I thought those antiwar demonstrators were all pinko chicken-shits, threatening our country and the whole goddamn free world with their marches and shit. That's before I found out what doing my duty was all about. Afterward — well, I just wished those demonstrators had ended the war about three fucking years before they did it."

We sat in silence for a few minutes.

"Those anti-contra demonstrators — I'd like to think they'll make a difference. At least they aren't waiting till the goddamn government commits American troops to Nicaragua. But hell, I don't know. You can bet your ass that we don't know the half of what's going on down there and how deep we already are. The bottom line is, if the government wants to wage war on Nicaragua and send American kids to die there, there ain't a goddamn thing we can do about it."

"Since we are having this little heart-to-heart," I said, "are you carrying a knife, Steel?"

"Me?" he asked in offended astonishment. "What would I be doing with a knife?"

"Were you carrying one at the time of the murder?"

"No, man, no way. I ain't that stupid, Cat."

I sighed. "Well, look, wherever you've got it stashed, promise me you won't even look at it until this whole thing blows over. Don't try to move it to a better hiding place, okay? Just leave it alone and don't go near it."

He didn't say anything at first.

"You are one tough bitch, you know that, Cat?"

"That's why you came to me and not Jessica Fletcher."

CHAPTER 7

A handkerchief lay on the table. Conspicuously embroidered in one lacy corner was the initial "C."

Standing before me on the other side of the table, leaning on his fists, was my least favorite member of the Cincinnati Police Department, Sergeant Fricke.

"I don't know why you think it's mine," I said airily. "C could stand for anything, really. Cincinnati. Catholic. Cop."

"Well, allow me to reconstruct my thinking, Caliban. A homeless pal of yours is wanted for questioning in a homicide. This particular pal happens to be evading the police. Another pal of yours, one of your tenants, in fact, shows up at the station whenever we try to talk to the homeless pal and says she's his lawyer and gets all hot and bothered if we so much as ask his name."

I didn't know what he was beefing about. I didn't know Steel's name, either.

"So we come across this hanky in the alley behind the St. Francis Soup Kitchen, where your pal likes to dine seven nights a week. We know it wasn't there before last night, on accounta we looked. So being the suspicious type that I am, I began to think maybe Miss Marble been—"

"That's Marple. Miss Marple."

"Well, excuse me, Miss Marple been hanging out in this alley with her pal Steel, chewing the fat and maybe holding her nose on accounta this alley don't smell like no perfume factory. And she's been using this hanky with a C on it for 'Caliban.'" He chewed his gum triumphantly.

I was going to have to speak to Franny about the wisdom of giving monogrammed handkerchiefs to a private investigator.

He leaned forward and glowered at me. "So where is he?"

"Who?"

"You know goddamn well who."

"If you're referring to my good friend Steel, I don't know where he is. As you know, he has no permanent address and no telephone number. He might be anywhere."

He might have been home in my basement, only he wouldn't accept my offer to harbor a fugitive from police harassment. I don't think he felt too comfortable underground.

"Goddamnit, Caliban, you're up to your neck in this, and I know it! If you're hiding that bastard, you goddamn well better come clean, or I'll have your ass in court!"

"Look, Fricke, I'm just an average citizen, a senior citizen at that. I don't know why you hold a grudge against me. I've never tried to do anything but help the police, like any citizen would. And just to show you how I feel, I'll let you come over and search my apartment — hell, I'll even throw in my car — as soon as you get yourself a search warrant. And in the meantime, stay off my goddamn case. I can see why you're grumpy right now. And I sympathize. You got a bellyful of Daily Doughnuts reacting to your on-the-job stress. You haven't got a shred of evidence against Steel, and if you try to arrest him now, the grand jury will laugh you out of the courthouse. So instead of going out to get more evidence, you figure it's faster and easier just to lean on Steel and hope he breaks down and confesses. But take it from me: it's not going to happen like that. So you might as well resign yourselves to getting off your butts and doing some hardcore investigating."

Another officer entered and whispered in his ear, the way they always do to make you nervous, like they just found some unpaid traffic citation and are impounding your car. With my luck, they'd found Franny's marijuana stash and were busy impounding the entire Catatonia Arms, the contents of my liquor cabinet included.

Fricke nodded, stone-faced, except this little vein in his temple was throbbing like a flea-circus acrobat.

"You got another young pal who is maybe your height, skinny, with long, light brown hair and wears Indian print skirts and no bra?"

"Maybe," I said. Sounded suspiciously like my daughter.

"You been warned, Caliban," he growled at me. "Now get outta my sight and take your little pal with you."

I found Franny marching up and down in front of the building, waving a sign that read "Free the Cincinnati 1."

"Okay, kid, I'm free. Let's go."

She looked disappointed. "But Mom, if I hang around here a little longer, the local media is bound to show up and cover the story. Then I can, like, talk about how the cops are harassing that poor homeless vet and preventing you from investigating the Fountain Square murder. You'll make the six o'clock news. It would be great publicity for the cause!"

"Franny, I'm not averse to using the press." In fact, I had called the Channel 12 troubleshooter on my first case. "But I have to be selective. The whole point of being a private investigator is to keep things private. Who's going to hire somebody whose face has been all over the news?" I put an arm around her shoulders. "Look, I'll make a deal: if they ever actually arrest Steel, you can picket all you want. You'll have a lot of company, believe me. Now where'd you park?"

Maybe because I thought I'd hurt her feelings, I proposed a nostalgic mother-daughter shopping trip, just the two of us, a fistful of credit cards, and a mall. In the old days, this situation would have brought out her acquisitive side. But now that she'd renounced capitalism, she didn't seem very interested in accumulating goods. Since I didn't have any more room in my apartment for them anyway, it was probably just as well. And the whole experience did have a ring of familiarity about it; we still argued, but we argued over different things.

"Yuck! Polyester! I can't believe they're still making so much clothing from plastic! I mean, when you think about the impact on our global environment — it just makes me sick!"

Even when we found clothes I thought would rank high on her scale of political correctness, I was wrong.

"Look, Franny! 'Made in Guatemala.'"

"Oh god, Mom, you don't want that! It's probably made by practically slave labor. Some wealthy industrialist type probably hires Native American workers for shitty wages and then collects, like, a two-hundred-percent markup when he sells the stuff they make. If you like that kind of stuff, I know a place where you can buy direct from a workers' commune."

Shopping with Franny was quite an education.

Lunch at the mall's food court wasn't much more successful. I was leaning toward Chinese fast food until my daughter warned me about the prospect of MSG poisoning. I resisted similar warnings about the stuff they put on lettuce to keep it fresh and bought a salad, only to be subjected to a disquisition on how much fat my salad dressing contained. Franny ate frozen yogurt and complained that she couldn't buy bottled water anywhere in the food court. I would have thought that all of those bottles would be bad for the environment, but what did I know?

All in all, the highlight of the shopping trip was when Franny added two new holes to her ears at the earring stand.

My next mistake was inducing her to stop at the IGA and allowing her to come in with me. I felt like I had to justify every goddamn item I tossed in the cart. To my daughter, no less.

"Mom, you're supposed to be *boycotting* grapes. Besides, haven't you read about all the toxic substances they spray on grapes these days? I hope you at least soak them good to, like, get most of the poison off them. Of course, the poor pickers can't do that."

I lost my appetite for grapes.

"You know, Mom, at your age, you really shouldn't be eating beef at all. I mean, even if you don't consider the animal-rights angle or how cattle ranching is wasting the world's resources, not to mention how it's contributing to global warming, don't you know what it's doing to your arteries?"

I grumbled and returned the roast to the case. I tried to trade it for a chicken and got an earful about salmonella poisoning.

"Mom, this spaghetti sauce has a shitload of salt and preservatives in it. You really ought to read the label, especially at your age."

I was feeling older by the minute.

In the dairy aisle, we bumped into Leon, who was buying milk for his mother. I felt unnaturally happy to see him. One thing Leon isn't is a critic.

"Hey, M-miz Cat."

"Hey, Leon, how's it going? I want you to meet my daughter Franny."

"This your d-daughter?" He stuck his hand out, like his mother had taught him. Leon was supposed to be mentally handicapped, but like I always say, mental capacity is relative. "P-pleased to meet you, m-Miss. You visitin' Miz Cat?"

"Leon's one of my operatives," I told Franny. "He's been active in all my cases."

"Really?" Franny looked impressed. "That's so cool!"

"That right, Miss. I be goin' out for b-baseball pretty soon, Miz C-cat. But I s-still want to be a operative, whenever I d-don't got no game."

"That's okay, Leon. We can work around it."

A skinny green-eyed blonde girl with braids, a little older than Leon, smiled as she approached us. It was Hope Smith, our neighborhood lawn care professional.

"Hey, Cat! Hey, Leon! What are you guys doing?"

"We're guarding the milk from an infamous gang of dairy thieves known to be operating in this area," I said. "What are you doing?"

"I'm spying for an infamous gang of dairy thieves," she said with a grin. "I'm supposed to tell them whether the milk's being guarded and how many guards there are, stuff like that."

"My daughter Franny. Hope Smith."

"Oh, hi! Are you visiting from out of town?"

It was beginning to occur to me that I could bribe enough people to ask Franny if she was visiting, emphasis on the "visiting."

"Hey, Hope, d-didn't I see you on T-TV?"

"I don't think so. When?" She frowned.

"It was this rally, d-downtown. I thought I s-seen you on the n-news."

"It wasn't me. I wasn't there."

"Wait, Leon. Are you saying that you saw the rally on the news?"

"Yes, ma'am. It was some p-pictures of folks m-makin' speeches and s-singin', and they was c-carryin' signs, too."

Television footage. Why hadn't I thought of that? Surely the cops had. I'd seen Curtis on the news myself. But who else was on that footage? Suddenly I wanted to know.

I wanted to know even more when I arrived home and found a note from Moses, taped to my door: the police had found Steel and picked him up again for questioning. Sometimes there's an ex-cop around when you need one.

CHAPTER 8

Jon Garfield, or Garf, Franny's friend, turned out to look nothing like a former president. For one thing, he was wearing an earring and a bandanna. He was tall, with long thick curly black hair pulled into a ponytail — a hairstyle not usually recommended for young men with receding hairlines. He wore wire-rimmed glasses, patched jeans, T-shirt, army surplus jacket, white sweat socks, and Birkenstocks. He talked a lot like Franny.

But the attribute that most appealed to me was his car, and by the time he showed up with it I would have handed my daughter over to Godzilla if he had owned a vehicle.

What kind of mother *is* she? you'll be saying. But I didn't want to be anyone's mother, of any kind; that was the whole point. When I had shipped Franny off to college — the first time — I thought I was retiring from motherhood and not a moment too soon. After all, I hadn't killed my children. I've never been investigated for child abuse. Any sins I'd committed would no doubt emerge someday in therapy, but until then I could breathe a sigh of relief and move on to activities far less taxing, debilitating, and demoralizing than motherhood.

I poured myself a gin and tonic and sat down at the kitchen table to contemplate the ID photos of Steve Sanders.

Moses had brought me a photocopy that the police had circulated when they were trying to identify him. In one picture they had put the cap and sunglasses on him, so he looked like a flasher. In the other one, he just looked like himself, I guess, only dead. Somewhere, Crosby, Stills, and Nash were singing about the long, long time before dawn.

Moses had found out that the Matthiases lived in Clermont County, though he'd indicated that if I started to harass them, he would deny ever having told me anything. I looked up some Clermont County numbers in the Cincinnati white pages, then looked up "Matthias." I found a "Matthias, Thom. and Linda" on State Route 48. I dialed the number.

A woman answered.

"Ms. Matthias?"

"Yes, who is this?" She sounded a little sharp.

"Ms. Matthias, my name is Catherine Caliban. I'm investigating the Sanders murder on behalf of a man whom the police suspect, and—"

"Look, I don't know why you're calling me, but my husband identified the body and that's all we know."

She hung up.

Maybe I needed to practice my persuasive style. I ran my index finger up the side of my glass and wrote in water on the Formica: "M-1, C-0." I dialed again.

"Look, whoever you are, you'd better stop badgering us. We—"

"I'm sorry, Ms. Matthias, I don't intend to badger you," I lied sweetly. "It's just that the police are trying to pin the murder on an innocent man, a homeless man at that. I'd so much appreciate any help you can give me." Code: *you're oppressing an oppressed person.* Luckily, I didn't have to introduce her to Steel.

There was a slight pause on the other end.

"What I'm telling you is that we have no help to offer, whether or not you are who you say you are. Neither one of us has seen Steve or heard from him for years, and we don't know anything about his death. Please don't call again or we'll have to inform the police."

She hung up.

Okay. She'd hung up on me twice and lied to me once. Moses's source in the PD said that the Matthiases had spoken to Steve on the phone from time to time.

I pushed "redial," just to see if it would work. I heard a ring on the other end. A male voice this time.

"Hi. This is the home of the Matthiases — Tom, Linda, Gwen, Bobby, Harmony, Malcolm, and Joanie. We can't come to the phone right now, but we really want to talk to you, so leave us your name and phone number and we'll get back to you as soon as we can. Have a nice day!"

"Hi," I said to the phone. "This is Catherine Caliban. I'm investigating the murder of Stephen Sanders on behalf of a suspect, a homeless man whom the police have questioned twice because he was near the scene of the murder. I'm trying to find out more about Sanders's involvement in the antiwar movement at Ohio State in the late 60s and I could really use your help. In fact, it would really make my day if I could talk to you about Sanders. I'm not a reporter, just someone concerned that a poor homeless man doesn't fall victim to a gross miscarriage of justice merely because of his poverty."

I spoke without taking a breath, afraid that the Matthiases had used up so much tape on their own names, I wouldn't have much left over for my message. I managed to recite my number and hung up. I left out the part about the poor homeless man having served in Vietnam, because I wasn't sure how they'd react.

Mel had brought me a number for the chair of the Central American Coalition, the group that had sponsored the rally. Mel moves in wider circles than I do, so her contacts were almost as good as Moses's in their own way. I mean, it goes without saying that if I ever want to throw a leftist lesbian potluck Tupperware party, Mel can supply the guest list. But she had other resources as well.

Another answering machine. I guessed the Back to Nature component of the Movement had been fully reincarnated in the technologically savvy environmentalism of the 80s.

Then I remembered that my own resident environmentalist had said something about going off to "do a mailing" at the Unitarian Church. That sounded political. Could it be connected to the Central American Coalition? I should have been listening more closely, but I found these days that I had reverted to a kind of automatic edit mode dredged up from my days as a mother.

St. John's Unitarian Church in Clifton has long been a center for political activity on the left. Some groups have office space or mailboxes there, and the congregation is always passing the plate for some worthy cause or other. It wouldn't surprise me to learn that the church was harboring Central American refugees in the basement. I hadn't been there for years but it used to be one of the regular stops on my circuit when I was trying to track down my wayward daughter.

Tonight on the left-hand side of the room as I walked in, I spotted my daughter sitting at a card table talking on the phone. Six other people, ranging in age from, say, sixteen to seventy, were lined up on either side of her, doing the same thing. On the floor to my right sat another twenty people, surrounded by paper. Perhaps ten other people were circulating, as if it were their job to add to the general confusion. In the background, faint beneath the buzz of voices, I heard music: Crosby, Stills, and Nash singing a Joni Mitchell song.

What I felt was a tap on the side of my head, followed by a blow to the kneecaps.

I looked down to see a Frisbee and a three-year-old on the floor at my feet.

The three-year-old had his face screwed up, as if he were thinking about crying. I did, too. So, being the older, more mature person, I swallowed it, smiled at the little demon, and picked him up.

"Boy! That would have been some catch!" I enthused.

"Oh, gee, I'm *so sorry*!" A young man rushed up, trailing three other kids of varying sizes. "I told them not to throw that thing in here. But my child-care partner couldn't come tonight, and I'm kind of overwhelmed. They told me I'd only have four kids to watch, but instead I have—"

He looked around in some confusion, counting.

"Wait. Where's Brittany?"

"She went to the bafroom," somebody volunteered.

"Nuh-uh. She went outside to play on the swings," somebody else countered.

My assailant had disappeared.

"Look, I'm fine, really. I can see you're—"

My child-care representative had disappeared.

"Hi, Mom!" Franny waved me over. "Want to stuff envelopes?"

"Actually, Fran, I came looking for anyone who might have known Sanders or could give me any more information about the rally."

She took a bite out of something that looked like a grubby foam disc. I think it was a rice cake.

"Why don't you ask Greg? Hey, Greg!" She shouted at a clump of people gathered around a computer terminal. "My mom wants to talk to you." That's my girl — two days in town and she's already on a first-name basis with the head of the most politically active group around. I'd be willing to bet that our telephone number was already being featured on half a dozen telephone trees.

Greg Gunderson was a short, slight guy with thinning blonde hair and beard and a genial smile. I went through my speech again about who I was and why I was interested in the case. He steered me toward a pair of antique folding chairs.

"You know Sanders?" I asked.

"No, the police asked me right away to come look at the body, but I'd never seen him before. Say, have you ever been to the morgue? Man!"

"So I assume none of the Coalition members knew him?"

"Just the Matthiases, as far as I know."

"The Matthiases are members of the Coalition?"

"Sure are. They do real good work for us. Of course, it's a long drive for them, but they come when they can."

"Did the Matthiases attend the rally on the 14th?"

"No, I don't remember seeing them. But we had a huge turnout, so I could have missed them."

"Do you think the murder was in any way connected to Coalition activities?"

"The police asked me that." He shook his head. "No, to be honest, we get our share of threats, but we don't pay much attention. Mostly it's some guy with a bee in his bonnet and a buzz on, calling up late at night to rant and rave about communism and patriotism."

"Is there anybody else here tonight that might be able to help me, do you think? Anybody, for example, who might've been at Ohio State and active in the late 60s?"

"Well, let me see." He surveyed the room. "There's Ann Fenstemeyer. You should talk to her. She was there. I think she even knew Sanders, though she didn't recognize him from the police photo. Come on, I'll introduce you."

My backside was more than ready to abandon the folding chair. My exaltation was premature, however, as I realized that to interview Ann, I would have to sit on the floor. I lowered myself ungracefully as Greg introduced me and told my joints and muscles to shut up.

Ann was a big-boned brunette with freckles and a broad smile. She was peeling address labels off of a sheet and slapping them onto postcards.

"Anybody offer you some tea?" she asked cordially as my butt made contact with hard wood. "I think we've got Citrus Surprise and Currant Chamomile."

"Thanks," I said. "The citrus one sounds nice." It also went with the gin I'd been drinking before I left home.

One of the circulating extras went off to get it for me.

CHAPTER 9

"What's going on here tonight?" I asked.

"We're working on our campaign to get Congress to reject the president's proposed contra aid package. The phone bank calls registered Democrats and tries to talk to them about the situation. And we're sending cards out, asking people to write their Congressional reps."

"That would be Dez Lewis, right? Isn't he already on your side?"

"Yes, but he needs to be able to say that he's acting at the urging of his constituents. And there are some other players involved as well."

"Did Lewis attend the rally?"

"Yes, he was there. Say, you want to work while we talk?" She looked at me expectantly.

"Sure, I guess so."

She gave me a stack of cards and one of those long strips of computerized labels, admonishing me to keep the cards in Zip Code order. I was beginning to worry that the task required math skills beyond my capacity.

"In some ways, it was like déjà vu — the rally, I mean. There was Dez up on the platform, just as fiery as ever, except we were all, what, fifteen, sixteen years older. And here we all were again, trying to prevent the government from getting involved in something just to keep the right-wing cowboys and defense contractors happy. It's like the song says about keeping the change. We blew it when we let Reagan get elected. But on the other hand, things aren't the same at all. We're all older and I hope we're wiser."

"Yeah, but some people don't get wise with age, they just get senile. Look at Reagan. Anyway, tell me about your involvement in the antiwar movement at OSU."

"Well, I joined the SDS in my freshman year — that would be 1965."

"Ah, those were the days," a guy sitting near us interrupted with a sigh. He had stray address labels stuck to his shirtsleeves.

"They weren't just working on Vietnam then, you know, but they'd staged the largest antiwar demo up to that point the previous spring. But that was the spring when King marched from Selma to Montgomery, and then Watts happened that next summer, so there was a lot going on. But I went to Washington to march in November, and Oglesby, the national president of SDS, was there."

"A prince of a fellow," put in our bestickered commentator. There was a sudden burst of laughter from the phone bank. Somebody must have gotten a live one.

"So that was 1965. Gradually, the SDS seemed to be moving toward supporting violent confrontation — at least, the OSU chapter did — and so I left and joined the SMC."

"Which was—?"

"Oh, sorry. The Student Mobilization Committee. And that's where I stayed till I graduated in '69. Meanwhile, there'd been this other collective formed, a splinter group from the SDS. It was really small and supposed to be kind of secret. I think the point was to keep it small so it could be secret. In fact, Dez Lewis was one of the founders."

"He was?"

"Yep. He was really active in the antiwar movement, you know. The Matthiases belonged — have you talked to them?"

I explained my communication problem with Linda Matthias and Ann nodded.

"Well, they learned in the movement not to trust anybody trying to get information."

"Ain't that the truth!" snorted our eavesdropper, slamming his fist down on his pile of cards.

"And, of course, if the papers get hold of that bombing thing — you know about that, right?"

I nodded. "More or less. Less, really, and looking for more."

"I don't really know much about it, because, like I said, I was already gone. I just know they were all framed and some of their friends did time for it. So you can see why they don't want to talk to anybody. It must've been hard for them even to decide to come forward and identify Sanders. Believe me, once you've been beaten or gassed by the forces of law and order, you don't want to have anything more to do with them. But they are really amazing people, the Matthiases. They've been active on peace and social change issues for a long time. More tea?"

I held my cup out, even though I thought it would have been improved by a shot of gin and an ice cube. A runner whisked it away.

"So did Sanders belong to this secret splinter group?"

"Yeah, but it wasn't secret like that. I mean, you knew who belonged and everything. You just weren't supposed to know what they did."

"Was that so they could, uh, engage in more violent activities?"

"Not violent ones, I don't think, just illegal ones. But in those days lots of crucial antiwar activities were illegal. Like helping resisters get to Canada. Or even advising people how to beat the draft, or maybe which doctor to see to get a medical exemption. And as far as the draft boards themselves were concerned, you could disrupt them without bombing them if you could steal their records. Now, of course, everything would be computerized, so if they start up a draft to send kids to Nicaragua, we'll just break into their computers and disable them with a virus."

"No shit?" I was taken aback. "Can you do that?"

"I can't, but we have computer wizards among us who can. Tom Matthias, for instance. Golly, half the teenage boys I know could do it."

"My son could do it," Mr. Stickers put in, "with his mouse tied behind his back."

"So Matthias and Sanders belonged to this group, and who else?"

"Well, Linda, of course, and Ginny. Only then they weren't Linda Matthias and Ginny Sanders. I forget what their names were. Talk about dumb!" She slapped one cheek and shook her head. "Us, I mean. The women of the left. Here we were, doing all the shitwork of organizing — typing the letters and flyers, making the coffee, keeping everything clean."

A man about my age leaned over and handed me a cup. "Careful, now, it's full."

"And in return we got to debate politics with the men, but when we disagreed on matters of policy or action, the discussion was over, and we'd get overruled and sent back to the kitchen. And in the end, some of us even married those jerks and changed our names!"

"You, too?"

"Sure! I told you I was a different person. PJ used to say that as soon as the war was over, she planned to start a revolution on the home front and she didn't just mean an economic one. 'When the workers rise up,' she said once after a few beers, 'we're gonna look around and realize there isn't a goddamn man among 'em.' Well, gosh, we were ripe for the feminist movement, but we were sure slow getting there."

"Who's PJ?"

"Oh, PJ — she was with AWOS from the beginning, that fall after Chicago." She pronounced it *ay-woss*.

"AWOS?" I echoed. It sounded like one of those high-tech radar systems they have on Stealth bombers — you know, the kind we pay billions for and it turns out they can't tell a MiG from a pig or a pigeon? Why the government ever sends men out shopping I will never know.

"Antiwar at Ohio State. But nobody ever called it that. They liked the idea that it sounded so close to AWOL, of course."

"So let me get this straight. This splinter group, AWOS, was formed the fall after the Democratic Convention in Chicago?"

"Yeah. It was Chicago, I think, that made some people say we had to work smarter, knowing just what we were up against. Well, here the cops had just rounded up the most famous activists they could find and charged them with conspiracy. I remember Dez Lewis said, 'Hell, if they're going to charge us with conspiracy and convict us of conspiracy, we might as well start conspiring!'"

"And he was the founder, Dez Lewis?"

"Probably the main one. But PJ was a founder, too."

"Wait — was she Phyllis Jeanette Silverman?"

"That's right. But she went by PJ. Dez was pretty cool with women. I mean, compared to most of the macho types we were surrounded with. He wasn't intimidated by women like PJ. You can bet the women turn out at the polls for him."

"Okay. So we've got this small splinter group, small for the purposes of conducting covert operations—"

"Well—"

"—Okay, sorry, secret activities. And already for members we've got Lewis, PJ, two Matthiases, and two Sanderses."

"That's six. Seems like they always had six, or that's what I remember. Of course, there were some fluctuations, too. Dez graduated in '69, when I did. So there must've been at least one other person, maybe more." She sighed. "The older you get, the harder it is to remember."

This was hardly news to me, proud holder of a Golden Buckeye card that could get me a shitload of discounts all over the state, if I could ever remember to use it.

"I don't suppose you have a yearbook from 1969, do you?"

She shook her head. "We counterculture types didn't go in for that sort of thing. We figured it was for people who wanted to remember battles on the gridiron, not in the streets, even though there was plenty of scarlet and gray in both places. But—" She smiled mischievously. "I have one from 1970. In fact, I have it here in the office. I was just showing it to somebody the other day."

"You do?" My little cat's ears pricked up.

She stood up in one graceful movement and maneuvered through the obstacle course of bodies and paper and left the room.

"You were right to come to Annie," Mr. Stickers advised me with a wink. "There's nothing she doesn't know about the antiwar movement, take it from me."

Ann returned, neatly sidestepping a tug-of-war between two kids who apparently wanted to read the same book. It was kind of heartening, really, to see a kid who cared enough about reading these days to fight over a book. Much less two kids.

"See, 1970 was the year they shut the place down. You know, after Kent State and all. Well, it started earlier, over the Cambodian invasion." She sat down next to me.

I felt a little dizzy, like I was suffering from a major memory lapse. I'd lived through the 60s, sure, and this stuff was all sounding vaguely familiar, but I was having a hard time dredging up anything I'd count as a clear memory. I resolved to cut back on the gin and took another sip of lukewarm herbal tea. Across the way, the book which had served as a bone of contention two minutes before lay abandoned, and the kid who had won the tug-of-war was pestering a little girl with a sucker.

Ann opened the yearbook across both of our laps.

"There's an index in the back, but you shouldn't be too disappointed if you don't find any names you recognize. The AWOS people tried to remain strictly low-profile, unlike some of the others who were competing to get their names on the evening news. But what makes this yearbook unique is the section on the strike. Here." She flipped to a well-thumbed page. "This is where it starts: April 24th. There's a rally in the Oval — that's this big green at the center of campus. They present a list of student demands to the administration and call for a strike on the 29th. So on the 29th at noon, the students walk out, and after that you get practically a blow-by-blow, hour-by-hour account. Fawcett — that was the president — he closed the University finally on May 6th, that's two days after Kent State, even though the place was crawling with National Guard troops by then. He reopened it on the 22nd, but on the 26th the students walked out again and he ended up closing it down for the rest of the year."

"So this was all because of the war?"

"No, not exactly. There were several issues, mostly related to student rights and racism. They were trying to get the University to fund a black studies curriculum—"

"So it wasn't the antiwar activists leading the strike?"

She opened her mouth to say something, then stopped, hands raised in midair.

"How can I explain this? It wasn't just one movement in those days. That's not what was going on. I mean, that wasn't what Chicago was about. It was racism and poverty and the war and government — all those things together. Individual groups worked on individual issues, but we saw it as all related."

She wore a look of concentration and her fingers flexed as she groped to translate 60s politics into the equivalent of "See Spot run."

"The antiwar movement and the Civil Rights Movement weren't the same movement, but they often acted in coalition. You see, the government was spending billions to fight this war overseas and the defense industries were getting richer, but the inner cities here at home were falling apart. And you didn't have to be a genius to figure out that the government was more interested in protecting rubber and oil interests in Southeast Asia and fattening up defense contractors at home than it was in solving the problems of the black ghettos.

"Meanwhile, the men who were most likely not to beat the draft and get sent to Vietnam were Black or Hispanic or Native American. And it was the young people who wanted a change, but we were fighting the military-industrial complex and the universities were part of that. OSU was making millions in defense-related research and development contracts — the Battelle Institute in particular. So the universities, *our* universities, had a vested interest in continuing the war, especially as long as the draft deferment for education protected their enrollments."

My head was beginning to throb. My system had been overloaded with information and herbal tea. I found myself longing for my gin.

"Well, here. You'll see it in the pictures." Her finger began to roam the page like a pointer on a Ouija board. "Like this one of a planning meeting for the spring Moratorium. This guy, he'd headed the Hall Defense Committee. Hall was a Biology instructor who was arrested and convicted for failing to register for the draft. This guy edited one of the alternative newspapers — I forget which one; they came and went and changed names all the time. This guy was head of the West Campus Students Association of All Mankind. They were working against housing discrimination.

"And then here's a picture of some SDS guerilla theater. Here's the president of the Student Mobe Committee, meeting with the head of the New Mobilization Committee, the Vietnam Moratorium Committee, and the Columbus Moratorium Committee."

I closed my eyes.

"The members of AWOS," I said. "Did they belong to any of these other groups, too?"

"Oh, I don't think so." She shook her head. "I guess some people were members of more than one group at a time, but you have to realize that there were political distinctions between all these groups. They weren't interchangeable. I mean, I guess it's hard to understand, but it was a big deal when the Student Mobe and the New Mobe agreed to work together on the Moratorium because they didn't see eye to eye. And AWOS — well, they were into their own thing."

Thank God, I thought. And there were only six of them. I was beginning to wonder how anybody found time to attend school and earn enough credits to graduate. If I met someone who'd done it, I'd bribe them to have a little heart-to-heart with my daughter.

"Can we look for AWOS members in the pictures?"

"Oh, sure," she said, and bent over the book.

Half an hour later, she'd marked six or seven more or less fuzzy pictures of Sanders and his future wife, Ginny; Matthias and his future wife, Linda; and PJ Silverman. And one more for good measure.

"Now here's somebody I'd really like to nail," she'd said, stabbing his face with an emphatic forefinger. "Dirty Bertie Baskam. Or Bertram Russell Baskam the Third, as his mother no doubt calls him. He was a sonofabitch then, as president of the neo-fascist Young Americans for Freedom, and he's a sonofabitch now, as a Cincinnati attorney with his eye on a federal judgeship. *And—*" She looked up at me and narrowed her eyes. "He was there that day. At Fountain Square. I saw him standing across the street, watching the demonstration."

CHAPTER 10

"Speaking of the demonstration," I said. "I suppose all the television stations sent camera crews that day."

"Yeah, but they're not going to let you look at their footage. They're real strict about that kind of stuff, don't ask me why. Seems to me any citizen should be able to file a request, have its legitimacy certified, and then be able to view their tapes. But it doesn't work that way. We shoot our own footage for our own archives."

"You do?"

A kid with a long blonde ponytail appeared behind Ann and gave her a bear hug.

"Mo-om, Peter's bugging me. He keeps getting my pile out of order, and he spilled grape juice on my labels."

"Well, tell him if he doesn't quit, you'll never ask him over to play World Peace again."

"World Peace?" I echoed.

"It's an alternative game for kids, all about peaceful conflict resolution. Nobody wins or loses. They love it."

"Okay," said the kid. "But if that doesn't work, can't I just brain him one?"

"Want to see our video footage of the rally?" her mother asked me, standing up.

"Hey, where you goin'?" Stickers wanted to know. "You were supposed to help me with the twenties!"

"Oh, put a sock in it!" she told him. To me she said, "That's just my ex-husband, Jeremy."

We made our way to a small room that served the group as an office. Taking up half the space was a video monitor and VCR on a stand. And to think that in the old days all you needed was a mimeograph machine.

She selected a tape from a nearby bookshelf and popped it in.

I've never been to a rally for anything, but I suspected it lost something in the translation to television. For one thing, the camera operator was none too steady, so the image wavered, kind of like a mirage. It could have conveyed excitement, I suppose, but instead it just made the whole business seem frenetic. There were lots of fast camera movements Franny started calling "swish pans" during the quarter she majored in film at USC. That must be because if you watched enough of them, you started to feel the contents of your stomach swish.

The image stopped dead in its tracks. It took me a minute to figure out that Ann had punched a button on the remote.

"There's Tom," she said, and pointed. "I didn't know he was there."

"Tom Matthias?" I leaned forward. According to my informant, Tom didn't know he was there, either.

"At least, I think it's Tom. It sure looks like him."

The man's head jerked and stopped then jerked and stopped again. He was turning to look at something.

"That's Tom, all right. You really should talk to Tom."

I sighed. Everybody told me what to do, but nobody told me how to do it. First, I had to get past the Dragon Lady.

"Do you see Linda?" I asked.

She shook her head.

I caught a glimpse of familiar-looking blonde hair, but it was gone before I could identify it. Hell, lots of folks I knew could have been there. As if to prove it, Curtis's face popped up in front of the camera again. What's that called — when someone has an instinct for where the camera is? Curtis had a career waiting in Hollywood. I even spotted Steel in the background a few times. He was limping a little, playing the wounded vet, not always on the same leg. He needed a continuity advisor.

She played it through several times and I got to see part of Dez Lewis's speech. But we didn't find anything else of particular interest and I suspected that Ann was beginning to get anxious about her address labels.

I left with the video and the book tucked under my arm. I had to make a food run on the way home, so it was nearly eleven when I arrived. I let myself into Kevin's place and studied the control panel on his VCR. Sidney sauntered in to watch. He loves television, and he loves to watch his mother make a fool of herself as a neophyte venturing into advanced electronics. My own television was an old cabinet model that Fred picked out for our tenth anniversary, romantic devil that he was.

I found the only slot big enough for a video and shoved it in. It popped back out. I shoved it in, the machine shoved back. Sidney jumped up on top of the VCR for a closer look and got whacked on the nose by the tape. He pawed at the thing, spoiling for a fight, and I let him. I figured he probably knew what he was doing. Between the two of us, we finally got the damn thing to drop. I sat closer to the TV than I ever allowed my kids to sit and studied the screen.

I was ready for Tom Matthias this time. He was wearing jeans and a nice leather jacket. He was standing at the back of the crowd and I watched him turn his head again. I pushed reverse and watched him again. It looked to me as if he'd spotted something — or someone — but I couldn't read his expression. Surprise? Doubt? Interest? The blonde hair went past again and I reversed it. It belonged to a teenager. The camera had caught her for only a few seconds and then only the back of her head in a partial profile. She reminded me of Hope Smith. I suddenly remembered that Leon had thought he'd seen Hope at the rally, so this must be the mysterious

Hope Smith lookalike. After all, the world was full of skinny teenage girls with long blonde hair. Ann's daughter, for one.

I ran the tape past the "We Shall Overcome" finale, but I didn't spot anybody else who looked familiar. I found it interesting that we hadn't seen Steve Sanders. Maybe the cops were right: he'd been incognito and had avoided all cameras.

Sidney was snoozing on top of the VCR, purring in harmony with its hum, until the tape clicked and began to rewind. He awakened, jumped down, and looked at me hopefully.

"Sorry, Sid." I gave him a pat. "I don't have time for a wildlife video tonight. Ask Uncle Kevin to run it for you tomorrow." Sidney loves those videos of big cats stalking small furry or feathery creatures and will sit transfixed for hours, as if following his team in an athletic competition.

Why was I bothering with this case, anyway? If Moses was right, Steel wouldn't be indicted, much less tried and convicted, on the basis of the circumstantial case against him. On the one hand, I could use the investigative practice. On the other, I thought of myself as a busy woman. I had other things to do with my time. Such as—? Well, I had curtains to wash and a kitchen floor to wax. I had a dripping faucet to fix. I had letters of condolence from Fred's relatives that I hadn't answered yet, almost two years after his death. I had a paint-by-numbers kit of two kittens that my friend Mabel had given me last Christmas and I hadn't even opened color number one yet. I had all those monograms to pick out of all those hankies Franny had given me over the years.

The next day I called Dez Lewis's office and got a tentative appointment for Friday afternoon. With members of Congress, everything is tentative, from their schedules up to the federal budget, never mind the promises they make before they get elected. Then I drove to Columbus to track down copies of the *Columbus Dispatch* from the summer of 1970.

You could put one of the smaller Ohio counties inside the perimeter of the Ohio State University campus and have space left over for Pataskala, Ohio. A friendly young man with dreadlocks pointed out the library tower and I spent the next hour circling the campus, trying to get closer to it. Just when I thought I was about to bump into it, it would pop up over my right shoulder about half a mile away. I finally parked the beige bomber in the garage and started hiking. This was not a campus for the elderly.

It was a sunny day, mild for late April, with the promise of warmer days to come. The campus was crawling with people. Now, I'm as sociable as the next person, but to tell you the truth, I was feeling overwhelmed. I was also beginning to realize how so many different groups could have been in business around here in the late 60s and early 70s. Now, fifteen years later, the place was a smorgasbord of humanity: preppy types wearing alligators, medical types wearing lab coats, hippie types wearing torn jeans and the lingering scent of incense, Black and white kids wearing African caps and colors, Indian men wearing turbans, administrative types wearing suits and heels, secretaries dressed like administrative types, graduate students wearing looks of concentration and the lines and shadows of advanced exhaustion. As I approached the tower, I passed a pond to my right. Dozens of people sprawled on its grassy banks, ducks glided across its surface.

Lucky for me, I am not intimidated by libraries. Because if I were susceptible to intimidation, this library would have intimidated me. But the way I figure it, my tax money supports this library just like it supports most of the libraries I frequent. So, what the hell?

Anyway, I didn't even have to ask where to find the newspapers because the sign was staring me in the face as soon as I walked in the door. And with all my vast experience, I didn't have to ask how to run the microfilm readers. I pulled the *Dispatch* and the Ohio State newspaper, *The Lantern*, for the summer of 1970 and went to work.

As in Cincinnati, the first *Dispatch* story appeared on July 15th, only this time with close-ups of all four of the people arrested. Tom Matthias had dark eyes and medium-dark hair, worn long and on the stringy side, and a full beard and mustache. There was a distinctive peak in his hairline and his ears were rather prominent. Linda Genovese Matthias, who'd recently married him, according to the story, had dark eyes and lighter hair, but in newsprint it was hard to peg as either light brown or dark blonde. She wore it in a braid. She had rather prominent cheekbones and appeared to have flawless skin, untouched by makeup. Michael McCafferty sported a head of long, thick, dark hair, but his face was clean-shaven. His eyes were light in color, their anger and defiance coming across even in newsprint, and his face was fuller than Matthias's. He wore a bandanna tied around his head. And the final defendant, mystery woman Phyllis Jeanette Silverman, was a striking brunette, with dark hair something like McCafferty's and dark eyes.

The four were charged with planting a bomb on the site of a local draft board on the evening of July 13th — a bomb that had been found and deactivated after the police had received an anonymous tip. The cops obviously weren't giving the press much to write about, so much of the story was devoted to the defendants and their antiwar activities. Even this subject had proven pretty resistant to the *Dispatch* reporter's efforts, since even AWOS's alleged activities were vague. "They're *real* passionate about the war," one friend was quoted as saying, "but I don't see them hurting anyone. I mean, it's not like they're really into nonviolence the way some groups are, but still — a bomb! That's just too heavy for them." "It's not their scene," said another, angrier informant. "It's just not their scene, man. They were trying to protect people from the violence of the f — war that the f — government is waging on the people of Vietnam and the people of America, so why would they be doing something violent?"

Other than that, I found out how old they were — all between nineteen and twenty-six — and where they were from. Tom and Linda Matthias had attended the same high school in Cleveland. Michael, who went by Mickey, was from

Cincinnati, and Phyllis, who went by PJ, was from Dayton. The article mentioned two former members of the group, Steven Sanders and Virginia Sasinowski Sanders, who now lived in Rochester. They had not been charged in the case.

I followed the story through the next several months. Bail had been set at one hundred thousand dollars for McCafferty and Silverman, and at fifty thousand dollars each for the Matthiases. Family members paid bail for all but McCafferty. At first, the three who were out on bail appeared at rallies in their behalf. Then, three weeks later, Silverman had disappeared in a stunning escape that had left the FBI baffled. As the days dragged into weeks, it became clear that the trail had gone cold: Silverman was officially underground.

On January 5th, 1971, a front-page headline told me that McCafferty had been convicted of the bombing; on January 9th, he had been sentenced to thirty years.

I read on, skipping sports, entertainment, ads for used cars, and Dear Abby. Where the hell was the follow-up report on the Matthiases? At first, they seem to have vanished as effectively as Silverman. Then I found it on January 17th, page three: all charges had been dropped. The federal prosecutor cited a lack of sufficient credible evidence to ensure a successful prosecution. He wanted to save the public the expense of a long and probably fruitless trial.

Since when? I thought. I never met a prosecutor yet who was overly scrupulous with my tax dollars. Okay, I never met a prosecutor, but I had never read about one like this. A sensational trial is to a prosecutor as a whiskey-stained piano is to a lounge singer or a photo-op to an aspiring politician. Even if you lost, you got to appear on the television screen every night for two weeks. Hell, he hadn't even charged them with the bombing, for chrissake; the charge was conspiracy. Any prosecutor who couldn't get a conviction on conspiracy, given the circumstances, ought to turn in his monogrammed leather briefcase. He hadn't plea-bargained; he hadn't done shit. I smelled a rat as big as J. Edgar Hoover's telephone bill.

Tom Matthias sounded pissed off. "I challenge them to try us!" he was quoted as saying. "Of course, there's no evidence, but that didn't stop them in Mickey's case!" I wondered what was behind the outrage. Annoyance, perhaps, that McCafferty had been the chosen martyr, not him? Righteous indignation that his name had been smeared and never cleared? Linda Matthias's response had not been recorded.

I read on through another six months, scanning every mention of antiwar protests until my eyes felt like burnt-out light bulbs. I caught two references to Silverman: both reported her as still missing.

I punched rewind in annoyance. Heads swung around as the machine screamed and I flushed guiltily, realizing that I'd violated one of the cardinal rules of microform etiquette. I let up on the button, and the scream dropped to a hum before giving one final snap. My fingers fumbled with the little string that goes around the reel and again with the box that the reel was supposed to fit into. I'd known I'd need manual dexterity to take up detective work, but I hadn't thought of it as a prerequisite for library research.

My eyes and my posterior lobbied to call it a day as far as the Microform Reading Room was concerned, but I knew that if I were a serious researcher, I'd unwind and rewind my way through another few miles of grainy black-and-white film. I compromised: I took myself out to lunch. In the bright spring sunshine, the cavernous chill of the library receded. A street vendor's hot dog improved my mood and I sat down on a bench to contemplate the Oval.

I tried to imagine it back in the late 60s teeming with angry radical types — tried to envision the SDS-sponsored guerrilla theater, the teach-ins, the be-ins, the Yippie iconoclasm that had preceded a decade and a half of Yuppie conformity, tried to reconstruct a time when half the campus didn't even care if the Buckeyes went to the Rose Bowl. I conjured up five thousand National Guard troops confronting four thousand students two weeks before Kent State.

But like I said, my memories of that time are pretty hazy. Franny says that after Kent State we curtailed her activities. Actually, the way she puts it, her father metamorphosed into a cross between a Gestapo commander and a CIA operative and threatened to confiscate her magic markers and Birkenstocks. Me, I have a vague memory that Fred flipped out at one point and proposed we check her into a Catholic boarding school in Maine, but I don't even remember when that happened. I do recall that for her fourteenth birthday we had a phone jack installed in her room, but by her fifteenth birthday, she was accusing her father of using it to monitor her calls. She was right, too. By the time the National Guard fired on the protesters at Kent State, Jason, her nearest sibling, was already safely out of business school and well into ruining his first marriage. Sharon, my oldest, was exploiting the war boom, according to Franny, profiting from the stock sales that fueled the military-industrial complex. They didn't speak for years, but Franny wasted a portion of her allowance sending propaganda to her sister.

Hell, I thought, I should have paid more attention. But I had been worn out with the effort to keep Fred and Franny from saying the kind of thing that caused permanent estrangement at best, and at worst those headlines about family tragedy. When you thought about it, I'd pulled off a goddamn miracle getting Franny to attend Fred's funeral in tears rather than picketing it in Birkies.

CHAPTER 11

Those detectives you see on television are always cruising around in their Trans-Ams, trailing suspects into bars and discos, muttering in code on their CBs, crashing around in heavy traffic areas on high-speed chases, blasting away with their semiautomatics. They bitch about the boredom of stake-outs, most of which last only as long as a commercial break, and congratulate themselves on their legwork.

Take it from me, legwork is a pool party compared to the eyework and buttwork of library research in the Microform Reading Room. Could it be that these macho masters of crime wimp out when it comes to serious detective work and send some underpaid woman staff member to do their research for them? Me, that's what I think, and I'd bet my Frigidaire on it.

So I spent another two hours squinting at back issues of the OSU *Lantern*, and then a motley collection of issues of papers called things like *Forum*, *UF*, *The People*, *Yes*, and *You-Niversity Press*. These last papers must have been the kind of thing Franny had in mind when she talked about the alternative press. Most of them seemed to be badly mimeographed and they ran to explosive headlines like "Travesty of Justice: Green Fired." Objectivity was clearly not the name of the game. But when I finished, I had a clearer picture of the last days of AWOS.

In fact, between the *Lantern* and a couple of alternative papers, I now knew in some detail about the evidence in the case against McCafferty and Silverman. I knew, for example, that the bomb found had contained some materials which had come from the basement of the house where all the AWOS members lived. I knew, too, that McCafferty and Silverman had accused the FBI and Bureau of Alcohol, Tobacco, and Firearms of stealing these materials and planting the bomb to frame them. Traces of gunpowder matching the powder used in the bomb — this had been in that innocent, bygone era before plastic explosives — had been found on an old jacket of McCafferty's. McCafferty had pointed out that he'd been arrested in a July heat wave and would have had no reason to wear a jacket while building bombs in his basement. But what about the fiber found stuck to a screw, fiber that had been matched to the carpet in McCafferty's Volkswagen? Most significant, however, had been two pieces of evidence: a partial fingerprint on the inside of the pipe used to house the gunpowder and several strands of hair caught on the edge of a drawer in the desk under which the bomb had been placed. Both had been identified by FBI experts as Silverman's. And since McCafferty, not Silverman, had been AWOS's resident mechanic, he was presumed to have constructed the bomb for Silverman to plant.

Silverman had never gotten her day in court. But McCafferty's attorney had done his best to unravel the government case with reason. If McCafferty had built the bomb, why was it Silverman's print they found on the bomb itself? And why on the inside of the pipe, which was more likely to have been handled by the bomb's maker? Clearly, the maker had taken the precaution of wearing gloves. Why would he have allowed anyone else to handle the components without gloves? The FBI conjured up a picture of two radicals, heads bent over their work, a kind of surgeon-and-nurse scenario plagiarized from *General Hospital*, with McCafferty barking orders and Silverman handing him instruments. I had to admit, I preferred the alternative scenario presented by the defense: the FBI looking to secure the case against both Silverman and McCafferty, and needing watertight evidence against Silverman, planting the fingerprint inside the pipe. I knew it could be done and I admired the subtle deviousness of it.

In fact, the whole case had the Bureau's fingerprints all over it, if you asked me: nothing too obvious, everything understated, but all of it adding up to a preponderance of evidence. A speck of gunpowder here, a fiber there, and an opportunity for a star-studded parade of experts to drag in their electron microscope photographs and their chromatography reports and their chemical analyses. By the time they were done testifying, they would have jargoned the jury into submission. Anybody this smart, the jurors would have said, must be right. Me, I wouldn't have bet a congressman's conscience on it. I hadn't sat through the Watergate hearings for nothing.

But where were they now, Silverman and McCafferty?

I realized that I was ideally situated to find out.

Some people specialize in tracing missing persons and they're not all listed under Private Investigators in the Yellow Pages. I was in a position to know. For ten years, not excluding this past one after I'd moved to Northside, I had received a Christmas card, booster calendar, and solicitation letter from a college Franny had attended for only one semester — a college from which she had parted on less than amicable terms. If you think hope springs eternal in your business, you have never met a college fundraiser.

So I ambled over to the reference desk and asked about the fundraising network at Ohio State. A librarian with the gleam of a library endowment in his eye answered all my questions and provided me with a copy of the campus directory. I turned down a tour of the CD-ROM terminals, which sounded like a hospital wing but turned out to be a covey of computers, and beat a retreat.

I considered calling Franny for advice. She'd lived and worked for so long inside universities she was a genius at manipulating their internal mechanisms. But I decided to trust my instincts.

"Hi! This is Catherine Caliban, in Career Development? Who's this?"

"This is Grace."

"Hi, Grace. Listen, I'm trying to track down current addresses on a couple of alums. You think you can find them for me?"

"Why don't you just call it up on the VAX?"

The vax? What the hell did my Electrolux have to do with the price of potatoes? I faked a sneeze.

"Sorry. What did you say?"

"The VAX. Why don't you use your PC?"

Why do I always have a suspicion that when people start speaking a foreign language around me, it has something to do with computers?

"Listen, to tell you the truth, I'm a new temp in this office. My supervisor asked me to get these addresses but she didn't tell me how to do it."

"They haven't explained about the VAX?" She sounded disapproving.

"Well, I think they expect the person I'm replacing to be back by the end of the week."

I crossed my fingers. I'd looked up the Alumni Office on the map in the front of the phone directory and found a likely office at some distance from it to identify myself with. The campus was huge, I'd reasoned. What were the chances that staff members who worked in nonadjacent buildings knew each other? With my luck, I'd just struck the president of the staff association. If she asked me who I was replacing, I was in trouble.

"Okay, I'll look them up." She gave a little sigh, just so I'd know it wasn't her job. "Give me their names and Social Security numbers."

Uh-oh.

"How about names and date of last registration? Will that do?"

So I gave her Silverman, McCafferty, Sanders, and Sasinowski and told her they'd last been registered in the spring of 1970.

"I've got a permanent for Silverman, maybe a mother or grandmother, nothing recent." She gave me an address in Dayton. For Sanders and Sasinowski, she gave me an address in Rochester.

"You got a permanent on Sanders?" I asked. I was getting into my character. "Mother in Cleveland?"

"Yeah." She gave me an address.

But she saved the biggest surprise for last.

"Okay. Here's an LKA for McCafferty."

It wasn't a federal penitentiary. It was an address in rural Hamilton County — not too far from Linda and Tom Matthias, not an hour away from the Fountain Square Parking Garage.

CHAPTER 12

That night I made two phone calls. The first was to Silverman's address in Dayton. I'd wangled the phone numbers from my pal Grace, saying that I didn't know if my boss wanted them or not, but I'd better have them, just in case. You know how unreasonable bosses are, I was saying, and Grace had understood and passed them on without a murmur.

The party on the other end was elderly and cranky. Maybe she was cranky because she was elderly, but maybe not. I ought to know.

I explained that I was looking for Phyllis Jeanette Silverman because an old friend of hers had been murdered in Cincinnati and I was investigating his death. This news did nothing to cheer my listener.

"Well, I wouldn't know about that. Mrs. Silverman doesn't live here anymore. She moved to a nursing home four years ago." She had a hint of an accent — German or East European.

"And are you a member of the family?" I asked brightly.

"Mrs. Silverman is my sister-in-law, not that it's any business of yours."

Everybody's business is my business, that's my motto when I'm on a case.

"I wonder if you could be so kind as to tell me the name of the nursing home where Mrs. Silverman is living. Then I won't bother you anymore." A veiled threat: if you won't, I will.

"No, I couldn't be that kind, and if you bother me anymore, I'll call the cops. You've got no business to go harassing a poor old woman with murder investigations or any other kind of investigations. Let sleeping dogs lie, that's my advice to you, Missus Detective. This family has had enough investigations to last a lifetime, but I tell you one thing: we survived Poland under the Nazis and the SS, we can survive the U.S. of A. under the FBI, the CIA, and the IRS. I sleep with a gun under my pillow."

She slammed the phone down so hard that Sophie woke with a start and fell off the shelf where she'd been napping. Her tail swelled up like a porcupine under attack.

"Sorry, Soph." I patted her dazed head. "I hope that gun's a revolver with an empty chamber."

It was early days to start calling every nursing home in Dayton, so I dialed Mrs. Steven Sanders, Senior, instead. This one sounded much more susceptible to my charms. Of course, she also had a dead son to talk about.

I asked if I could drive up to see her the next day.

"Are you with the police?" she asked, puzzled.

"No, ma'am, I'm conducting a separate investigation on behalf of a homeless veteran whom the police have questioned. But I don't imagine you care who solves the crime, as long as somebody does, isn't that right?"

"I guess not." She paused. "You're not FBI?" she asked, with the kind of weary resignation that said she didn't expect me to tell her anything if I were.

"Certainly not!" I said crisply.

"Well, I don't know why anybody else would want to drive all the way up here. The Cincinnati police haven't volunteered. But I guess if you want to come, come on ahead. If you're FBI, I can't stop you anyhow."

I can't say that I wanted to drive all the way up there, either, but I preferred my interviews face-to-face. Plus, there might be other things I wanted from her — old photographs, for example. Blackmail material under the mattress. Refugees in the closet. Hell, I didn't know. But AWOS might be only part of the picture, and a small part at that.

Grace hadn't come up with a phone number for McCafferty and Ma Bell didn't have one, either. I tried the Matthiases again, just for fun, but the line was busy. So I was settling in for some mindless television, when I heard a crash from the basement.

Maybe loud nocturnal noises disturb you. Maybe they strike terror in your heart. But if you lived in a building with four other people, three cats, and a hyperactive beagle, you wouldn't think twice about anything short of a gunshot. And during walnut season, when the trees drop their fruit on the neighbors' tin-roofed garages, a gunshot wouldn't faze you, either. So I didn't react until I heard a muffled groan.

I snapped on the light in the hall and was headed for the basement door when the front doorbell rang. I paused, then answered the door. It was Curtis.

"Hey, Cat, how you doin'?"

"Fine, Curtis, how *you* doin'?"

"Fine, Cat, jus' fine."

"That's good." I waited.

"Now, Steel, he ain't doin' so good."

"No?"

"No, ma'am, he ain't doin' so good. Fact of the matter is, Cat, he down in your basement right now, layin' on the flo', which is where he landed after he tripped over one of them barbells.

"Now, I tole him not to do this here, but you know how he do, Cat. First, he got to come 'under the cover of darkness.' You know how he talk when he like this. Then, it ain't enough he already wearin' camouflage, he got to smear this black muck all over his face till he look like some kinda nightmare. But that ain't enough, he got to go break in your basement window 'stead of ringin' the do'bell like a normal person. I tell you, Cat, if he don't get hisself killed over this business, he gone drive me crazy."

"Well, let's go inspect the damage."

My intruder was already up and hobbling, to the delight of Winnie the beagle, who added her barks to his curses. My little watchcat Sidney was inspecting the broken lock on the window with curiosity.

"Damn, Cat, I fuckin' near killed myself on a fuckin' barbell. I think I broke my foot. What do you want to leave that crap lying around for?"

Shame was a commodity in short supply.

"I was testing my low-cost, low-maintenance security system," I said. "Looks like it works. And if you so much as mention the word 'lawsuit,' I'll call Mel down here to drop the other one on you. So get over it."

"That's right, Steel," Curtis put in. "This jungle warfare shit givin' me a headache, man. Now whyn't you take care o' your business with Cat, and then we can leave through the front door?"

"Front door, my ass. They probably got this house staked out."

"Back door, then. Any door, I don't care, so long as it got hinges and a handle."

"So, what's going down, Cat? Any news?"

"Yeah, plenty. It's just not coming together yet. I spent the day in Columbus, reading about AWOS — that's the antiwar group Sanders belonged to — and running down addresses. Tomorrow I'll see Sanders's mother. I want to find out more about other people in Sanders's life, especially more recently. I need to know what relationship he had to the anti-contra movement, if any. I need to rule out other possibilities. It's just that, so far, every time I pick a thread that unravels, one end is in AWOS and the other one in Cincinnati."

"So you thinkin' one of these AWOS folks snuffed this Sanders dude, Cat?" For all his complaining, Curtis loved a mystery as much as the next person.

"Maybe. Or maybe someone outside AWOS who's got a grudge against them. You ever heard of a Bertram Russell Baskam, Steel?"

"Nah, name don't mean nothin' to me." He rubbed his ankle gingerly.

"How about the other members? Phyllis Jeanette Silverman, Michael McCafferty? They're the ones who were indicted for a Columbus draft board bombing. Virginia Sasinowski?"

He shook his head. "Don't none of 'em ring a bell, Cat."

I studied his face. "You better not be bullshitting me."

"Yeah, like I broke in here and busted my foot just so's I could put something over on you, Cat. Give me a break."

"Say, Cat." Curtis frowned with concentration. "You think someone set Steel up? You know, framed him — like they done in that movie. You know the one. Got that mean-assed-lookin' white dude in it, at a ski resort in Colorado."

Never believe for a moment that the have-nots of the world don't keep tabs on the haves. You want to know what the haves have, just ask the have-nots.

"I don't know," I said doubtfully. "They would've had to act fast to set him up. It does bug me that they cut the man's throat, though. I mean, your average murderer would've stabbed him. So why cut his throat?"

"'Cause it's quick and it's silent, man." Steel's eyes glinted. "And it's surefire."

"He right about that, Cat," Curtis put in. "You don't got to go pokin' around countin' no ribs, nor eyeballin' the man to see where his heart at."

"But not everybody could do it."

"You mean, it couldn't be a woman?"

I withered him with a glance. "Get a grip, Curtis. The barbells belong to Mel."

"Yeah, but Mel use them martial arts, the kind where you pray and bow a lot, and she don't b'lieve in cuttin' on people."

"Could *you* do it?"

"Well—"

"See what I mean? Lots of people know the technique in principle, but not in practice. Besides, you've got to be willing, you know? So the question is, who would be willing *and* able?"

"Someone work at the slaughterhouse?"

For those of you unfamiliar with Cincinnati, this wasn't as silly a suggestion as it might seem. Cincinnati, once dubbed "Porkopolis," is a meatpacking center. Curtis had correctly noted that we had living in this town a higher than average share of folks who killed animals for a living — folks familiar with knives and not embarrassed to use them.

"Okay. Let's re-enact the crime. Say Curtis is Sanders and Steel wants to kill him. How's he do it?"

"I sneak up behind the sonofabitch, and then—" Steel grabbed Curtis and demonstrated.

"In an empty parking lot? He'll hear you coming."

"Not if they singin' and carryin' on overhead," Curtis argued. "Maybe I don't."

"We was trained to move quiet," Steel said sulkily.

"Okay. Maybe he doesn't hear. But you pull him into a corner where people don't usually go, right? I mean, it wasn't next to a parking space, where he was found. So why isn't he struggling? Moses says there was no sign of struggle."

"'Cause I got my knife at his throat." Again, Steel demonstrated.

"Yeah, Cat, and I'd be thinkin', man, this dude gonna take my wallet and split, if I jus' be cool." He demonstrated by going limp and Steel dropped him. "Hey!"

"Man, you didn't tell me you was going to do that! Sorry."

I gave Curtis a hand up.

"Okay, so we know it didn't happen that way. But let's try it if they talk first. Say I'm Sanders. And either I meet you by arrangement or you just follow me and call out my name. So I turn around, and—"

"How come I'm the one who's always playing the goddamn murderer, Cat? Curtis says I'm paranoid, but the cops ain't the only ones keep casting me in this role."

"Because you're the one trained to use the knife the way the murderer did, for chrissake. And since you're the one in the hot seat, I thought you might be willing to give me a little help while I'm busting my ass to save your skin. But hey, if it's too much for you, don't do me no favors!"

"All right," he grumbled. "I'm just sayin'—"

"So now we're face-to-face, and we talk. So how you gonna get me to turn around so's you can cut my throat?"

"It ain't that easy, Cat. I can't just turn you around from where I'm standing."

"Right. So—"

"He got to piss you off, right, Cat? And then you turn your back, and wham!"

"Right! And so far he's doing a pretty good job of pissing me off, so I say, 'Fuck off!'" I shouted the last two words at Steel, and turned on my heel.

"You sonofabitch!" He growled, stepped forward, and grabbed me, fist holding an imaginary knife at my throat.

I heard a crash behind me and Steel loosened his grip in astonishment.

"Mother, run!" I heard a voice shriek from the top of the basement stairs.

"Franny?" I looked up at her in surprise. "You home already?"

My daughter stood brandishing a fire extinguisher, a crazed look in her eyes. Behind her stood Garf, his earring glinting in the light from the kitchen, mouth open, eyes wide.

In a sweep of the room, he took us all in, frozen in place like we'd been caught stealing pumpkins.

"Nice to see you again, Miz Caliban," he said. "Later, Franny." And he beat a retreat.

CHAPTER 13

Sanders's mother lived in a house eerily like the suburban split-level I had occupied in my previous life as a housewife. She served coffee in a family room reminiscent of the one we'd had, only it didn't have Jason's gym shoes in the middle of the floor, or shreds of Sharon's pom-poms clinging to the upholstery, or Franny's propaganda scattered about.

The woman herself was a little too made up for my money and she hadn't yet reconciled herself to Loving Care instead of Lady Clairol. She was my age, with hair as black as mine was white, powdery pink cheeks, black eyes, and eyebrows drawn in by a Japanese calligrapher. She wore the kind of pastel-orange pantsuit that Sharon would have approved of, but all that black and orange had kind of an odd effect. I kept getting distracted by her pastel-orange nail polish, wondering how she'd found just the right shade instead of concentrating on who'd murdered her son.

I sipped my coffee slowly. I'd already discovered that one of the disadvantages of my line of work was that people were always offering you a drink, mostly nonalcoholic. One of those little nervous, yappy dogs that looks like a pointy eared possum on stilts was sniffing my ankles. Sadie could have taken him out in one swipe, and by the look on his face when he got a nose full of cat hair, he knew it.

I'd murmured my condolences with as much sympathy as I could muster, but it seemed to have gone over all right. I asked her if she had any theories about the case.

"Well, I don't know, it was such a shock. He'd been doing so well lately. And then, he was so optimistic all of a sudden. I know nobody wants to credit a mother's instincts and they'll just say it's spite on my part, but what else can I think? She was the only enemy he had." She shook her head to emphasize this last statement.

"She?"

"Ginny, I mean. You know about her, I assume. Why, the whole business was just shameful! Shameful! I guess I must be pretty naive, Mrs. Caliban, though I wouldn't have said so before. After all, I raised him myself after his father left me for that little gold-digger in his office. Nowadays, you hear so much about it, all that AIDS business and all. And I knew the kids were into all kinds of things then, but not that! And then to steal her own child! And I wouldn't ever see her again — me, her own grandmother!"

"Um, I think you need to fill in some of the details for me, Mrs. Sanders." I interrupted her before she could throw in another personal pronoun I couldn't identify.

"Why, Ginny! I'm talking about Ginny! Well, there are words for her kind, but I don't like to use them, of course. Well, you can imagine what it felt like to go everywhere — the grocery store, the bank, my bridge club — and know that everybody knew she'd left my son for—" She took a deep breath, as if steeling herself.

"A woman?" I ventured. I think the reference to AIDS tipped me off, not because it made sense, but because I was beginning to see how her mind worked.

She closed her eyes and exhaled. "Well, I could see how it was going to be at the wedding. Not exactly how it would turn out, of course. Nobody in their right mind would have imagined that! But anybody who wears blue denim to her own wedding — well, it was bad enough that she was pregnant at the time. But blue denim — I ask you!"

She wasn't asking me, actually, which was probably just as well, because I would have opened my mouth and stuck both Adidas in, pointing out that her son must have made some small contribution to the pregnancy.

"He'd always been so ambitious, too. That's what I couldn't get over. I never thought Ginny was much of a wife for an ambitious man. But what do mothers know?"

I let that one pass as well. My mother had thought Fred and I made a perfect couple.

"What was it your son did? What was his occupation?" I had decided to try to impose some kind of order on the interview.

"He sold insurance," she said. "He was very good at it. He made Salesman of the Year three years in a row and when he died, he was about to be made vice president."

Well, hell's bells, I guessed I'd have to check out all the damn runners-up for Insurance Salesman of the Year or VP. But who would have thought a former activist would be selling insurance in western New York? I mean, I guessed they were all doing something somewhere, but insurance?

"And you say he'd always been ambitious. In high school, do you mean?"

"Oh, yes. He was practically a straight-A student, and he was treasurer of the student council for two years running. He just had so many activities, I couldn't keep up. And then he worked at the Kingburger after school and on weekends. You see, I was divorced and we didn't have much money, and he needed the money for college. He got a scholarship and one of those government loans for college, but still — you know how hard it is."

"Were any of his high school activities political in nature?"

"No, they were just normal high school activities." That was an odd way to put it, but I knew what she meant. "That's why I was so surprised when he became involved with this

Vietnam business. We'd never even discussed the war, but I don't think he'd ever thought much about it until he went down to OSU. Well, if I'd known what kind of place it was going to be, I would have tried to talk him into going someplace else — maybe Bowling Green or the University of Cincinnati."

Kent State? I thought.

"Someplace less — political. But it was like anything else, once he got involved, he became a leader. Oh, I don't know. Now, sometimes I think maybe the kids were right — about Vietnam and all. It doesn't seem to have made much difference in the end — all that money and all those lives wasted over there. I know he tried to explain it to me. He was getting lots of useful experience, he said. Well, anyway, he met Ginny through that group, and oh, she was a mess! Not bad-looking, but she didn't make any effort to make herself attractive."

This from a woman clearly on a first-name basis with her Avon Lady. I reached for a Fig Newton on a nearby Melmac plate because it was the only thing edible in sight. Eating always helps me concentrate. It also keeps me from saying things that will get me into trouble.

"You know how they were in those days. She had this stringy long hair, falling all in her face, and these little wire-rimmed granny glasses. I never saw her in anything except blue jeans or those dresses that looked like potato sacks."

"Did Steve's appearance change in any way during this time?" Cat the cagey.

"Well, now, let me think. He did grow his hair out and, of course, he grew a beard and a mustache, but he kept them very neatly trimmed, I thought."

"And he'd worn a beard ever since?"

"Oh, no! In fact, I was very surprised to see he'd grown it out again because he hadn't said anything to me about it. No, I believe he shaved it off right after they moved to Rochester."

"Can you tell me about the scar on his face? Did he have that in college?"

"Oh, yes, he's had that since — let me see — sophomore year in high school. He was riding on the back of a motorcycle and the boy who was driving lost control. The other boy still has a limp, I believe."

"Okay. So he joined this group — AWOS, I think it was called. And who did he meet besides Ginny?"

"Well, there was Desmond Lewis — he's that congressman from Cincinnati, you know."

"So I hear."

"And there was another quiet boy for a while, a Jewish boy. I don't remember his name, but I liked him and he didn't stay too long. And then there were the two that got arrested."

"Michael McCafferty and PJ Silverman."

"Yes, now I don't mind telling you, I almost fainted when I saw that story on the news! I always knew that Mickey was a wild one, but to think how close Steven came to being mixed up in all that! Why, he could have been blown to smithereens!"

Instead of which — I took another bite of Fig Newton. The possum was lying by her feet; he had one eye closed and one eye glued to my cookie. "What did Steven tell you about that?"

"Well, I called him right up and asked him if he knew that those friends of his had been arrested. He'd been so surprised! He said he had no idea they'd been planning something like that! You see, he and Ginny graduated in June and got married — well, *he* graduated, seems to me Ginny didn't finish. And then they moved to Rochester. Well, it turns out they got out just in time!"

"You said that Mickey was wild. What gave you that impression?"

"Oh, well, you could just look at him and see it. He had this wild black hair sticking out all over the place and these crazy eyes." Her own eyebrows plunged dramatically, knocking a fine shower of mascara off of her lashes. "You could just tell he might do anything! And the language he used! Well, the language they all used, except for Steven!"

She closed her eyes again for dramatic effect and I munched my Fig Newton.

"And PJ? What was she like?"

"Well, she was just a spitfire. She was Jewish, too, you know. I believe her grandmother had a lot of money. It didn't surprise me to hear that she was mixed up in that bombing. But, to be fair, she could be charming when she wanted to be and she could be very funny. That sounds like an odd combination, I know, that angry intensity and humor, but I have to confess, she could make me laugh!"

"How about the Matthiases, Tom and Linda?"

"Now, I liked them. I never believed that they were involved in that bombing, though how it could go on in the house without their knowledge, I don't know. Tom was real polite and Linda was sweet. I always thought she kind of held things together. Of course, they weren't married at the time. Not when I knew them."

"It sounds like they all lived in the same house, is that right?"

"Let me see. The boys lived together at first, and I believe PJ lived with them — in her own room, of course. I don't really know when Linda and Ginny moved in. Steven kept that pretty quiet, as I'm sure you can imagine. Well, when I realized, I tried to talk to him about it, but he said he and Ginny were getting married anyway, and you know they never listen to their mothers. I've never really gotten used to these new attitudes toward marriage, Mrs. Caliban, have you? I worked hard at my first marriage, but just because it didn't work, I didn't give up on the whole institution! And when my second husband came along, why, he shared my belief in the importance of marriage."

I wasn't going to comment. After Fred died, I become an abstainer myself. Anyway, she wasn't really talking about marriage, she was talking about sex, and I seriously doubted whether we were going to see eye to eye on that subject.

"Did Steve become involved in the McCafferty trial at all?"

"No, he had the new house and job and baby and all, so he was really too busy. And, as I say, he was pretty shocked about the whole thing. I believe he sent Mickey some money, though."

"Did he know what had become of PJ Silverman?"

"You mean, when she disappeared, or later? Well, he heard she disappeared, of course, but he didn't know anything about that. I mean, he didn't know where she was and never heard from her, though he told me if he did he would advise her to go back. And then, he was very upset by her death."

"Her death?" I squeaked. A crumb hit the carpet and the possum caught it on the first bounce.

"Didn't you know? Steven thought it was so sad, the way she died out in that little house — really a shack from what they said — all alone. The gas lines were so old and there was some kind of explosion and fire."

"When did this happen?"

"Let me see — I believe it was 1975. I seem to remember that it happened around Hayley's birthday."

"Where did it happen?"

"Somewhere in Athens County. That's all I know."

"Did Steven keep up with his other friends from the movement — I mean, from AWOS?"

"You know, that police detective asked me that. I can't really say for sure. He heard about PJ's death, and he'd been real close to Tom Matthias, but you know how it is when you've got a new job and a baby. Then later on, when Ginny left, I think it kind of put a strain on relations, the way divorces sometimes do."

Ideas fluttered around my head like fireflies.

"Tell me about what happened when Ginny left."

"Well, it all began when she decided to go back to school — that's what Steven said. She started taking classes at the University of Rochester. Hayley was in kindergarten — that's my granddaughter. And that's when Steven noticed a change in her. She was taking some kind of feminist class, I think.

Well, you know what that can lead to! First thing you know, why, she's all dissatisfied with everything — Steve, the baby, housework, and I don't know what-all. So I guess they started fighting a lot. I thought maybe, since Ginny's own mother didn't seem very interested, I should try to give her a little advice, you know. But these days, nobody wants to listen to a mother, much less a mother-in-law.

"Then one day, when Hayley was nine, Steven found out about this woman Ginny had been — well, *seeing*, you know. And they had this terrible argument, and then next day when Steven got home from work, Ginny had left and taken Hayley with her. And he never heard from her again! Just — sometimes — he'd get a card or a phone call from Hayley." Her voice quavered. "And sometimes, on my birthday or Christmas, I'd get a call, too. Well, I guess it only happened maybe three times in all these years."

The possum was camped out on my foot, waiting for another breach of etiquette on my part.

"Did he try to trace them?"

"Of course, he did! But it's expensive, you know, Mrs. Caliban, though my husband was very generous with Steven. I guess I never realized how easy it is to just disappear without a trace. The postmarks on the cards were always from big cities, mostly New York or Boston or Chicago. The detectives seem to think maybe she got other people to mail them, people who were going to those places.

"We'd never given up hope of finding them. It broke my heart, Mrs. Caliban, to think of my granddaughter living that kind of life! Steven always said that if we got her back, Hayley could come to live with me and I've kept a room ready for her all these years. She's fifteen years old now — can you imagine? But who knows how her mother has corrupted her!

"The hard part is — Steven was getting close. He told me so the week before he died. The last time I spoke to him, why, he was so happy and confident! 'Air out that room, Mother,' he told me. 'I should have a surprise for you soon now.' Oh,

I got a surprise, all right!" Tears were painting little mascara trails down her cheeks. "I got the surprise of my life!"

On my way home, I passed the exit that would have taken me to Akron and Kent. Much as she had tried my patience in close quarters, at least I still *had* my daughter, I thought.

On the radio the boys sang an a cappella score for my mental movie, asking me what I would have done, what I would do now.

CHAPTER 14

I opened the refrigerator door and stepped back in horror. Maybe I was in the wrong refrigerator, in the wrong house, in the wrong dimension.

"Your co-op order came, Mrs. C." Kevin popped his head in the door.

"Not my co-op order. I think I got the Dalai Lama's by mistake. What is this crap?"

I tentatively poked a pale, spongy cube wrapped in cellophane. Kevin looked over my shoulder.

"I think that's tofu. Is it in between the organic wheat germ and the seaweed?"

"Who are we expecting for dinner? Charlie the Tuna and his Japanese cousin? This stuff looks like mold."

I picked up another package and squinted at it in disgust.

"Well, you're not far wrong."

"Shit, Kevin, if I want mold in my refrigerator, I can grow my own. It's bad enough that the Beano is edging out the pina colada mix on the pantry shelf. Stand aside!"

I was taking aim at the garbage can when my eyes fell on the kitties' bowls. I crossed the kitchen and swooped down on one. It held a congealed mass in which orange and green predominated.

"Now, don't worry, Mrs. C. They're all right. I fed them some leftover sole when I got up and they were perfectly happy."

"Kevin, this extended motherhood is driving me crazy. It's not natural for mother and daughter to live in the same house at our age! What am I going to do? I'm a desperate woman."

The phone rang.

"Is Fran there? Oh, well, this is Tammy, her contact on the CAC telephone tree? Would you please tell her there's a meeting at the Unitarian Church at seven-thirty tomorrow, and she should bring markers and poster board? Oh, and she should call all the twigs on her branch. Thanks!"

"Kevin—"

"Now, Mrs. C, you just need to get your mind off your troubles. Tell me how the investigation is going."

"Terrible! I've got too goddamn much information and my brain has shut down! I haven't eaten red meat all week and my neurons are deteriorating." Okay, so a hot dog is red meat. I lied. Go ahead, turn me in to the Vegetarian Mafia.

"Now, now. They're probably just going through withdrawal in the absence of artificial hormones and additives and other toxic substances. What did you find out from Sanders's mother?"

"Well, skipping the makeup tips and censoring the homophobia, I found out one, that PJ Silverman died in an explosion and fire in Athens County in 1975. I have to check it out, but she's probably out of the running as a murder suspect, though not, perhaps, as a murder victim."

"Right. Explosions and fires are always suspicious."

"Two. Ginny Sanders, who never got her OSU degree, by the way, left Sanders for another woman, took their daughter, Hayley, with her, and disappeared in 1979."

"Knowing, no doubt, that she'd never be granted custody as a lesbian mother."

"Right. But according to her ex-mother-in-law, she was about to be found. Which is why Ginny is Mrs. Sanders's favorite suspect."

"Wait. Are you saying Sanders was in Cincinnati to look for Ginny?"

"Well, it looks that way. Either that, or he was going to see people in Cincinnati who knew where she was."

"The Matthiases, for example."

"Right." I went back to the refrigerator and started rummaging. I found some organic peanut butter with little puddles of oil on its surface and a beer. The beer looked like regular beer, so I popped the top and took a cautious swig. "Or McCafferty, who seems to live out in Newtown. Which may give us as many as four former AWOS members living in the greater Cincinnati area." Back behind the rice cakes in the pantry, I found some regular saltines, a little stale, and introduced them to the peanut butter. Not bad.

"A fifth member, Desmond Lewis, the congressman, is based in Cincinnati and attended the rally that day. I talk to him tomorrow, if I'm lucky. There was another member, but she can't remember his name."

Sidney showed up and started lobbying for peanut butter, so I smeared some on his paw. He sniffed at it like the master taster for Friskies.

"But you want to hear something funny? Everybody who knew them thought that Silverman and McCafferty were innocent, that they were framed. Everybody, that is, except Sanders, who told his mother how shocked he was to learn what they'd been up to."

"Well, but maybe that's just what he told his dear old mother."

"Maybe. But he didn't get involved in the trial at all. And after all, he and Ginny got out just in time. The others were arrested the very next month, for chrissake!"

"You think they were tipped off?"

"It looks suspicious, doesn't it? And how come they didn't come back and picket the courthouse and work the press and fundraise and all? I haven't been hanging around Franny all these years without picking up a thing or two. Activists don't just deactivate, unless they go underground, and the Sanderses weren't underground. The business about the new job and the baby is a load of crap. This isn't Ward and June Cleaver we're talking about. This is the Columbus Six, am I right?"

"You're right, Mrs. C. Kind of looks like they hung their friends out to dry, doesn't it?"

The doorbell rang. Standing in the hallway was a gypsy in dark glasses, with dramatic black-and-white streaked short hair and a woven basket slung over one shoulder.

"Mrs. Caliban? I'm Patty, from Patty's Natural Foods in Clifton? Your daughter Franny left her checkbook in the store earlier."

My daughter's pusher. I narrowed my eyes at her and contemplated the prospect of buying her off.

She was holding Franny's checkbook out to me.

"Thanks," said Kevin, who had come up behind me. "We are ever so grateful, aren't we, Mrs. C?"

He nudged me between the shoulder blades with his elbow. I cracked a smile like a death's head. "Thanks."

She went away and I turned back to Kevin.

"But then what if the bombing was a setup? Lots of people thought it was and we all know that Hoover's henchmen were capable of it. But why drop charges against the Matthiases? It would be one thing if the Matthiases were part of the setup, working undercover or something. But it was Sanders and Ginny who really got away."

"You think the Bureau bungled the job and just didn't come away with enough evidence against the Matthiases?"

"Well, I guess they screw up now and then, like everybody else. But it's hard to believe they would screw up so badly that two of their targets, much less four of their targets, got away. I mean, what was it about Silverman and McCafferty that made them so much more dangerous than the others?"

The phone rang.

"Hi, this is Brenda, Fran's yoga instructor? Will you please tell her that class is canceled tomorrow night because of the CAC meeting? Thanks a million!"

"I don't know, Mrs. C. Sounds pretty complicated. You get a picture of the pre-dead Sanders?"

"Sounds like you've been hanging around with those Operation Rescue bozos." I handed him the photographs I brought back from Cleveland, one with beard and one without.

The phone rang.

"Hello, um, is that Miz Caliban? My name is Pat McNaron and I'm with the People's News Service. I'm supposed to interview Franny about this commune in New Mexico? I thought maybe I could catch up with her at the CAC meeting tomorrow night, or else after the demo on Saturday. Would you tell her that, please? Hey, thanks! Have a great day!"

"Why do I feel like Joan Baez's social secretary?"

Kevin was squinting at the photographs of Sanders. "So do you think his friends wouldn't recognize him?" He looked up at me.

"I don't know. It's possible. With the beard, he looks like every other bearded guy you see."

"Not every. There's Garf. Anyway, his eyes are kind of interesting."

"Touché." Garf didn't look like anybody I'd ever seen. "Obviously, I need to talk to the Matthiases and McCafferty. So that's my next step. I'll have to go calling on the Matthiases and try to take them by surprise."

"Do I have the name of your bail bondsman? You going out there tonight?"

"No, I've done enough driving for one day." I yawned and stretched. "I'll go tomorrow night."

"You can't go tomorrow night, Mrs. C. You have a family dinner to attend."

"Oh, yeah," I grumbled. "I repressed it. The only thing I look forward to is the look on Sharon's face when Franny turns down her boeuf bourguignon. Say, Kevin—"

"Yes?"

"Got any refined sugar at your house?"

CHAPTER 15

Congressperson Desmond Lewis looked like a model for a jeans ad in *Rolling Stone*. He had blow-dried sandy hair, on the long side for Congress, I'd say, and contact lenses. When he smiled into your eyes and gripped your hand, you were supposed to forget that he had made you wait an hour and a half while he lunched with the mayor and opened a new Kroger store out on Reading Road. He almost did.

Lewis had a nicely furnished office in the Fifth-Third Bank building downtown — just over the Fountain Square Parking Garage, where I'd left the beige bomber. For those of you unfamiliar with the Queen City but familiar enough with fractions to wonder at this name, it was the inelegant result, no doubt negotiated by a committee, of a merger of the Fifth Bank and Third Bank. The outer office sported what appeared to be natural fiber rugs that had cost more than my car when it was new, couches and chairs in brightly colored corduroys, and artwork by some local artists I recognized. The inner office featured more of the same, in addition to an oak desk piled high with papers. On the wall across from me as I walked in were three shelves glimmering with Rookwood pottery.

At least, I assumed it was Rookwood. I didn't know much about antique pottery, but the exquisite colors, combined with the prominence of the display, convinced me that these pieces had to be products of Cincinnati's most famous art pottery.

"Do you collect, Mrs. Caliban?" Lewis asked, noting my curiosity.

I shook my head. "I collect small, rambunctious animals instead."

He nodded appreciatively. "One reason my pottery is here at the office."

"But I don't think I could afford it, anyway." Attack Cat. Start asking the tough questions — it catches them off guard.

"I know what you mean. Most of these were gifts from my mother. I once attended an auction with my checkbook in hand, but the bidding started at the price of my first campaign, so I resigned myself to being a spectator." He shrugged.

He had me thinking about his mother and her money.

"Lewis," I mused. "Is that Lewis Hardware?"

He grinned. "Lewis Funeral Home."

"No kidding!" I said. Maybe I could chat him up on the subject of rigor mortis. "Was that an asset or a liability when you ran for office?" I sat down on a comfortable sofa and he sank into the armchair opposite, then popped up immediately and felt around in the seat. He held up a Lego construction that looked like a psychedelic version of two nuclear reactors mating.

"My son Randy." He sat down again. "An asset or a liability? Well, it gave me name recognition, I suppose. My family had buried lots of people's friends and family over the years. On the other hand, the people who'd benefited most directly from our services weren't eligible to vote."

"Doesn't your family object if you joke about things like that?" I wondered.

He shrugged. "I get my best material from my dad. But I don't often use it in public. Now what can I do for you? Talk about Steve Sanders, right?"

"Please. Did you know him well?"

"Not too well. He wasn't part of the original group. We formed AWOS, PJ, Mickey, and I, in the fall of 1968, after Chicago."

"PJ Silverman and Mickey McCafferty?"

"That's right." He did one of those Kennedy things with his hair, brushing it back from his forehead. "And by the end of that fall — let's see — Ginny had joined, and Tom and Linda, too. That's Ginny Sasinowski, Tom Matthias, and Linda Genovese. Of course, Tom and Linda later married."

"Someone told me you always had six members. Is that right?"

He laughed. "Sometimes we had six. And then we said it was a rule: just six, no more, no less. But, hell, we were always making up rules and breaking them in those days. We had a secret code once, too, but it was too complicated, so nobody could remember it."

"So when did Sanders join?"

"He came in the spring — maybe April or May. After the Chicago Eight were indicted. Lennie Dwyer joined at about the same time."

"Dwyer?" I made a note. "But he was gone by the summer of 1970, right?"

"Yeah, don't know when he left, though. But he's here in town, so I guess you could ask him."

"He is?" Damn, I thought, retired conservatives moved to Florida and retired radicals moved to the Queen City. "How would I find him?"

"He's a lawyer now at one of the downtown firms. You can probably look him up in the Yellow Pages."

"So you graduated in '69, right?"

"That's right. Went to Washington to work for the Mobe."

"Some mobilization committee, right?"

"Yes, the Student Mobilization Committee, that's right."

I was confused. "But I thought that AWOS and the Mobe were two distinct groups? And from what I've been told, they didn't necessarily see eye to eye."

He shrugged. "No, but then, there were sometimes distinctions, too, between the national organization and the local campus chapters. I wanted to continue doing antiwar work. I couldn't get interested in anything else at the time. I agreed with enough of the Mobe's platform. I mean, that's the name of the game, right? Compromise."

He should know, I thought. But had that been the first step he had taken on the road to mainstream politics — Kroger openings and campaign barbecues? I wondered what his AWOS comrades had thought of his rise to political prominence. I decided that he might not be my most reliable source on that.

"So can you tell me what you know about Sanders?"

He started rolling his tie around his index finger as he considered. Endearing, I suppose, but a nervous habit? Was he nervous?

"He was an ambitious son of a gun. He came on strong, with lots of ideas. He impressed people."

"You?"

He smiled. "You're a cagey woman, Mrs. Caliban. Well, yes, I suppose you could say that I was impressed. And maybe some of the friction between us came out of jealousy — I was leaving and he was taking my place. Not that we had battles or anything, just civilized disagreements."

"Did you question the depth of his commitment to the cause?" I was remembering what Sanders's mother had said about how apolitical Sanders had been in high school.

He had unrolled his tie and now started on a new roll. "Hmm, did I? I suppose so, but it wasn't anything I could put my finger on. And after all, the group went on to do great things while he was there. So, like I said, maybe it was some kind of jealousy that he was replacing me. That's often the problem with these activist organizations, you know? The founders identify so strongly with them that their sense of who they are is all wrapped up in the organization. Ego starts to interfere with the common cause. That was certainly true in the antiwar movement. And there I was — graduating and leaving what had been the most exciting four years of my life. But, hell, I didn't own AWOS, nobody did. That's easier to say now than it was at twenty-one."

Thinking about past brushes with the PTA, Little League, and the band mothers' organization, I concluded that some people had trouble saying it at thirty-five and forty-five.

"You say the organization did great things. Exactly what was it that the organization did?"

He let go of his tie roll and did that Kennedy thing with his hair, giving me his most appealing smile.

"You know, Mrs. Caliban, if I didn't know better, I'd think you'd been sent by my political opponents to dig up some scandal on me."

That pissed me off. Here I was, just an aspiring detective trying to do my job, minding my own business, which involved poking my nose into everybody else's business.

"I was under the impression that your scandalous past as an antiwar activist was a matter of public record. It's the only reason my daughter maintains her voter registration in Hamilton County, so she can vote for you," I said coolly. "As for me, I don't think you know me at all. If you did, you would know that I am investigating a murder in which a friend of mine is implicated and your scandalous past interests me only so far as it connects with this murder, and otherwise, not at all."

Okay, so I lied again. I love scandal. It gives me something to talk to Kevin about.

"Hey, I'm sorry if I offended you. I apologize. And you're absolutely right: I haven't made any secret of my involvement in antiwar activities, including activities that were sometimes on the far side of the law. As for what I know about you, I wouldn't be talking as freely as I am if I hadn't asked around about you. Word is you're one tough — uh, woman — and you pick all the right causes."

"I pick cases, not causes." Actually, they picked me.

"That's what they said you'd say." He laughed. "But seriously, Mrs. Caliban, I'm trying to be as candid with you as

I can be. So I'll tell you what AWOS did. We helped draft resisters get to Canada if we couldn't help them get deferments. We served as part of an underground railroad for politicals — that's activists who had been charged with criminal activities. I'm not talking murder, now, but people like the Berrigans who were involved in what we considered legitimate protest."

"Not draft board bombings."

He blinked. "Not usually, no."

"And you worked independently of all the other groups?"

"Not entirely, no. We were part of a vast network. Many of the people we helped belonged to other groups with higher visibility."

"So you had a lot of experience in making people disappear. I presume that was helpful when McCafferty and Silverman were charged. But why didn't they both run?"

"They each made their own decision on that, or so I hear. I did talk to both of them after the arrest on more than one occasion. Mickey decided to stand his ground and fight and PJ decided not to. They were both legitimate decisions."

"And did you maintain contact with PJ after she disappeared?"

"That's *very* hard to do, Mrs. Caliban. Most people don't realize what it's like to go underground. There are spies and informants everywhere and you have to assume that anyone you were close to previously is being watched."

I did some watching of my own. "Tell me about PJ's death."

He frowned. "God, what a waste!" He paused a moment and looked out the window. "What I heard was that she was living out in this cabin in rural Athens County — no electricity, just gas for fuel and a well for water. No neighbors. Nobody really knew her, though she'd been seen in Athens a few times. There wasn't much left of the place after the fire, but I guess the cops didn't think there was much to burn in the first place. They decided that she'd been trying to light the gas stove and it malfunctioned."

I caught my breath.

"And exploded," I said.

His eyes met mine and he nodded.

There were two goddamn many explosions in this script — the one that didn't happen, and the one that did.

CHAPTER 16

As it turned out, I didn't do any investigative work until Sunday. I spent Friday night at that goddamn family dinner and Saturday recuperating from it. The only investigating I did was introspective: how had Fred ever managed to persuade me that I wanted to have kids?

Allow me to set the scene for you. Flushed from hours spent in close consultation with Julia Child, my older daughter, Sharon, is wearing an apron and pretending not to notice that Ben, her terrorist-in-training, has seized the opportunity of five minutes to himself and made Play-Doh cookies for dessert, leaving behind a trail of fluorescent crumbs ground into the carpet. Sharon has turned a deaf ear to all suggestions from her mother that killing the fatted calf would be an empty gesture given her sister's dietary proclivities, and the aroma of dead cow meat in wine sauce is curdling the expression on Franny's face. Frank, Sharon's husband, is openly sulking in a way that leads me to assume that Ben's five minutes of destruction occurred on his watch. After a hard week at work, he obviously thinks that five minutes of childcare constitutes an undue burden and wonders why they spent all that money on the Disney Channel if it couldn't keep one three-year-old enthralled for the duration of a single cartoon.

Jason, my middle child, appears similarly preoccupied; he doesn't see why his lovely but efficient wife, Corinne, made him wear a tie to a family dinner for Franny, who is wearing a T-shirt, no bra, an Indian print skirt, and sandals. Corinne, as usual, is looking determinedly cheerful in a Marimekko print dress which the baby has decorated with strained carrots. Her stepson, Jay, who is thirteen, is off in a corner playing with some kind of hand-held computer game. He is the only contented person in the room. His nine-year-old sister, Melissa, advertises in every line of her posture, every nuance of her sullen expression, and every utterance that leaves her lips that she is missing a once-in-a-lifetime MTV special on the hottest rock group in the solar system. Frank is mixing my drinks weak.

I am in for a long night.

The men retire to another room to discuss whatever it is men discuss when they are trying to avoid women. I sit down on the couch and try to distract Melissa from her misery.

"How's school, Melissa?"

"Okay."

"Whatcha been up to?"

"Nothing."

"Nothing? Well, what have you been studying in school?"

"I don't know."

Three strikes. Melissa goes off to bug her brother, who is, in her view, too happy when she is so miserable.

"So, Mother," Sharon says brightly. "I see where the police arrested several Northside men who were operating a child pornography ring."

This is a not-too-subtle dig at my neighborhood, which Sharon considers a training ground for *Miami Vice* types. I don't dignify it with an answer, but Franny does.

"How's your friend Julia, Sharon?" Julia has been married to a middle manager at Procter & Gamble, whom she has finally charged with assault and taken to court.

"She's doing pretty well, I guess," Sharon says. "They've taken the splint off her arm and she should be able to walk without crutches in another month."

"I hope she's in a support group," Franny says.

"Well," says Sharon. "I don't think everybody feels comfortable talking about their personal problems with a group of total strangers."

Why not? I wonder. I'd feel a hell of a lot more comfortable talking to a group of total strangers than to my children.

Sharon is back on her Florida kick.

"Franny, don't you think Mother should move to a condo in Florida? The weather would be so much easier on her at her age."

"Look, Sharon, I don't want to hear any more about any goddamn condo in goddamn Florida," I say before Franny can get a word in edgewise. "I'm not that keen on sunshine and citrus and I don't play dominoes or Bingo. I'm not going to spend the rest of my life sitting around on my ass, swapping medical emergency stories with a bunch of old farts. If you and Frank want a place to stay while you're whooping it up at Disney World, get your own goddamn condo."

"Yeah, Sharon," Franny chimed in. "And what makes you think Mom would ever consider moving to a state that's so politically backward? I mean, it's practically Neanderthal!"

You get the idea.

We sat down to dinner, and after a brief but thoroughly graceless grace muttered by the resentful Melissa, I looked down at my plate. Little chunks of pink meat swam in congealing wine sauce. I could practically hear them moo. I admit it: I lost my appetite. Worse: I felt the gin rising up in my stomach.

I focused my attention on my salad — normally the part of the meal I avoided.

Eventually, I got caught.

"Aren't you hungry, Mother? You aren't eating."

"I guess not, hon," I said weakly.

Franny looked at my plate, then shot me a glance. She smiled and said nothing.

Damn that kid! I was supposed to be influencing her, not the other way around.

A suspicious loud noise issued from the baby, who looked astonished. Melissa spilled milk on Jay's computer game. The ice cream inside the Baked Alaska melted and leaked out through a crack. And Ben serenaded us with Christmas carols.

I went home.

I felt so bad I didn't even register how strangely the cats were acting. Sadie, my little disaster barometer, was camped by the front door; she meowed loudly as soon as I crossed the threshold.

"Oh, God, Sades, turn it down," I moaned. "Mother is two meows away from a nervous collapse."

Sophie sat motionless in the middle of the kitchen floor, her body pointed toward the back of the building. Sidney sat, also motionless, on the windowsill that overlooks the parking lot and sometime basketball court, staring out at the darkness.

Franny wisely refrained from comment on my reaction to dinner.

"Poor Mom!" she said. "Why don't you sit down and put your feet up and I'll mix you a drink?"

A well-trained kid, when she remembered. If only she'd get her own apartment, I thought, maybe I could put up with her better. And, I added, as my eyes closed, her own refrigerator.

CHAPTER 17

Saturday I was hungover, in more ways than one, and the weather matched my mood — bleak and rainy. I spent a lot of time in my favorite chair, reading Sue Grafton and wondering whether there was any kind of underground railroad for mothers who wanted to disappear. I had visions of them sitting around in a circle in some church basement in Omaha, wearing polyester and jogging shoes, voices trembling with emotion: "Hi. I'm Emily, and I'm a motherhood survivor." They would probably pool what pitiful financial resources they had, converting their pennies into unmarked bills destined for a defense fund in Richmond, Virginia, where a mother was on trial for child abuse after shattering her kid's eardrum by secretly turning up the volume on his Walkman to teach him a lesson.

The phone disrupted my reverie.

"Mrs. Caliban? This is Ms. Radway, at General? We have your daughter Frances—"

General what? General Electric? Was she picketing them again?

"Pardon me?"

"I'm a nurse at University Hospital — formerly General? We have your daughter Frances here in the Emergency Department. She's been involved in a car accident, and—"

"A car accident?" So much for Mothers Anonymous; I was back on the job. "Is she all right?"

"She's conscious. We're treating the superficial injuries now, but we'll need to do X-rays and more tests—"

"Can I speak to her? Is she okay?" I could hear my voice squeak.

"We'd like you to come down, if you can."

Five minutes later, Moses was trying to calm me down as we headed out in his white Ford Fairlane.

"What if she's lost a lot of blood?" I wailed tearfully. "She's a vegetarian, Moses. What if she's anemic and the blood she has left isn't strong enough, or whatever?"

"Now, Cat, you know she ain't anemic. She's got too much energy to be anemic. And if she's lost blood, they'll give her a transfusion."

"A transfusion?" I squeaked. "A transfusion? What if she gets infected blood and develops AIDS or something!"

"Now, Cat, come on, now. You best stop imagining things that might go wrong. We'll know soon enough what kind of shape she's in. You know that girl's got a hard head — just like her mother."

Franny's hard head was wrapped in a bandage and lying on a pillow in a hospital bed when we saw it. She had an IV attached to one hand. Her eyes were open and she gave me a shaky smile when she saw me.

"Hi, Mom. Hi, Moses."

"Honey, what happened? Are you all right?" It was a stupid question, even stupider the third time around with the answer so obvious in front of me.

She rolled her head from side to side and glanced around. Then, raising her unencumbered hand she gestured feebly for us to come closer.

"The brakes failed," she whispered.

"Oh, Franny!" I looked at her, dismayed. "Is Garf all right?"

"Not on *Garf's* car, Mom. On *your* car. I took your car, don't you remember?"

I stared at her, aghast. "My car?" I echoed. Flooded with guilt, I searched my memory. "I guess it's due for a tune-up, but the brakes? I haven't had any trouble with the brakes!"

"Shhh, Mom, keep your voice down," she stage-whispered. "You never know who might be listening."

I glanced around in bewilderment. What did the orderlies care about my brakes?

"Don't you get it?" she demanded. "Somebody must've, like, cut your brake line or something. *You* were supposed to be lying here instead of me. Here — or the morgue."

"What! Fran, how hard did you hit your head?" To tell you the truth, she scared me. I was afraid the blow to her head had affected her whole personality. Maybe she had a different identity now — one of Charlie's Angels, say.

"Hold on," Moses cut in. "Franny might have a point. Tell us what happened, Fran."

"Hold on, yourself," I grumbled. "Franny, how bad are you hurt?"

"Not too bad, Mom, considering." She gave me a look. It occurred to me that she was not too badly injured to play the situation for all it was worth. I relaxed. A little.

"The doctor says I might have a mild concussion, so I'm waiting for X-rays. They also want to X-ray my spine. I mean, I don't have any, like, internal injuries or anything. I mean, my blood pressure's okay, so that's how they know I'm not bleeding internally."

"So now tell us what happened," Moses urged her.

"Well, I was going up to Colerain to buy poster board and I decided to go the back way on Kirby. And it was just after that, like, fork in the road where the stop sign is, you know? And I was trying to brake before this curve and I pushed the pedal all the way to the floor, and, like, pumped it even, and nothing happened! So I knew I didn't have any brakes at all, and I was having trouble on the curves and I didn't want to hit anybody, so I kind of picked, like, a soft spot in the side of the hill off to the right, and just kind of aimed the car at it. I felt the car skid, and then the impact. I was, like, trying to do this visualization thing, you know — where you imagine yourself someplace else doing something else — and I imagined that I was thrown into this really soft snow bank. The car's pretty messed up, though," she concluded abruptly.

"That's okay, Fran. I've been wanting a new one, anyway. Listen, I don't think you're supposed to be talking this much if you have a concussion."

Ten minutes later, as they were whisking her off for X-rays, her voice was trailing down the hall. "Mom! If you've still got Diane, you better take her with you from now on!"

Diane was my little .25-caliber automatic. She was cute as a button and, according to Kevin, about as deadly. Kevin had given her to me during my last case, with the caution that outwitting or outrunning my assailants would prove more successful than trying to outgun them with a Diane. She was the best he could do on short notice. Kevin seemed to think that my best bet was to cripple the wood-be thugs with laughter by pulling a Diane on them. I had assured them that it was all in the aim. There are some parts of the male anatomy that no man wants even a .25-caliber slug in.

Meanwhile, down in the hospital cafeteria, I was weeping into my cup of weak tea and questioning my choice of careers.

"I mean, I have to face facts, Moses. If I keep at it much longer, my whole family could be wiped out. Ben was kidnapped on my last case and now Franny's been hurt. And I'm not even counting the bozos who have taken potshots at me. And I'm not even *licensed*, for chrissake!"

"Now, Cat. You just upset. You got to do something with your life. What you going to do instead? Sell insurance? Be a librarian? Be an Avon Lady?"

"Well, they all seem safer options than the career path I'm on right now."

"That's just it. They're all safe, but you don't want safe. You had safe most of your life and you're bored with it. You just got to play smarter, that's all. Develop your sense of danger."

"Sense of danger?" I frowned in concentration.

"That's right. That's what keeps cops alive out on the street. That's what kept your friend Steel alive over there in Vietnam. You got to recognize that in your line of work the bad guys are going to go after you. They don't want the murder solved. And even the folks who haven't killed anybody yet don't want you poking around in their business. That's where your sense of danger comes in. You learn to watch your back."

"Yeah, but damn, Moses! Seems like my whole goddamn family has to develop this sense of danger! Ben and the baby are too little and I don't think Sharon's prepared."

"Well, you right about that, Cat. Families are the hard part. But in the meantime, you got an investigation under way and somebody out there just tried to kill you."

"You don't think I was just low on brake fluid?"

"Now, Cat, what have I been saying?"

"Right. Sense of danger. Right."

"Now, when did you last use your car?"

"Yesterday afternoon, when I went to see Dez Lewis."

"And you got back when?"

"Around four."

"And you didn't move it after that?"

"No, Jason insisted on picking us up to go to Sharon's." Why people think grannies like to be crammed into a car with kids is a mystery to me.

"And he picked you up when?"

"At six."

"Uh-huh. And I left at 6:30 for my lodge dinner. Kevin went to work at, say, four or five. And the girls?"

"They were out, too. I think they went to a concert, but they were gone by the time Jason came."

"So I got home at about 10:45 and you got home just after that. I know 'cause I heard you."

"Yeah, but Moses, does it have to be that complicated? I mean, you're making this sound like one of those Agatha

Christie train schedule things. Don't you think whoever it was just waited till we were asleep?"

"Well, if you don't want my help—"

"God dammit, Moses, don't pout! That's the last thing I need! Look, I apologize. We'll do it your way."

"I'm just trying to be methodical," he grumbled, his feathers still ruffled.

"Hey! You know what? I just thought of something. The cats were acting really strangely when we got home last night. Sadie was trying to tell me something, Sidney was watching the back of the building, and Sophie was crouched in the middle of the kitchen floor. I bet you're right, Moses. I bet the perp was there while we were all out. Maybe even still there when we got back!"

He looked mollified. "Come to think of it, Winnie was pretty excited last night, too, Cat."

"You know what else? Mickey McCafferty — the only member of AWOS to serve time over the bombing — was always described in the press as some kind of mechanical genius."

"Yeah, but I wouldn't jump to any conclusions, Cat. You don't need no PhD in auto mechanics to cut a brake line. A rat can do it."

"A rat *did* do it. And I'm gonna catch the sorry-assed bastard."

Franny, it turned out, was being kept overnight for observation because of the head injury. The X-rays didn't show any broken bones, but the doctor predicted some possible back and neck problems from the whiplash.

Meanwhile, I was planning to take my sense of danger on the road. All I needed was a set of wheels.

CHAPTER 18

Even with a bandage wrapped around her head, Franny had her mind on her work and threatened to break out of the hospital unless I represented her at the Central American Coalition demo that evening. Some right-wing group was holding a black-tie, hundred-dollar-a-plate dinner at the Westin to raise money for the Nicaraguan Contras. The speaker was some hotshot contra leader who had the CIA in his hip pocket, according to my daughter. He was also a fascist paramilitary swine who lived high off the hog in the U.S., eating and sleeping at luxury hotels all across America — also according to my daughter Franny.

I was a little more on top of the situation in Nicaragua than I had been with Vietnam. And given my age, I've been hearing dire predictions of commie infiltration and falling dominoes a hell of a lot longer than my daughter had. So far, I couldn't see that that much had come of it, except a couple of wars we didn't even win and a shitload of casualties on all sides, not to mention that the countries that everybody was fighting over got pretty much destroyed in the process. If it had been my kid killed in any of it, I would probably have bombed the fucking Pentagon by now.

Plus, I was concerned about the finances. I knew the president wanted some big congressional allocation for the so-called freedom fighters. But last time I looked, we had a whopping big deficit which, if dropped from a high-flying plane, would take out most of the Midwest. Any housewife will tell you that if your bank balance is minus four hundred, you don't go out shopping for a new refrigerator. Why this simple economic principle doesn't register with the president and Congress I don't know, except that so few of them have any experience with household management.

In short, I was willing to go down to the Westin and put in my two cents.

The rain had ended in midafternoon, and it had turned into one of those beautiful spring days which serve as preludes to summer. The temperature was in the upper seventies and a stiff breeze tugged at the multicolored flyers some people were passing out. A few gray clouds lingered on the northern horizon and overhead the sky was striped with the trails of two jets, heading home to Wright-Patterson Air Force Base in Dayton.

I had, at Franny's insistence, tried on one of her T-shirts; it featured a map of Central America being trampled by several men in fatigues and read: "It's ten o'clock — do you know where your Marines are?" But I'm a lot bigger than Franny up front, and on me, the map of Central America stretched out to look like Antarctica in a funhouse mirror. So I traded it for a cotton short-sleeve and some cotton blend trousers. I was wearing my Adidas in case there was trouble. Mel drove, which was an experience in itself, and I did the parallel parking. We also parked Diane in Mel's glove compartment; I didn't want to get arrested with an unregistered firearm for which I had no permit. That kind of thing might weaken my application for a PI license.

We followed the chanting voices and soon found ourselves on Fountain Square, across from the Westin. There was a lot of shouting going on, even though there wasn't anybody much to shout at. Most of the dinner guests were parking underground in the Fountain Square Garage and then taking the underground walkway to the Westin. I was willing to bet they were tripping all over their evening gowns in a rush to get past the scene of the crime. But the television cameras were out in force, so the crowd was playing to the cameras.

Speaking of cameras, I bumped into Mr. Television, Curtis, when I stepped back to avoid getting poked in the eye by a sign being wielded by a particularly enthusiastic demonstrator.

"Hey, Cat!"

"Hey, Curtis. You working?"

"No, ma'am. We demonstratin'."

He showed me his sign. On one side, it said: "Street People United Against Military Spending." On the other, it read: "How many plates could *we* buy for $100?"

"That's nice, Curtis," I said. "Catchy."

"Well, you know, Cat, since all this trouble come along for Steel, we've been talkin' about this Nicaragua business. Seems like the government just want to get they hands on folks' money to give away to some army overseas don't even belong to us. Charity begins at home, Bill say, and then he ax do we want to get involved. So we say, sure. Not Steel, though. He hiding out."

Bill McGann was the fearless organizer of Street People United.

"Come on, Curtis." Trish appeared at his elbow, tugging on his sleeve. "That contra guy's arriving in a big white limo. I got me some tomatoes left over from the market. I'ma go throw some at him. Hey, Cat!"

I followed them through the crowd, which had surged forward at the appearance of the white limousine. A man wearing a tuxedo emerged from the car, and turned, as another man clambered out. The second man looked Hispanic, and his dress uniform jacket was weighted down with some kind of military hardware I hoped I hadn't paid for. Two other men emerged and as they turned toward the hotel, pointedly ignoring the crowd, a gust of wind raced down the street and caught the first man's toupee, tossing it gleefully in the air like a cat with a mouse, and swept it into the streets.

My reflexes catapulted me into the street before I could think about it, I had recognized the man: hirsute or hairless, he was none other than Bertram Russell Baskam III, erstwhile leader of the Ohio State chapter of the Young Americans for Freedom.

I caught the hairpiece under my foot before it could blow away again. I was only vaguely aware of brakes squealing and horns honking.

I was across the street with my prize before you could say Daniel Ortega, to thunderous applause from my side. On the sidewalk, I stood my ground, and let him come to me.

Dirty Bertie was flushing to the roots of his thin reddish-brown hair. He had a thin face, too, and light brown eyes the color of baby poop, which he hid behind thick black-framed glasses.

"Mr. Baskam? I'm Catherine Caliban." I held out the hand that wasn't holding the toupee. "I'm looking into the murder of Steve Sanders."

"Is that so?" He gave me a limp hand and let it lie there until I got tired of holding it and turned it loose. "Well, I appreciate your assistance, Mrs. Caliban. And now, I'd like to return to my party." His voice had that kind of whine in it that some kids perfect in grade school and never get rid of.

"Well, I realize that, Mr. Baskam. The thing of it is—" I put one hand, the one holding the hairpiece, on my hip. "—I could use some assistance myself. I understand you knew Steve Sanders from your college days at Ohio State. You were on opposite sides during the Vietnam War, I understand."

"That was a long time ago, Mrs. Caliban. I doubt if I'd even recognize Sanders now. Now, if you'll—"

"Didn't you?"

"I beg your pardon?"

"Didn't you recognize Sanders when they ran his picture in the Cincinnati papers?"

"Obviously, I didn't or I would have come forward and identified him."

"And what did you think when you found out who it was?"

"I didn't think anything. What was I supposed to think?"

"But you were there the day it happened. Or rather, you were here — at Fountain Square."

"Yes, Mrs. Caliban, I was here, on this side of the street across from the Square. I never crossed the street. I had no desire to get any closer to the disturbance that was being made there. I have no desire to continue this conversation now." With that he reached over and snatched his hairpiece out of my grasp.

"And if those people are your friends," he continued, "you may tell them from me that they are making a shameful and embarrassing display of American discourtesy toward a distinguished foreign visitor."

"They're just young Americans, most of them," I countered, "exercising their freedom."

CHAPTER 19

In order to borrow Moses's car, I had to borrow Moses with it. So the next afternoon found us cruising around Clermont County in a white Ford Fairlane, with Moses behind the wheel and me in the navigator's seat. This arrangement was a mistake.

"We're coming to a fork. Which way?"

"What do you mean, a fork? I don't see a fork on the map."

"I mean a fork. A fork is a fork. Like the one we just passed."

"So what road are we on now?"

"How would I know that? Ain't no signs and I ain't the one holding the map."

"Are you sure you turned right back there where I told you to?"

"I turned the way you told me, Cat. I did everything just like you told me, only now we lost in the wilderness, coming up on another fork. You lucky I went to church this morning, got put in a charitable mood."

"You don't have forks in the goddamn wilderness. Pull over."

"I don't know how a woman could be married all those years and not know how to read a map," he grumbled, pulling into that oasis of the suburban wilderness, a Stop 'n' Go. "Didn't y'all go on family vacations?"

"Yeah, but we spent a lot of time being lost."

"I can believe that."

"It wasn't my fault, though. Fred never listened to me. Whatever I said, he'd do the opposite. So after a while, I stopped looking at the map. Seemed like our chances were just as good if I made it up. So I kind of got out of practice."

Moses took out his pen and marked the route on the map. We reviewed right and left, just to make sure that our definitions coincided, then set out again. We ended up turning off a rural road into a long driveway leading up to an old farmhouse, complete with a barn out back. We parked and tried the front door.

An attractive teenager with short-cropped blonde hair and green eyes answered the door, a Walkman attached to her head. She looked vaguely familiar. Had she also attended the demonstration on the 14th?

"Dad's out back," she told us.

"Gwen! I'm on the phone," I heard a woman's voice call as the door was closing.

A man was halfway to the house when we intercepted him. He had dark-brown eyes and medium-brown hair with a hairline receding from a widow's peak. He was clean-shaven and dressed in jeans and a T-shirt identical to the one I'd tried on the day before. It looked a lot better on him.

"Can I help you?"

"Mr. Matthias, I'm Catherine Caliban and this is my associate, Moses Fogg. We're looking into the murder of Steve Sanders. I'm representing a homeless man that the police have been questioning in connection with the murder. May we have a few minutes of your time?"

"Sure, I guess so." He didn't look alarmed or suspicious, just — what? Weary? Puzzled? "Do you have any identification? The press have been pretty pushy, you know."

Before I could speak, Moses whipped out his wallet and passed something to him.

"You're police?" He frowned.

"Retired. These days I work with Ms. Caliban on her private investigations."

He seemed to accept that and led us to a patio area, where we sat down. Moses took out a notepad, preparing to play his role as my sidekick.

"Nice place you got here," Moses observed. "How much acreage?"

"Just thirty," Tom said. "It's not really a working farm, we just grow enough to sell at the local farmers' market. I always wanted a farm, thought it would be a good place to raise kids. My wife's the farmer, though. She grew up on a farm, and so she has the know-how to manage the place."

"So I gather you don't make a living off the farm?" I tried to convey interest, not suspicion.

"No, I'm a computer consultant. I help out when I can, but unfortunately, I travel a lot. Linda and the kids do most of the work."

"Oh, right. You went out of town, I think, the day after Sanders was killed."

"That's right. I didn't see the news that night because I was busy getting work done that I needed to take with me."

"But not too busy, I gather, that you didn't put in an appearance at the rally that afternoon. But that's not what you told the police."

"Initially, no." He looked uncomfortable and shifted in his chair. "They gave me a chance to change my statement after they saw the news tapes. It was stupid of me, really. Maybe it was stupid of me to come forward in the first place and identify Steve. That's what Linda said. But — he was a friend and I couldn't let him go unidentified and unclaimed. Still, I recognized that it might put me in an awkward position if I confessed to attending the rally. I only stopped by on my way home. I was there ten minutes at most, just as things were winding up. But I knew those were probably the wrong ten minutes. And I was right."

"And you still maintain that you never saw Steve at the rally?"

"No, I never saw him, as far as I know. But even when I saw his picture, I wasn't absolutely sure. Except for the scar, he wasn't that distinctive-looking. And it sounds like he was wearing a cap and sunglasses at the rally, so I really doubt I would have recognized him."

"What did you think of Steve? You said he was a friend."

"Well, sure. I mean, in college he was a good friend and we went through a lot together during the antiwar movement. He was a real leader and I had a lot of respect for him. He had good ideas. I don't believe in capital punishment, of course, but I hope they find the guy who killed him."

I was startled by the scrape of a chair as Moses stood up next to me. Where the hell was he going? Then I spotted a tall woman closing the patio door behind her. She was wearing an Indian print skirt and sandals. She had long, light brown hair, permed into an impressive main. Her dark eyes flashed angrily.

"Tom, you don't have to talk to anybody about this," she said to him.

"I know I don't, Linda. But these people are representing a homeless man that the cops have been harassing about the murder and I don't see any harm in telling them what I know. I don't know much, but I don't have anything to hide."

She ran a hand gently through his hair. "I just don't like digging up the past," she said, more sad than angry now. "We've had enough trouble."

"My wife, Linda," Tom said to us. "Ms. Caliban and Mr. Fogg."

"I understand your concern, Ms. Matthias, and believe me, all I want to do is clear my client," I assured her.

"I understand that, Ms. Caliban. But you have to remember that we lost two friends, and nearly lost our own lives, to manufactured evidence."

"Can you tell me more about that case?"

"I could, but I don't see what bearing it has on this case."

"I don't know, either. But I'm trying to figure out why Sanders was killed. And at a protest rally, too."

"I can't figure that out," Tom said. "I keep wondering what he was doing there, unless he was looking for us or for Ginny. But if he was, why didn't he call us when he got to town? We have an answering machine."

"Were you still in contact with him?"

"Not close contact," Linda said. "Maybe a phone call once a year."

I didn't remind her that she was contradicting what she had told me on the phone.

"Are you in contact with Ginny?"

"No," Tom said. "We haven't seen her since she left Steve. I hope she's okay. And I keep wondering if she's heard about his death."

"Do you have any reason to believe she's in Cincinnati?"

"No. Why?"

"Because Steve said something to his mother that led her to believe he might have located Ginny."

"Well, Cincinnati's a big city," Linda said, "and we're not exactly within the city limits. Still, it's odd that she wouldn't call if she were here, just to let us know she's all right. She should know we would never give her away to Steve."

The patio door opened again and a kid, this time male, stuck his head out.

"Mom, Jeff wants to know if I can come over and play his new computer game."

"In a little while. Right now, we're busy."

The head disappeared.

"Did you consider Steve a friend as well, Mrs. Matthias?"

"Of course. I mean, Tom and Steve were naturally closer than Steve and I, but of course he was my friend."

"How would you describe him?"

"Well, let's see. He was very intense and he had lots of ideas. Everybody respected him."

"And did they like him?"

"Well, people who agreed with him did. Sometimes there was a clash of wills, or egos, among the men. But I would assume his real enemies wouldn't be found among the antiwar activists, and certainly not among the AWOS members."

"And how did you feel about Ginny?"

"Oh, we liked her, we both did." Tom looked at his wife and she nodded. "In some ways, she was the more practical of the two."

"It didn't keep her from getting pregnant," Linda pointed out.

"Yeah, but she wanted to be a mother. I'll bet she makes a great mother."

Another head, female, appeared at the patio door.

"Mom, Bobby won't get off the phone and I'm supposed to call Nadine about our history project."

"Tell him five more minutes, and I'll personally pull the plug," Linda told her.

"Speaking of mothers, you seem to have quite a crew," I observed.

"Five," Tom said with obvious satisfaction. "We both wanted a big family."

"We like to say it keeps us young." Linda smiled at him.

"I'm curious about the other AWOS members. Most of them seem to live right here in Cincinnati."

"I really don't see why you're focusing on AWOS, Ms. Caliban." Linda's smile changed to a frown. "That was a long time ago. Surely a lot has happened in Steve's life since his college days."

"That's true for us," Tom agreed.

"But you're members of the Central American Coalition, the group that sponsored the rally."

"I suppose that's true." Linda shrugged. "But we're members of lots of things."

"And is murder a regular occurrence at events sponsored by those other groups you belong to?"

"I see your point," she said wryly. "But it's hardly a regular occurrence for the CAC. And anyway, Tom and I didn't kill him, and none of the other AWOS members was there."

"Except for Dez Lewis."

"Well, yes, but surely you don't suspect a congressman."

I suspect everybody, sweetie, I said to myself. That's a detective's lot.

"What about Mickey McCafferty? Was he there?"

"Mickey?" Tom asked, apparently surprised. "No. Why would he have been?"

"Well, he lives around here, for starters. And he was another antiwar activist who, like you, might be drawn to the CAC and its cause."

A little girl wandered out onto the patio and came and stood between her parents.

"Mom, I'm bored."

Tom hoisted her onto his lap.

"Mom and I are busy talking right now, Joanie. But when we're finished, maybe you could help me with the horses, okay?"

She nodded and cuddled against him, looking at us shyly.

"About Mickey and the CAC cause," Tom said. "Mickey would say that the only cause he's interested in these days is himself and his '58 Chevy."

"You mean he's bitter?"

"Who wouldn't be? He spent ten years in prison for something he didn't do. A good guy, and now he's an auto mechanic with a federal record and a parole officer."

"Anyway," Linda added, "he's very careful not to mess up his parole. You're not allowed to protest anything on parole."

"You say he's bitter. Was he angry that Steve and Ginny left just before the arrests and never came back to support him during the trial?"

"It wasn't just before the arrests," Linda said.

"Sure, he was angry," Tom said. "He had a right to be, and frankly, I couldn't understand why they never came. We knew Ginny was having a difficult pregnancy, but still."

"Were you angry? You were arrested, too."

"Hell, yes," Tom said. "But like I said, we thought there must be some explanation. Anyway, we remained friends. And we didn't suddenly avenge ourselves on Steve fifteen years later. And neither did Mickey, believe me. He wouldn't jeopardize his parole that way."

"Why do you think the charges against you were dropped?"

Tom laughed. "That's one of life's little mysteries, isn't it? We always figured the guy assigned to plant evidence against us was a trainee who washed out."

"Aren't you curious? Couldn't you send for your FBI file now and find out?"

"Yeah, I guess we could. We've talked about it, but somehow we never get around to doing it."

"Those files are so heavily censored anyway," Linda said. "I had a friend who sent for hers and it was just pages and pages of heavy black lines. She couldn't tell anything from it."

"I'd like to talk to Mickey."

"We can't tell you how to get in touch with him." Tom frowned. "The best we can do is offer to call and see if he'll talk. He's pretty reclusive, so I doubt he'll say yes. He doesn't even have a telephone at home."

"I'll take what I can get," I said. I wasn't about to tell them that I already had McCafferty's address.

"I like Uncle Mickey," Joanie offered, sensing, the way kids do, that one of her favorites was being slandered.

"We all do, honey," Linda said, "even when he's gruff with us, isn't that right? Sometimes he sounds like a growly old bear, but we just ignore him, don't we? We know he's really a teddy bear."

The little girl nodded and flashed me a smile.

"Can you tell me about PJ?" I wondered what they could tell me in what had become a G-rated conversation.

"There's not much to tell," Tom said. "She went underground and ended up in that godforsaken, run-down little cabin in Athens County. Cops figured the stove was old and hadn't been maintained. She probably tried to light the pilot."

"But was she in touch with you while she was underground?"

"At first she was," Tom said. "But then we lost track of her. That happens, you know. People who go underground don't have a fixed address."

"We were very sad to hear about her death," Linda said, and looked it.

Joanie wriggled off of her father's lap and approached Moses.

"What are you writing? How come you never talk?"

"I'm taking notes on what other people say. I'm a writer," he said solemnly. "Are you a writer?"

"I can write my name. Want to see?"

"Maybe when everybody finishes talking, you can write your name for me. Okay?"

"Okay." She looked pointedly at his lap. He lifted her onto his knee. I heard his bones creak three feet away.

"So was Dez Lewis a friend of yours, too?" I pursued.

"Sure. Still is. He and Mickey and PJ founded AWOS. Everybody liked Dez. He had charisma — that's how come he could succeed as a politician." Tom smiled.

"I understand there was some friction between him and Sanders."

"Some," Tom conceded. "But you're going to have a hell of a time convincing anybody that a U.S. congressman left a big rally, slipped downstairs to a parking lot, and cut the throat of the guy he used to have political disagreements with in college."

"And Lennie Dwyer? What about him?"

"He wasn't with the group very long," Linda volunteered. "I know he has a law practice in town. We run into him every now and then. I always liked him. Tom did, too, didn't you, Tom?"

"Yeah, I wished he'd stuck around. We still run into him every now and then. He does pro bono work for some good causes."

"And Bertram Baskam? He's a local attorney too, now, I hear."

"That twerp!" Tom ejaculated. "If he had any spine, I'd nominate him to be your chief suspect."

"He could have hired somebody, I suppose," Linda suggested. "That's the way he'd do it. He wouldn't want to get his hands dirty. But he and Steve were big enemies in the old days. Steve hated his guts and I'm sure the feeling was mutual. And he probably has the contacts in those right-wing paramilitary organizations to hire a dozen hitmen. Come to think of it, I think he makes a great suspect. He's the kind of person who would assume he'd never get caught, or else he'd buy his way out."

Joanie yawned in Moses's face. "What's a twerp?" she asked.

"Don't ask me," he said. "I don't even know how to spell it."

Gwen appeared at the patio door. "Mom, is Joanie with you?"

"Yes, honey, she's here." Gwen withdrew.

"Tell me something," I said to Tom, ready to wrap up the interview. "I'm kind of curious. Steve went from AWOS to selling insurance. Lennie went from AWOS to a career as an attorney. Dez Lewis joined mainstream politics. And you became a computer consultant." I left out the dead and missing in action. "What happened to the counterculture?"

"We grew up," Tom said, smiling sadly like a wistful Peter Pan.

That was the part Franny hadn't yet managed. Did I really want her to? I tried to suppress the question but it popped up anyway: did I really want her to join the mainstream?

Moses and I set out, Moses having turned the map upside down so we could follow his trail back.

"But I can't read the street names upside down," I complained.

What I needed was a new car all my own. And damned if I hadn't just found myself an auto mechanic to give me advice.

CHAPTER 20

"Mom! Patty offered me a job!"

We had picked up Franny on the way home and her spirits didn't seem dampened by her stay in the hospital.

"A job?" I echoed. "But what about school? I thought this was just a visit — like spring break, or something."

"Mo-om! Spring break was ages ago. Anyway, Garf and I are both doing independent studies this semester on the Central American situation. Santa Cruz'll probably let us do an internship with the Central American Coalition this summer and I can work at Patty's health food store to earn money. Isn't that great?"

The full horror of my situation was sinking in. One: my daughter was planning to live with me all summer. This wasn't even May yet. We'd kill each other off by the Fourth of July. Two: my daughter was planning to work at a health food store. I was about to trade refrigerators with Adele Davis. I shouldn't have bribed that woman when she came to the door — I should have shot her and pleaded temporary insanity brought on by tainted tofu.

I went home and took a nap. Maybe when I woke up I'd discover that I'd been having a bad dream.

Instead, I woke up to the doorbell ringing and a sharp pain in my stomach. I heard a thump as whichever cat it was hit the floor and scuttled off, either to hide or answer the door. I hoped it was the latter. I rolled over and closed my eyes. The doorbell rang again.

"All right, all right, put a lid on it," I grumbled.

Hope Smith, our neighborhood lawn care professional, was standing there. She was rubbing the back of her leg with her foot and twisting the tale of her T-shirt in her hands.

"Hi, Cat. Can I talk to you? Is this a good time?"

"It's better than when I was asleep, but since I just woke up, I won't guarantee my mood. Come on in."

"This is kind of like a professional consultation."

Looking pale and troubled. Another lost cat? Teenagers didn't usually consult me about their romantic difficulties. "Step into my office," I said. "Step over the guitar case and pull up a chair. Want a Coke?"

"No, thanks."

"So what can I do for you?"

"Well, it's kind of hard to start." She was staring at her hands.

"Want to start at the beginning?"

"I don't think so." She thought. "Mom doesn't know I'm here. But I just had to talk to someone." She thought some more. "Remember when we were in the grocery store that day and Leon said he saw me on TV, at the rally?"

I nodded.

"I was there. With Penny. Mom wouldn't go."

Penny Stokes was her mother's partner. Is that the right word? I can't keep up. But for those of you who are my age and wondering, I don't mean business partner.

"You told Leon you weren't there."

She nodded. "I lied."

"How come?"

"Because he was my father." She looked up at me through tear-filled eyes.

I was a little slow on this one, I admit; it took me a minute. "Steve Sanders was your father?"

She nodded again. We were both doing a lot of nodding.

"Then you're — Hayley Sanders?"

"Uh-huh."

"And your mother is Ginny Sasinowski Sanders, not Val Smith?"

"You always change your name to something with the same initials, see." She licked a tear off her upper lip.

"I see." Ginny. Virginia. Valerie.

I felt for a minute like the earth was shifting under my feet. But when I thought about it, the whole thing seemed pretty logical. Virginia Sanders ended up living near her old friends. Her politics probably hadn't changed, but she might be wary of public appearances. I had always considered Hope mature for her age. Now I knew why.

First things first, I supposed. I pushed a box of tissues at her. "Honey, I'm so sorry about your father."

"It's okay," she said, her voice trembling. "I wasn't that close to him. Except I don't think he should've died that way."

"Did you see him at the rally?"

She shook her head. "Nuh-uh. But I keep wondering if he saw me." She sniffled. "I mean, it kind of gives me the creeps to think that he might've been watching me the whole time."

"Do you think he would have recognized you?"

"I don't know. I mean, he hadn't seen me for six years. But what was he *doing* there in the first place if he wasn't looking for us? See, Cat, it's all confused right now, you know? I feel bad about him, and a little sad, and at the same time I'm mad at him that he might have tracked us down. And I'm scared that he came so close. And I guess I can't help being relieved that he didn't find us and get me away from Mom and Penny."

"That's okay, honey. Those are all perfectly understandable feelings. Were you afraid he might have hurt you or your mother?"

"No, not really. I mean, I saw him get violent with her once or twice, but he wasn't usually that way. But he would have taken her to court and you know how that would turn out. And the courts probably would've come and taken me away even before they decided anything and shipped me off to my grandmother."

God, she was young to understand so much.

"Why did you want to talk to me?"

"Well, I heard that you were working on it — you know, Dad's murder. Leon told me you were trying to protect this homeless man. And I know what a good detective you are. I guess I thought you'd figure out about us eventually."

She must think I'm psychic, I thought.

"Anyway, if anybody found out about us, they'd suspect us. And then they'd go after Mom. I mean, I don't want this poor homeless guy to be framed for a murder he didn't do, and I don't want Mom to be framed for it, either. But I know Penny and her are worried sick about everything. And I'm worried, too. Well, I thought I should just come and talk to you and, like, offer to help if I could. Oh, I don't know, Cat. I just want it all to be over and everybody to be safe and I don't want my grandmother to find us!"

I went over and put an arm around her and let her cry for a while.

"Will your mom be mad that you told me all this?"

"I don't know, Cat. She might be. But I don't think she knows what to think, or what to do anymore. I think they've started talking about moving again. But I'm tired of moving and I like it here! It's been good for Mom here, too. I mean, the lesbian community has been really supportive."

"You must have led a pretty hard life in the past few years." I sympathized.

"Well," she said ruefully, "it's been an adventure. For the first year, I was Harry. That was a major, big-time challenge! We dyed my hair and cut it off short. But I couldn't have any friends."

"Didn't you like your father?"

"He was — oh, I don't know how to say it. He was hard to live with. He was just so critical all the time. Mom couldn't ever do anything right. And he wasn't very affectionate with me. I don't think he really wanted to be a father. It gave me a stomachache, lots of times, just to be around him."

"So you and your mom and her — lover — ran off together?"

"No. Barb didn't come. She couldn't face it, she said. I mean, we didn't hate her for that. We understood. It was a big sacrifice to make."

"And Penny's willing to make it?"

She nodded, smiling. "She's terrific! You know she's expecting? Only we usually say *we're* expecting."

"Congratulations."

I wasn't going to ask, but my sophisticated young informant told me anyway.

"It's a sperm bank baby. We think it's nice because the baby will be a complete surprise — we won't know what to expect. Anyway, it's safer legally."

"I see." I was getting quite an education. "Hope, tell me something, if you want to help. Is your mother still in contact with the people she knew in her college antiwar group? That would be Tom and Linda Matthias, Mickey McCafferty, Dez Lewis, or Lennie Dwyer?"

"We see Aunt Linda and Uncle Mickey. I've heard about the others, and they talk about them, but I've never met them."

"Do you know why you haven't met Linda's husband, Tom?"

She shook her head. "Not really. They say he travels a lot. We never meet anybody at home, anyway. We always go out somewhere. Everybody's careful. I've only ever met two of Linda's kids."

"Honey, I think I better talk to your mom."

"She's home now."

"Well, but don't you think you'd better prepare her? Why don't you go have a talk with her and ask her to call me?"

"Okay."

I put a hand on her head and stroked her hair.

"And don't worry about this, Hope. We'll get all this sorted out and make sure we protect you from your grandmother."

She smiled up at me bravely through liquid green eyes — green eyes that suddenly shocked the hell out of me. Which two kids had she met?

CHAPTER 21

It was still light when I reached the Smith-Stokes house. Moses had loaned me the Fairlane, but not without a big song and dance about how it was his last remaining asset. The house was one of those tall brick Northside houses in the process of renovation. Two cats were chasing fireflies in the front yard. A very fine house, indeed.

Val looked as if her last lesbian friend in the world had gone straight and moved to Miami. Her face was pale and haggard. She motioned me into an armchair, rightly judging that my joints would object to the futon and the beanbag chair. I was offered — guess what? — herbal tea and declined. She and Hope took the futon, and Penny settled gracefully into the beanbag chair. It had the effect of making me tall all of a sudden.

Val Smith, a.k.a. Virginia Sasinowski Sanders, had kind of a triangular face defined by prominent cheekbones and a delicate chin. Her wavy blonde hair was streaked with gray and pulled back carelessly with a hairband. Her bangs fell randomly across a narrow forehead and occasionally over her expressive blue-gray eyes, now reddened somewhat. Penny, her partner, was a substantial brunette with very short dark hair streaked with some kind of artificial red, and an earring collection in both ears that my daughter would have killed for. She worked as a nurse, but she would never have been hired to play one in a TV commercial. She didn't look pregnant, but damned if she wasn't knitting something.

"I hope you're not mad at Hope," I began, deciding to use the names I knew them by.

Val seized her daughter's hand.

"Of course not." She sighed. "I know this has all been hard on her. I understand the need to talk to somebody. God, do I understand it! So maybe this is the best thing. But I hope you can appreciate that living like we do, we have to be very careful about who we trust."

"I understand that. As you know, I'm not really a professional yet, but I do already have a client." At least, I was supposed to have a client, though come to think of it, I hadn't seen him in several days. "But I'll keep what you say confidential and if it turns out to have any significant bearing on the murder, I'll consult with you before I reveal anything to the cops. Okay?"

"Okay. So what can I tell you?"

"Well, I guess I'd just like to hear your story."

"My story. Okay, where do I start? I met Steve in the spring of 1969 when he joined AWOS."

"You were already a member?"

"Yes, I joined in the late fall of '68. Steve and I became involved in the summer of '69 — that's when several people took a house together. Mickey and Steve and PJ lived there at first and I was still in the dorm. But late in the fall, I moved into the house, too."

"Into Steve's room?"

"No, I had my own room. Everybody did. We all squabbled too much to share rooms. Even Steve and I did. You'd think I would have known from that that I shouldn't marry the guy, but in some respects, I was still pretty naive. Then in the late spring of '70, I found out I was pregnant. Steve was graduating, so we decided to get married. At some point in there he lined up this job in Rochester. So we got married in June — June 5th — and moved to New York. God, what an idiot I was!"

"Not a complete idiot, Mom!" Hope objected. "You got me!"

"Hear, hear," Penny murmured.

"That's right, sweetie." Val hugged her. "It was the only thing your dad ever did for me and he didn't do it on purpose, believe me!"

"So you moved to Rochester. And a month later, your friends were all arrested for planting a bomb."

"That was such bullshit! I couldn't believe it when I heard it! And I couldn't believe how lucky we were to get out just in time!" She said this with a straight face.

"But you didn't go back."

"I tried to tell Steve we had to go. And he kept saying we would. But it was never the right time for him. He was so busy with his new job. 'Fuck the job,' I said. 'Our friends need us!' 'I know, I know,' he'd say. 'We'll go next week, as soon as I finish working on this account.' And then I was having some trouble toward the end of my pregnancy, and then it was too late to go. Later, of course, I realize that he'd never intended to get involved, the bastard! In one of our biggest fights that year I left him, I accused him of abandoning our friends along with his political commitments."

"What did he say?"

"He got really angry and started spouting a lot of crap out of *Father Knows Best*, about how we'd had a kid to think of then and couldn't be as irresponsible as we'd been before, and he was tired of being poor all the time. And as usual, he accused me of not thinking clearly or understanding the situation. Maybe *I* hadn't cared if I delivered the baby in prison, but he had. He was always pulling that mental superiority bullshit on me, but by then it didn't work anymore."

"So Hope was your only child?" I had to ask.

"Yes, thank goodness! And thank goodness she was as bright and sensitive and resourceful as she was or we wouldn't be sitting here together today."

She gave her daughter's hand a squeeze.

"When you ran away, did you let any of your old friends know where you were?"

"Not at first. Not for — oh, maybe two years. Then I called Linda one day, when I thought Tom would be at work. If Tom had answered, I would have hung up."

"So you didn't trust Tom?"

"Well, he was a friend of Steve's, and I thought he'd have a hard time keeping a secret."

"But not Linda?"

"Linda was always the steadiest one of all of us. She kind of played the peacemaker role and kept us all together. So yes, she could keep secrets. She probably knows lots of secrets about all of us."

"Was it Linda who suggested you move to Cincinnati?"

"Yes, but we didn't actually move here until 1982. And we didn't move here just to be near Linda. Penny wanted to go to nursing school, and then I was offered a job at the EPA. Mickey was out of prison by then."

"And how come Mickey moved here?"

"Well, he grew up in northern Kentucky, so it wasn't that far from home for him and I think he wanted to be close to Linda and Tom."

"And you?"

"Yes, me, too. I'd always liked Mickey."

"But you don't keep in contact with Dez Lewis or Lennie Dwyer?"

"No. Lennie wasn't with the group that long, although I liked him well enough. But I wasn't close to him. I knew Dez better and I'll always consider him a friend. But he lives a public life. He's a rising politician. It would be dangerous for both of us if I contacted him."

"Dangerous?"

"You never know who's got him under surveillance. It could be his enemies, or it could be the FBI. That's one thing the antiwar movement taught me: you just never know. If the Bureau has me or Hope on a list, and I'm sure they have, I'd lose Hope to her grandmother and probably end up in prison for kidnapping her. Then his enemies will say that Dez has been colluding with me all along and they'll try to damage his reputation. See what I mean? It's better for both of us."

"So you don't attend rallies?"

"No. I do what I can behind-the-scenes, but Penny is the one who goes out in public." They exchanged an affectionate smile.

"You know, it seems to me kind of odd that so many of the AWOS people ended up in Cincinnati, even though they don't all keep in touch with each other."

"Oh, I don't know. Dez comes from here and so does Lennie Dwyer. I think his dad taught at the medical college. Mickey grew up in northern Kentucky, but he lived in Cincinnati for a while during high school and his dad worked for Cincinnati Milacron. Tom got his first job here after college and they bought the farm, so when he opened his new business, they stayed here. He had lots of business contacts and Linda liked the climate better than Cleveland's for raising vegetables. We came here because of the nursing college, and Linda, and the lesbian community and the job opportunities. So it's not that surprising that we all ended up here."

"So what's your theory on who killed Steve?"

She shook her head. "I don't have a clue, Cat, I really don't. I mean, I could've killed him a few times, so I know he's capable of making somebody angry enough, especially, I guess, a woman. But if his current girlfriend did kill him, I'd testify in her behalf, if I could. But it doesn't sound like a very likely scenario for a domestic dispute, does it? I mean, if I were going to kill him with a knife, I would have stabbed him in the chest with a kitchen knife — *in* the kitchen. Now I sound like that Clue game. But you know what I mean — I wouldn't have cut his throat in the parking lot."

"Does the method or location suggest anything to you?"

"Nothing you haven't thought of, I'm sure. They keep talking about who was at the rally, but you wouldn't have to go to Fountain Square to use the Fountain Square Garage. For one thing, there's that underground passage to the Westin. For another, you could drive in and out of the garage without being seen by anyone on the Square."

"For that matter," Penny spoke up, "you could walk into the garage and out without being noticed. You could take the elevator down from the Skywalk and the Skywalk's connected to half of downtown, starting with the Fifth-Third Bank building."

Where Dez Lewis had his office. But Lewis had been on the speakers' platform.

"Penny, I gather you didn't see Sanders that day."

"Not that I know of."

"Would you have recognized him if you'd seen him? If he were wearing a hat and sunglasses, say."

"I don't know, Cat. I'm not all that good with faces. I've seen pictures of him, sure, but he's not very distinctive-looking."

"Except for that scar."

"Yes," Val said. "That scar. That must explain the beard. But who the hell was he hiding from? Me?"

"Maybe he didn't want to tip you off before he had talked to the police or his lawyer. Can you think of anybody else he'd be hiding from? Dez or Tom, for example? They were both there."

"Tom was there?" Val frowned. "But why would he be hiding from either of them? It doesn't make any sense. Hiding from me makes more sense, I guess. I just don't know, Cat. I have thought, sometimes—"

"Yes?"

"Well, it sounds stupid, I know, but I didn't always like Steve's business associates."

"You mean, you thought there was something shady about them?"

"I don't know if 'shady' is the right word. But yeah, maybe it is. I know they were insurance executives, and let's face it, they were a hell of a lot more conservative than the people we'd been hanging out with. But occasionally somebody would come to the house, not one of the usual crew he worked with, somebody I didn't like the looks of. Mirror-sunglasses types. Like narcs or something. That only happened a couple of times in the first year or two we were married, and I hadn't thought about it in a long time, but when Steve was killed — I don't know, one day I remembered it. He'd told me they were there on insurance business, but I didn't believe it at the time and I don't think I believe it now."

"What kind of business do you think they were there on?"

"I don't have any idea. Monkey business, I told the baby, since she was the only one I could talk to about it. Once she went looking for the monkeys. It was a good thing she couldn't talk yet!"

Hope laughed at herself.

"Did Steve ever divorce you?"

"I don't know. His mother once said he did, told Hope that when she called one Christmas, can you imagine? But that doesn't mean it was true."

"That means you probably inherit everything, including all his private papers. But the police will have all that stuff impounded. I suppose we'll hear eventually if they find anything interesting."

"I doubt that I inherit, Cat. Steve's smart enough to have made a new will. He probably left everything to his mother outright, or in trust for his daughter."

"So he never had any other children after you left?"

"I really don't know. I doubt it. Steve wasn't 'into' children, as he told me once."

So who was the green-eyed girl who looked so much like Hope, the one I knew as Gwen Matthias?

CHAPTER 22

If you ask me, shopping for a car is about as much fun as a hysterectomy. I can't think of another single transaction in which I am so certain I'm being cheated. Even if I don't wear the polyester pantsuits my daughter Sharon keeps foisting on me, I swear a buzzer goes off the minute I step on the lot — it's the goddamn Grandma Alert. Soon I am surrounded by smarmy salesmen with damp hands and beady eyes, steering me toward the Coupe de Villes with one fist in my pocketbook. They go blank when I talk about blue books and fuel injection, and they don't even take my Golden Buckeye card. It's enough to drive a woman to drink, et cetera.

But my call to the body shop Monday morning confirmed my hopes that the beige bomber had stalled for the last time. I told him that I had no intention of strewing its ashes over the parking lot out back, so they could sell it for what they could get, subtract their tow, and send me what was left.

"Could you tell me what went wrong with the brakes?" I asked.

"Sure could, lady. Listen, you ought to call the cops. Some bastard's gone and cut your brake line. A clean cut, too — it wasn't no accident."

"But shouldn't they have failed right away if that was the case?" I thought of all the stop signs and traffic lights between here and Mount Airy Forest.

"Yeah, that's right! So they was real clever. What they did was, they cut most of the way through, see? But after a couple of bumps and maybe ten minutes of road vibration, the whole line gives out, see? And there you are: no brakes! Clever, see what I mean?"

I called the insurance company, who said they'd be in touch.

I'd decided to mix business and torture, so I sat down with a Greater Cincinnati Yellow Pages and a map. Sidney promptly flopped down on the map and began to wrestle with one corner. By the time Kevin wandered in about eleven, I had a shredded map and the name of the auto shop where Mickey McCafferty worked: Jack's Rapid Repair on Plainville Road in Mariemont.

"What's your plan, Mrs. C?"

"There's nothing to eat in there, unless you're Bugs Bunny."

"Now, Mrs. C, I heard a rumor that you didn't exactly clean your plate at dinner the other night. Anyway, I was looking for some of that granola Franny bought the other day."

"She's getting to me, Kevin. I can't face eating Elsie the Cow anymore."

"That's okay, Mrs. C," Kevin yawned. "It's probably better for you, not to mention Elsie. She's right about that."

"But where do I draw the line? With Wilbur the Pig? Chicken Little? Plants have feelings, too, you know. I read a story once about a plant that went into shock when its friend fell off the shelf."

"They like music, too, but only some kinds. Heavy metal is definitely out."

"I'm serious, Kevin. She leaves these animal-rights magazines around. I'm sure she does it on purpose. Do you know anything about how they raise pigs these days? Or calves for veal?"

"I know, Mrs. C, it's strong stuff. I'm not a vegetarian but I think it's a viable option. And not just from the animal-rights angle. Red meat isn't that good for someone your age. But what I say is, take it at your own pace. Most people don't change their diets overnight, even if their daughters move in."

"You just said that four-letter word."

"Sorry, even if their daughters visit. I think you should definitely read more and give it some thought. But don't try to do everything at once or you'll be miserable. Just try to find some healthy things that you like. Like pasta, for example."

"And pizza?" I said hopefully.

"There you go. Of course, substituting cheese for beef isn't always so great if the cheese is high in fat. You just have to watch that stuff if you want to stay fit and feisty for your detective work."

"Speaking of which—"

"Yeah, how's it going, Mrs. C?" He'd found the granola and poured himself a bowl. Sidney gave it a sniff, then got that expression cats get when they look like they're going to sneeze. Kevin poured him a little puddle of milk on a plate and he went to work on that.

"It's pretty complicated," I said. "It could have been any of them, really. Between the ones who acknowledge that they were there on the scene and the ones who could have been, they're all suspect. Except for the one who died, and I'm even wondering about her."

"Well, let me put it this way. Suppose you're wanted by the FBI and you want to disappear. How do you do it?"

"On television, they go for a swim. Then they have a boat pick them up offshore and go off to live in South America or Tahiti or someplace."

"Well, this wasn't a swim. It was a gas explosion and fire."

"But they must have identified the remains somehow."

"What remains? How much was left, do you think?"

"I don't know. But there had to have been something. Teeth, for example."

"Right. That's what I've been thinking. Isn't that how people usually get identified? I mean, let's face it: no fingerprints."

"Is this what y'all consider appropriate breakfast conversation?" Moses appeared at the door with Sophie in his arms and Winnie at his heels. "Cat, can I borrow some laundry soap?"

"You can see what's down there. Now that Franny's around, I don't guarantee anything. She probably wants me to wash the clothes in spring water and baking soda. Say, Moses, how easy would it be to fool a forensic pathologist about the identity of somebody who'd been in an explosion and fire?"

"Well, that might depend. If they've got bones — even one bone, if it's the right bone and pretty much intact — they can probably estimate height. If they've got teeth and a tentative ID, they can check dental records. Hey, I thought you had enough suspects, Cat. What you trying to do, increase the pool of candidates by resurrecting the dead?"

I picked Winnie up in my lap so she could see over the edge of the table.

"I know, I know. I'm probably just trying to overcomplicate things. But if I wanted the FBI to close my case, I wouldn't just leave my wallet on the beach and swim off into the sunset. I'd leave them some remains. And it seems to me that the best way to prevent them from identifying those remains would be to set off a gas explosion over them."

"You got a devious mind, you know that, Cat?"

"I love it," Kevin enthused. "If they didn't work it that way, they should have."

Winnie yawned in my face, sending a warm puff of dog breath my way.

"So what's next?" Moses asked.

"First, I'm going car shopping. Then I'm taking my prospective purchase to a certain auto mechanic I've been wanting to meet."

"You taking Diane?"

"No, I'm taking Kevin."

"You are?" Kevin was surprised.

"You know how you love to go shopping with me," I reminded him.

"Clothes shopping, Mrs. C. I love to go clothes shopping with you. Car shopping involves close encounters with a bunch of unsavory characters."

"Come on, Kevin. Ple-e-ease? I'll do your dishes for a week and I promise not to use steel wool on your seasoned skillets this time."

"Well, all right. What are you going to buy?" I could see the gleam of interest in his eye.

"I don't know," I said. "Something more reflective of my sparkling personality than a beige Pinto."

"Oooh, how about one of those sporty numbers, with a sunroof? Or a convertible?"

"You best be thinking about something that ranks high on safety in *Consumer Reports*," Moses said.

"It'll have to be used, anyway." I sighed. "So we'll just have to see what's out there."

"Let's start with the newspaper." Kevin pulled it toward him along with the cat that was serving as a paperweight.

Moses retired, like the coward he was. Winnie stayed on to put in her two cents, and to finish Kevin's granola.

CHAPTER 23

We arrived at Jack's Rapid Repair some four hours later in a spiffy little blue Rabbit with four-on-the-floor, sunroof, and air conditioning. Already I was in love. I had forgotten what it was like to drive a car that goes when you put your foot on the gas pedal. We had the radio cranked up and were singing along with "Marrakesh Express." I fervently hoped that Mickey McCafferty wouldn't find anything wrong with what I was already coming to think of as "my car." It could really color my opinion of him.

Jack's was a standard-issue cement-block garage, with Salvation Army reject furnishings in the waiting room, along with a supply of dog-eared hunting and fishing magazines and a snack machine featuring corn nuts and peanut butter crackers. The woman behind the counter littered with paper and greasy auto parts was watching a soap opera on the dusty television next to the snack machine. We asked for McCafferty.

Mickey McCafferty appeared, wiping his hands on one of those red rags auto mechanics use. Since the rag was as dirty as his hands, it didn't seem to be doing him much good. He still had the long, thick, curly dark hair of his college days, dark eyebrows, and light blue eyes that even now appeared permanently angry. He wore no beard or mustache, but I wouldn't exactly call him clean-shaven, either; his chin and jaw were covered with dark stubble. He was on the short side — taller than me, but shorter than Kevin — and muscular. The height was a problem, I thought, but he sure as hell would have had the strength to cut somebody's throat.

I told him only that a friend had recommended him and I wondered if he'd look over the car I was thinking about buying. He didn't ask questions, just followed me out to the car. He looked under the hood, then asked me to "start her up." He looked under the hood some more, then asked if I wanted to go for a test drive.

"Sure," I said, feeling my stomach lurch.

"Can I go too?" Kevin said, feigning enthusiasm.

"Sure," I said.

McCafferty headed out like he knew where he was going. He didn't say anything, but he played with the controls for the air conditioning and heat and the cigarette lighter.

We reached Ault Park. He started around the circle, then pulled off the road. He reached over before I could respond and opened the glove compartment. Satisfied, I guess, he slammed it shut.

"So what do you really want, lady?" he asked, pulling a pack of Camels out of his pocket.

"I want to know who killed Steve Sanders." Like him, I skipped the preliminaries. I assumed he'd been forewarned and didn't need them anyway.

"Why?" He lit a cigarette from the car's lighter, frowning.

"I represent two parties who are afraid they'll be accused."

"Two?" He frowned again. He kept his eyes on the front windshield. "I thought you were supposed to be representing some homeless guy."

"I had a long talk with Val Smith last night," I said. "She's very frightened. She knows it's possible to be convicted for something she didn't do."

He didn't say anything for a minute. "So what do you want from me? I didn't do it, but whoever did deserves a medal, in my book."

"You didn't like Sanders?"

"I hated the bastard's guts. But he wasn't worth going back inside for."

"Why didn't you like him?"

"He was a fake, as fake as they come. Wanted to be a big shit in the movement, always full of fucking plans, and then Kent State happened, and the sorry-assed bastard bailed out. Should've known then." He muttered the last sentence under his breath.

"Known what?"

"That he was a phony. Shit, I kept waiting for him to show up at one of our rallies. You know what he did? Sent a fucking check for our fucking defense fund. He didn't want to be on the front lines when the pigs were using real bullets instead of teargas."

"Had you seen him or spoken to him since he left?"

"Spoke to him on the phone a few times after the arrest. We've never gotten along that well. Tom was the one who bought all that self-proclaimed hero-of-the-movement crap. Tom and the girls. Me, I'm not into heroes."

"PJ ran. How come you didn't?"

He smiled bitterly. "How could I? I had a *cause*, man. I knew I couldn't win, but I had to give the bastards a run for their money. Use the trial for publicity. Try to expose the kind of subversive crap they were pulling, running a goddamn police state. The FBI in collusion with the ATF, the fucking Columbus police, the campus police, the National Guard. Who knows?"

"Were you angry that Silverman walked away?"

"Are you fucking crazy? Walked away?" He waved his hands and I heard Kevin shift heavily in the backseat. "You think it's easy, what she did? Listen, lady, she served her time just like I did. Living underground is a hell of a lot like living in prison. Only difference is you don't know where your next meal is coming from. She had her reasons for doing what she did. We all do what we have to do, you know?"

"Was she your closest friend in AWOS?"

"Yeah." He stared out the front window. "Goddamn near killed me when I heard she died. Out in the goddamn woods, alone. *That's* the murder they should be prosecuting."

"You mean—" I caught my breath.

"I mean she was murdered, wasn't she? They drove her underground, forced her to live that way. They might just as well have lit the fucking match."

"You're obviously still in contact with the Matthiases. Did you resent it when the charges against them got dropped?"

He shrugged. "Luck of the draw. It's like Tom's always said — they must've sent an idiot to plant the evidence against him and Linda."

"And I guess they didn't have the mechanical skills you did."

"Yeah, right, lady. Mickey the Mechanic — that's me. Shit, you know how fucking easy it is to build a bomb? Tom had built radio sets with his dad when he was a kid and Linda — hell, she'd been around farm machinery all her life. Steve — he had a lot of those home maintenance-type skills, you know? Wiring plugs, stuff like that. But me, I'm the genius, so I'm the one gets nailed. Of course, Tom and Linda were both pissed off when the charges were dropped. And they worked like hell on my case — for all the good it did."

"So you get along well with them?"

Again the bitter smile. "About as well as I get along with anybody these days. Tom's the real thing — an idealist. Course nowadays, he's Mr. Computer, but who am I to squawk? They're still politically active. And Linda is still living out her Earth Mother fantasy."

"Was Linda ever involved with Sanders?"

He thought a minute. "Look, lots of people were involved with lots of people in those days. That's all I want to say."

"Fair enough. What about Dez Lewis? You still in touch with him?"

"I talk to him every now and then. He wrote a letter in support of my parole — did you know that? It was a risk for him, but ol' Dez never was one for backing away from a risk."

"So you liked him?"

"We founded the group together — him and me and PJ. Sure, I liked him."

"What about Lennie Dwyer?"

"Lennie's my lawyer." He pitched his cigarette butt out the window. "He's done all right by me. Kind of a stiff-necked bastard, but he's okay."

"And then there's Val. You keep in touch with her, too."

"That's right. Another reason I'm pissed off at Sanders — what he did to Val."

"What did he do to her?"

"Oh, he wanted her around to massage his ego, and when she stopped doing that, he got pissed off. He would've waged a hell of an ugly custody battle — not because he wanted the kid, but because he didn't want Ginny — Val — to have her. And it wouldn't have occurred to him that the whole business might harm the kid. He was just such a fucking egomaniac!"

"So would you say you're closest to Val?"

"Yeah, me and Val are pals." He lit another cigarette and thought for a minute. I didn't interrupt him. "Sometimes I wonder what would've happened if Dez hadn't left when he did. Dez was smart, and, well, more than smart — perceptive. He didn't like Steve that much from the beginning."

He paused again and then looked at me for the first time in the conversation, narrowing his eyes and studying me. "See, the rest of us, we were so fucking naive. Plot-counterplot. That's what we thought. Us versus Them. But it wasn't that way at all. It was like sleight of hand. They say, 'Watch this hand.' So you watch the other one. But while you're watching the fucking hands, you get kneed in the balls or kicked in the ass. We thought we had it all figured out. But there was always this goddamn third joker in the deck."

He stuck the cigarette between his lips and turned on the ignition.

"I gather you're not politically active now."

"Can't afford to be. Can't afford to exercise my fucking civil liberties or I'll get my ass thrown in prison again." He suddenly grinned at me around his cigarette. "By the way, nice car. You should buy it."

CHAPTER 24

Lennie Dwyer was a busy man, but when he found out what I wanted to talk to him about, he offered to meet me at Arnold's at 6:30.

That gave me all day to run errands in my cute little blue Rabbit.

First, I had to take Franny to the chiropractor. She was experiencing a lot of pain in her back, which, added to the pain in her head, made her pretty miserable. She wasn't getting much sleep, I could tell, even with the prescription Tylenol, and I was feeling guilty this morning for all of my recent unmotherly thoughts.

"Asshole!" I cried, as a balding man in a dark-gray Pontiac cut in dangerously close to my baby-blue fender. "Fucking driver's license probably expired when he last had hair."

That's when Franny dropped her bombshell.

"You don't swear as much as you used to, Mom."

I didn't? That couldn't be true. Surely my language was every bit as colorful as it had always been! But what if it was true? Was I losing my edge without Fred around to serve as audience?

I stopped at a stoplight, chewed on my thumbnail, and worried. I liked profanity. It was useful. It startled people and got their attention. Especially people who tended to look through you if you were white-haired, short, and female.

"I do wish you wouldn't use 'fucking,' though," she continued chattily.

Of all my children, *Franny* was nominating herself for chief censor?

"What's wrong with it?" I asked, genuinely puzzled.

"Well, you know, it suggests violent sexuality. It always makes me think of, like, sexual violence aimed at women, you know?"

"Gee, Fran, I guess all profanity comes from something unpleasant. I don't think it means the same thing once it becomes profanity."

"Maybe not, Mom, but doesn't it bother you that, like, so many of our cuss words defame women? Like 'son of a bitch' and 'bitch' and even 'bastard,' which reflects more on your unmarried mother than on your father."

"Have you been taking women's studies classes again?" I asked suspiciously.

"Mo-om!" She rolled her eyes. "I'm just saying."

"Well, if I want to cuss, what's left that I can use, in your opinion?"

"Well, there's words like 'shit' and 'bullshit' and 'crap' and 'asshole.' Those are all gender-neutral."

I wasn't about to point out to my personal animal-rights rep that the bulls — all male — might have some objections to her list.

"And 'hell' and 'damn' and 'goddamn' and 'chrissakes' — all those religious ones are okay."

That was easy for her to say; the only church she had any ties to was St. John's Unitarian. But at the moment she was looking pained, as if the effort to convince me was making her headache worse.

"Okay, Fran, I'll think it over. I can't promise anything, but I'll think it over."

Damn, since my daughter had come to visit, I sure was having to think over a hell of a lot of things.

In the chiropractor's waiting room, I had a choice between *Organic Gardening*, *Natural Health*, and *Highlights*. There was soft dulcimer music playing in the background and a fish tank of exotic fish. When Franny emerged, she was looking a little less peaked. She stopped to make another appointment with the chiropractor and one with the hypnotherapist.

Then I dropped her off at her new job in Clifton. If looks could kill, mine would have shattered the plate glass in the window of Patty's Natural Foods.

"Don't bring anything else home, Fran," I cautioned her. "We don't have any room in the refrigerator."

I decided to take myself out to lunch at the Alpha, up the street from Patty's. Their food was supposed to be healthy, but they used real butter. Plus, they had a bar. It was my kind of place.

The rest of my afternoon you wouldn't be interested in. It's like I always say, in detective novels you never see the boys picking up their dry cleaning or buying stamps at the post office or scouting for insecticides at the lawn and garden center — insecticides for insects, I mean, not the old Agatha Christie tin of exotic wasp poison left in the greenhouse after somebody has been served a poison sandwich. Anyway, I tooled round in my new baby-blue Rabbit, and I felt like a new woman. I even bought some tomato stakes, just so I could practice putting the back seat down.

At a quarter to six, I stopped by the St. Francis Soup Kitchen, looking for my client. I found him sitting morosely at a table in plain sight, eyes fixed on nothing, eating mechanically.

"He gone all fatalistic, Cat," Curtis told me, shaking his head. "He eat every meal like he think it gonna be his last."

"I really don't think you've got anything to worry about, Steel." I took the folding chair opposite. "My investigation has turned up a shitload of suspects with better motives than you've got. Way I see it, cops'd be crazy to pin it on you when they've got so many better prospects."

"The cops *are* crazy, Cat. Don't you know that by now?"

"Yeah, well, I live with one, and he may be crazy, but he ain't stupid. Anyway, the cops have access to all of Sanders's private papers. I'm guessing, from what one of my sources told me, that they might find something in there that could blow this case wide open, so to speak." I was a little uncomfortable with incendiary metaphors these days.

"That true, Cat?" Curtis said eagerly. "You mean, like, this Sanders dude coulda been running from the mob?"

"Not quite like that, Curtis," I said. But what the hell did I know? Thinking back on what Val had told me, I had to concede it could be true. Maybe Sanders sold life insurance to the Mafia and he hadn't paid a claim fast enough.

By the time I left, Steel was looking a little more like his old self— more surly than cheerful, but at least not catatonic. I, on the other hand, was feeling less and less committed to this case. From what Val had said, Sanders had some rather unsavory acquaintances. The more I thought about it, the more unrealistic it seemed that somebody had surfaced out of his distant past to do him in. By now, the cops probably had their own list of suspects and none of the AWOS crew was on it. It was probably a list of names like Louis and Vinnie and Mack the Knife.

CHAPTER 25

Still, curiosity, if nothing else, made me want to meet the final living member of AWOS.

When I arrived at Arnold's, Kevin was working behind the bar. No, scratch that; Kevin was kibitzing with a city councilmember and somebody in a three-piece suit who looked like a banker. The banker appeared to be drowning his sorrows. I didn't feel too sorry for him, though; unlike some of the people caught in the Home State crisis, he obviously still had some liquid assets.

Kevin caught my eye and nodded toward a table shoved into a corner under the stairs.

Lennie Dwyer was a slight man, probably too short to cut Sanders's throat unless he had stood on a chair or unless Sanders had bent over backward to let him do it. He wore red suspenders, a red bow tie, and wire-rimmed glasses. Sartorially speaking, he did not look like he was vying for a Republican appointment to the bench.

Margo, one of Kevin's waitress pals, brought me a beer and another bottle of Bass for Dwyer.

"Have you talked to Mickey McCafferty since I spoke to him yesterday?" I asked, once the preliminaries were over. I decided to be direct.

"No, why? Should I have?"

"No, I just wondered."

"Mickey doesn't have a phone, Mrs. Caliban. If he had a phone, it would be bugged, he says, and he might be right. Generally speaking, Mickey doesn't trust phones very much, Mrs. Caliban."

"I see. Well, as I told you, I'm looking into Steve Sanders's murder and I wanted to speak to anyone in Cincinnati who knew him. Right now, that seems pretty much limited to people who knew him during the antiwar movement in the late 60s."

He nodded. "AWOS. We seem to have quite a contingent here. I'm assuming, then, Mrs. Caliban, that you are looking to nail one of us for the murder." He smiled at me benignly.

"No." I smiled back. "I'm looking to nail the murderer so that the rest of you can stop worrying and get on with your lives."

"Are we worrying? Now you surprise me, Mrs. Caliban." He looked genuinely surprised. "Of course, McCafferty is worried and he has cause to be. He was railroaded once before and makes a convenient target." He left it at that.

"Well, Tom and Linda seem worried, or at least, Linda does," I said.

"I see." He took a swig of his Bass. "Linda is worrying on everybody's behalf, especially Tom's. Linda was always worrying. Now she thinks the family is under attack."

"The family?"

"AWOS. She's worrying that the police will think one of us did it. She's also probably worrying, if I may be allowed to speculate here, that one of us did do it."

"Is she worried that Tom might have done it?"

He thought that over. "My first instinct is to say that Tom didn't do it, isn't the type, and Linda would know that. I only saw him violent once and that was when a counter-demonstrator took a swing at Linda. But when I think back on that incident, I'd have to say that yes, he'd be capable of it. But who wouldn't, if it comes to that?"

"Cutting somebody's throat? I wouldn't, for one. Would you?"

"Oh, I think you underestimate yourself. Given the right circumstances—" He shrugged. "You know, what most people don't stop to consider is the advantage of that technique — apart from the obvious ones, I mean. You don't have to watch your victim's face. One quick slash and you shove him down, face forward. No, Mrs. Caliban, that technique has a lot to recommend it."

"Are you speaking from experience?" I had to say it. I couldn't help myself.

"Imagination. And a certain callousness nurtured by an addiction to murder mysteries. Most people, I'll grant you, can't sit in a bar with a total stranger and discuss murder methods, but anybody could if they spent as much time immersed in murder as I do."

"Who do you like?" Okay, I know I was getting sidetracked, but again, I couldn't help myself. Besides, you can tell a lot about a person if you know who he reads.

"Robert Parker. Elmore Leonard. Tony Hillerman. Kinky Friedman. The locals, of course — Valin."

"No women?" I asked accusingly.

"P.D. James," he said promptly. "Martha Grimes. And that Chicago woman — Paretsky. So you might say I have an academic interest in the Sanders murder, Mrs. Caliban, as well as a professional one."

"But not a personal one?"

"You mean, was Sanders a friend of mine? He was at one time, but not a close friend. I joined AWOS in the spring of '69 and he was pretty new at the time, as I recall." He reached up to adjust his glasses, leaving a wet fingerprint on the lens, so he took them off and wiped them on a napkin. "They were interested in someone with legal expertise and I was in my first year of law school."

"So you were older than the others?"

"Not by much. Anyway, my mother was an attorney and I worked for her sometimes when I was growing up, so I probably had more background than the average law student, and Dez recruited me for the group. I stayed until the next fall — fall of '70. I left the group in November." He put his glasses back on.

"Did you have a falling-out with them?"

"No, nothing like that. It was just — how can I describe it, Mrs. Caliban? I liked the people individually, but the group dynamics were a little strange for me. It was an oddly incestuous group — really a lot like a family. Not wholly dysfunctional, either, but strange. Passions and jealousies always simmering under the surface, things going on you didn't know about, but things that affected the political work nonetheless. I decided I wanted to work with a larger group where everything would be more out in the open. So I joined the New Mobe."

I nodded. The group names didn't throw me anymore, as long as I wasn't being cross-examined about their politics. But I was more interested in the group he'd left — and in the passions and jealousies part.

"Tell me something about the relationships in the group."

"Well, while Dez was around, things seemed to go okay. He kept things focused and he was a brilliant negotiator, so fights never lasted long because he resolved them."

"Fights between whom?"

"Oh, anybody and everybody, really. PJ and Mickey were always squabbling, but those weren't really serious fights, that was just how their relationship operated. Mostly, they were allies against the others. Dez and Steve didn't always see eye to eye. PJ and Steve were always fighting. Tom and Steve were allies usually and Linda went along with Tom most of the time, unless she was mad about something else. Then she opposed him on everything."

"Something else?"

"Something personal, I mean. They were high school sweethearts — did you know that? But Tom was a good-looking guy and Linda could be jealous. Ginny and Steve had a rocky relationship from the beginning. I never could figure out why she went and married the guy. That was one breakup

I predicted years in advance. Anyway, you get my meaning. Two people would fight. Then two people would console the two people who were fighting. Then before you knew it, the two people who were doing the consoling would be fighting. I tell you, Mrs. Caliban, it got to where I needed a scorecard every time I arrived at that house for a meeting. And during the meetings, I always got the impression that there were at least two conversations going on, the one I was hearing and the one everybody else could hear, the silent one."

He went to adjust his glasses again, got them wet again, and took them off again to dry them.

"When Ginny and Steve got married, she was pregnant. Did you know that?"

"Well, I was gone by then, remember? But I was invited to the wedding and the pregnancy was openly discussed there." He put his glasses back on. "In fact, if I recall, there was some mention of it in the ceremony — of the baby, I mean, not the pregnancy. It was more than the usual allusion to fruitfulness, you know — maybe a blessing on the baby. They wrote their own ceremony, of course."

"Do you know if anybody else had a baby by Sanders?"

"No." He looked astonished. "Why?"

"Just asking. Because of the estate," I lied.

"Oh. Well, not that I know of, but as I say, I left in November."

"If you were invited to the wedding, you must maintain cordial relations with the group."

"Oh, sure. We kept in touch. In part because of my work with the New Mobe. But I would have, anyway. I like those people, Mrs. Caliban. I just didn't want to live with them or work with them."

"Were you surprised when Silverman and McCafferty were arrested?"

"Not surprised," he said thoughtfully. He reached for his glasses, smeared them, and started the whole process over again. At this rate, we would run out of napkins.

"In those days, we weren't surprised by anything the Feds did to keep us under control. Even Kent State wasn't so much a surprise as a shock. In the movement, we'd been expecting things to turn uglier for some time. You can't call out armed troops and expect nothing to go wrong. And we'd watched Chicago on television. There'd been lots of drug arrests among antiwar activists, not all of them legitimate. Dez Lewis can tell you about that.

"It kind of surprised me that they'd gone to that much trouble to get at AWOS, though. I mean, maybe they were more vulnerable because they were so small, but you'd think that ATF and the Bureau would have bigger fish to fry."

"So you don't believe they were guilty?"

"Hell, no." He waggled his empty bottle at Margo. "Bombs in the basement? Let's get serious, Mrs. Caliban. Hoover was reading from the same script he'd had back in the 20s and 30s. Anarchists in the basement. Commies behind every bush. Give me a break." He smiled at Margo as she collected his empties.

"Why do you think they dropped the charges against Tom and Linda?"

"Who knows? Could've been what they said — they didn't have enough evidence to convict. Somebody missed their cue there if that was the case, but we'll never know. They probably got transferred to South America. Could've been that somebody had connections."

"Connections? But weren't the Matthiases angry when the charges were dropped?"

"Well, Tom was, anyway. Or said he was. Linda seemed more relieved, which was the sensible response. Oh, I'm not saying that either of them had a hand in it. But they both came from fairly prominent families in Cleveland. Tom's dad is an attorney. I think he even served on the city council a term or two. Linda's dad is a businessman."

"I thought she grew up on a farm."

"She grew up on her grandparents' farm, but when her grandfather died, her dad used the land to build a subdivision.

So by the time she was in college, he was already a successful real estate developer. She wouldn't have to have known about all the efforts in her behalf and neither would Tom. They wouldn't want to have known, either." He reached for his glasses and I sat on my hand to keep it from grabbing his arm.

"I gather that you weren't McCafferty's original attorney."

"Hardly. I was still in school. No, he contacted me in 1977 and I went to see him then."

"And three years later you got him out."

"Almost four years, really. And I wouldn't say I got him out. Dez Lewis helped a lot and so did his own record."

"Do you think prison changed him?"

"How could it not? You've met him. He's a bitter man, Mrs. Caliban. But he was always a curmudgeon, so I wouldn't push that too far."

"You don't think he killed Sanders?"

"And risked going back inside? Not a chance."

"Were you in contact with PJ after she disappeared?"

He shook his head. "No. We weren't that close and I doubt that she kept in contact with many of her old friends. It would've been too dangerous for her."

He started to peel the label off his Bass bottle.

"I can still remember exactly where I was when I read about her death in the paper. My wife was working late, so I'd sat down in my favorite reading chair to wait for her. I'd fixed myself a drink and picked up the paper, figuring we'd go out to eat when she got home. When she got home, she found me sitting there bawling like a baby. I really felt that loss, Mrs. Caliban. What those guys did to PJ — and to Mickey — *that* was a crime."

I studied him a minute, trying to decide if his emotion was genuine.

"I understand your father teaches at the medical college," I said abruptly. "What's his specialty?"

"Pathology," he said, startled.

I left him wiping his glasses, waved goodbye to Kevin, and drove to the med school library. I couldn't stand the suspense. In the directory, I found a listing for a "Dwyer, Bernard M.," in Surgical Pathology.

At first, I was disappointed. Then I flipped back to the front of the book to the listing for "Pathology and laboratory medicine" and I started to smile.

Surgical Pathology was located on the thirteenth floor of the Medical Sciences Building. It shared the thirteenth floor with Autopsy Pathology. For the layperson, there was a translation of this term in parentheses: "Morgue."

CHAPTER 26

When I opened the refrigerator next morning, the first thing I noticed was that my daughter had shoved a new jar of "natural" grape juice onto the top shelf. My unnatural orange juice had by now been forced back into the recesses and out of sight and I didn't have the energy to go looking for it, so I reluctantly pulled out the grape juice and poured myself a shot.

To tell you the truth, I wasn't feeling all that hot. It might have been the nachos and margaritas I'd consumed the night before. I eyed the grape juice with reluctance, and took a swig. It wasn't bad. I took another swig. It tasted pretty much like normal grape juice. I took a third swig. I decided I missed all the chemicals and preservatives I was used to and threw the rest down the drain.

I went back to the refrigerator to hunt for the butter and finally found it buried under the bean sprouts. By now, I was pretty steamed, I can tell you. So what I did, I pulled everything out of the refrigerator and reversed the order. I put all of Franny's junk back in the back and all of my unhealthy alternatives in the front.

Call me perverse, but that's what motherhood does to you. And any mother out there who hasn't pulled some equally childish stunt to get back at her kids ought to check herself into the nearest psychiatric ward, if you ask me. One day, all that pent-up aggression will work its way to the surface and she'll be doing thirty years to life and making license plates.

My friend Mabel had talked me into going shopping with her. Mabel was about to go visit her friend Iris in one of those senior condo colonies in Florida and she didn't think her wardrobe was up to it. From Iris's accounts, the Golden Glow was a pretty swinging place, and I guess Mabel was afraid she'd need a tennis dress for tennis and golf shorts for golf and her old polyester standbys would look embarrassingly gauche.

So about eleven o'clock we headed out to Florence Mall. Now, you might think I was turning my back on the case, and to tell you the truth, I was thinking about doing just that. But we detectives need time to process what we've learned. And in order to process, you need to distance yourself from things so that your unconscious mind can work without your conscious mind always butting in. The boys go to the track. Me, I go shopping. It costs about the same in the end.

We started at one end and worked our way to the food court in the middle. I was feeling a little better and the prospect of eating something while liberated from my daughter's scrutiny was too good to pass up. I ate a slice of pizza and a salad from the salad bar, passing up the reduced-calorie slime for the original ranch dressing. For dessert I ate one of those chocolate chip cookie sandwiches with icing in the middle and on both sides. I drank a Diet Coke just to persuade myself that I wasn't completely out of control.

Then we waddled off to finish our circuit of the mall. Mabel was one of those shoppers whose taste you'd have a hell of a time figuring out if you just looked at what she took into the dressing room.

"This isn't me, but I love it anyway," she'd say.

"So try it on. How do you know it isn't you if you don't try it on?"

Plus, she never wanted to hurt the salesperson's feelings. She'd try on anything they offered her, no matter how hideous or unsuited to her.

"Ugh!" she'd say, wriggling into a sea-green polyester suit.

"I don't know why you bother," I'd say. "Even I feel sorry for the polyester they killed for that one."

"But what if she bought one just like it for her mother? Or even for herself, to wear on her next job interview? I wouldn't want to be the one to disillusion her," she'd say.

You can see how it went.

By the time I hit home, I was feeling off again. I stretched out on the couch. Sophie was miffed that I wouldn't let her sleep on my stomach, but that was the most questionable part of my anatomy right now. I lay there and thought about the case. By now, the cops probably already had the murderer under surveillance. He probably had nothing to do with AWOS or with Vietnam or with Nicaragua. He was probably some business executive or organized crime boss.

What difference did it make if, as I suspected, PJ Silverman was still alive? I didn't even care whether she lived in Cincinnati or Jakarta. I had no business tracking her down even if she was alive. I sure as hell didn't want to sic the FBI on her.

I didn't think the cops would ever figure out about Val Smith. I hadn't figured it out, and I like to think that I could run rings around Sgt. Fricke, intellectually speaking. Probably physically speaking, too, if it came to that.

Only not right now. Right now, I was feeling worse by the minute. Was there some kind of flu going around? I probably caught it from my grandchildren at that goddamn family dinner.

The word "dinner" made my stomach tighten up, so I hoped Franny wasn't expecting anything when she got home.

I got up and went to the medicine chest to see what I had along the lines of a stomach settler. I took a couple of swigs of Pepto-Bismol, closing my eyes against its putrid pinkness. It came right back up and brought some other things with it.

God, this must be the flu, I thought. All of a sudden, everything was lobbying to move up or down, so I took turns sitting on the toilet and leaning over it.

When Franny arrived, she found me sitting on the bathroom floor, crying.

"My god, Mom! Are you all right?"

What did she think? I wasn't thin enough to be bulimic.

"Let's get you to bed," she said.

"I think you better move the bed in here," I said.

She tried to get me up, but my muscles felt like overstretched elastic.

"It's okay, Fran," I said through my tears, worried about her back. "I like it here."

"You can't stay here, Mother. I'll call Garf."

"Don't you dare!" I warned her. "Call Mel."

With Mel's help, I got to bed and lay there feeling sorry for myself. Al went into high gear and made chicken soup, which I am ashamed to confess I threw at her. Well, I threw it at somebody, I'm not sure who, because I was having trouble focusing by then. That made me feel even sorrier for myself, which made me cry some more, which no doubt improved my vision enormously. Mel tried to take my temperature, but after gagging on the damn thermometer, I threw it out the window. At least, I threw it in that direction.

After a while, somebody new came in, somebody that smelled medical. Moses was there, too; I could hear him. Goddamn, I wished they'd all go away and let me die in peace and turn off the damn lights on their way out.

Now I was hearing things, too. There was this whine in my head. Boy, this virus I had packed a hell of a wallop; it was probably one of those mutants that had originated at some nuclear test site and migrated east — something the elderly don't have the genes to cope with.

I was trying to tell everybody to get out of my room, but I seemed to be having trouble making myself understood. So what else was new? I would apparently go to my grave misunderstood. I was trying to tell Moses to tell Kevin to take the cats, when somebody lifted me up and set me on this platform and strapped me down and wheeled me away. My eyes were doing really weird things now; I kept getting these flashes of red light. Then I heard a slam and the whine started up again, and we were moving fast.

Goddamn, I said to myself. My first ambulance ride and I can't even enjoy it.

I can't tell you much about the rest of the evening, only if you get a chance to hang out at an emergency room under similar circumstances, take it from me: don't. What they do is, they figure out what is most likely to kill you in your condition and they do that. Me, I was choking already and they wanted to shove a goddamn tube down my throat. And for once, I wasn't in any position to argue. Then they stuck me with needles and asked could I feel anything. Hell, yes! I wanted to scream, but I couldn't speak because my mouth was full of plastic tubing.

Then they changed their minds and removed the tubing and knocked me out, which was a big improvement on the situation, except that while I was out they hooked me up to a goddamn ventilator, which gave me a sore throat that lasted for days.

Later, I found out that a few other people spent a rough night as well. Like the Health Department official who got awakened in the middle of the night, and Mabel and the owners of the food stands where we had eaten our lunch, whom the Health Department official had awakened.

Well, I guess it's one way to get your refrigerator cleaned out, but I don't recommend it. Around 9 a.m., the Health Department, which had scoured my garbage, identified the culprit: the damn all-natural grape juice was supporting a healthy colony of *Clostridium botulinum*, and my taste for preservatives was the only thing that had saved me from death by botulism.

CHAPTER 27

What did Patty of Patty's Natural Foods have against me? Okay, I was a meat eater, but her reaction seemed a little extreme.

Franny was mortified, but I hastened to assure her that I didn't really think it was some nefarious plot to put me out of commission, permanently or otherwise. No, the whole episode just confirmed my suspicion that all those chemical additives are there for a reason.

Patty herself tried to disabuse me of this notion when she came to visit me in the hospital on Thursday, toting a huge vase of roses.

"I can't tell you how sorry I am, Ms. Caliban. But honestly, I don't think anybody knows how it happened. We checked every last bottle in the shop and all of the others were clean. I suppose the police asked you if the seal had already been broken when you opened the bottle?"

"They asked me, but I don't remember."

"I want you to know that all of our suppliers are highly reputable. We wouldn't deal with them otherwise. Natural food companies usually have higher standards than the mainstream companies. Their processing procedures usually exceed the specifications of the USDA."

"Well, I guess it just wandered in off the street then," I said testily. My throat still hurt from the tube I'd swallowed and the rest of me didn't feel much better.

"I know how you must feel," she said sympathetically. Her eyes said she could tell by the way I looked but was too polite to say that. My eyes said, *no, you don't, cookie*, but I was too polite to say that. "If I may, I'd like to leave this hundred-dollar gift certificate for you. It's inadequate compensation, I know—"

I stared at it in horror. A hundred-dollar certificate for health food?

I was burning it in the trashcan when Penny Stokes stopped by in her nurse's uniform.

"It's a good thing they called me last night," she said. "Lots of people mistake botulism for the flu."

"How did you know it wasn't?" I asked.

"Your eyes. Your eyelids were drooping and your pupils were responding to the light. That made me think it wasn't just influenza."

"I guess I have you to thank for the tube down my throat," I grumbled. I wasn't really in the mood to receive visitors.

"First, they had to make sure it was all gone," she said, nodding cheerily. "Then they had to help you breathe for a while. Don't worry, Cat. It doesn't last nearly as long as pregnancy."

"Oh, well, that perks me right up."

Kevin called.

"Oh, thank god, Mrs. C. It's good to hear your voice."

"How can you tell it's *my* goddamn voice you're hearing? I sound like a toad in heat."

"Sounds just like you! So, what kind of cookies do you want — oatmeal or chocolate chip?"

"Oatmeal!" I croaked. "No, wait, that'll hurt my throat. Look, why don't you just skip the cookie dough and bring me the chocolate — the kind that melts in your mouth? I didn't make it this far to choke on a damn raisin."

A nurse appeared at the door with Curtis and a sour look on her face.

"Mrs. Caliban, is this — gentleman — a friend of yours?"
"Curtis? He's my brother." What a jerk.
"Hey, Cat, how you feelin'?" He was carrying a bouquet that had a contraband look to it and it was stuck in an empty Ripple bottle. From the smell you could tell that Curtis had made the sacrifice and emptied the bottle so he could use it.
"Hey, how'd you find out so fast?"
"Al seen Trish this morning and told her. Hey, you think somebody tried to kill you?"
"Well, if they did, they picked a hell of an indirect route. Anybody could've drunk that stuff."
"Steel, he callin' it biological warfare."
"I feel like a goddamn battlefield, that's for sure."
Mabel arrived at about this time, looking pretty chipper for somebody who'd been up half the night answering questions. She was wearing one of her new outfits. Curtis was telling her she looked terrific in blue.
The sour nurse came in to take my temperature with a thermometer in one of those plastic cases that looks like a dinosaur's Popsicle.
Moses arrived in a bulky all-weather coat that made me glance out the window to see if we were having a tornado or something. Then Sidney popped out from under it, took a flying leap, and landed on the bed, purring loudly.
"I woulda brought Winnie, but I told them, one at a time."
I gave Sid a kiss and a cuddle, and he curled up on my lap under the covers. My mood was improving.
"So how long you in for, Cat?"
"You're asking me? The person least capable of constructing the night's events? I don't even know what day this is."
"Well, haven't you seen a doctor?"
"Yeah, I saw some doctors. None of 'em said anything useful that I can remember."
Moses sat down with a deck of cards to take advantage of me in my weakened condition.

"So, do you think this business is related to that other business?" Moses looked at me over his bifocals.

"You mean, is the bacteria in my grape juice related to the cut brake line? I don't see how. The brake line was cut when my car was sitting behind my house."

"And—?"

I narrowed my eyes at him.

"Are you trying to tell me somebody could've come into the house and poisoned the grape juice?"

"Are you discarding that card or you just waving it around to get a breeze going? Well, isn't it possible?"

"It's possible. Anything's possible. It's possible that my daughter secretly works for the KGB, but I don't think so."

"Why not?"

"There's too many people around our place — and, uh, animals."

"You referring to my vicious carnivorous watchdog and your lethal feline bodyguard?"

"Well—" I could feel Sidney's purr vibrating along my thigh bones. "Okay. Say somebody sneaked in and poisoned the grape juice. When did they do it? Franny told me this morning that she only brought the juice home on Tuesday afternoon, and I know she did, because I had already told her there was no more room in the refrigerator. So supposing they watched the house Tuesday night, saw their opportunity, slipped past our four-footed furry alarm system, picked the lock on my door, and got in. Why poison in the grape juice? Anybody could have drunk it. I mean, they should've put it in my gin if they wanted to make sure they got *me* this time."

"Well, I don't know much about bacteria, Cat, but—"

"When they fixed the brakes, at least they fixed the brakes on a car usually driven by me. Except for sneaking around the house at night, I don't see any pattern in the modus operandi. Unless you think they thought that since they didn't get me before when they tinkered with something that belonged exclusively to me, they would take a different tack this time and tinker with something that didn't."

"Well, it's your Frigidaire."

"Not lately, it isn't."

"Anyway, you're wrong about there being no pattern."

"Look, I know you're dying to call 'Gin.' Just do it and get it over with and then tell me what's on your mind."

"Okay." He made his sets and laid his last card down. "This is not a person who shoves a gun in your face and blows you away. What these attempts have in common, if they are both attempts, is the anonymity. That's why they're so messy in the first place. If you pointin' a gun at somebody, you know who's going to fall if you pull the trigger. That means you got to look at them."

"Somebody — it was Dwyer — said that about the Sanders murder," I reflected. "About not having to look at someone if you cut his throat."

"Well, that's true, I suppose, but you have to get a hell of a lot closer than you do if you cut a brake line or leave a bottle of poisoned grape juice around. See, that's the other thing about these last two — the killer didn't even have to hang around the scene of the crime."

"I guess the police ought to dust my refrigerator for prints." I sighed.

"They already have."

I looked at him in horror. "And where else?" I demanded.

"Lots of places." He shrugged. "Don't worry, Cat. Kevin and me already cleaned it up. You can't hardly tell they've been there."

"So you don't think the throat cutter, the brake line cutter, and the poisoner are all the same person? Hey, maybe that's the connection. The first two crimes involved cutting implements."

"I ain't saying they are and I ain't saying they ain't. I ain't even saying we got three crimes here. I'm just contemplatin' the possibilities. So let's contemplate the possibility that the juice was deliberately poisoned and the bacteria was introduced before it left the shop. How many people know about Franny's new job?"

"You seen Franny's CAC phone tree? I'd say anybody on a branch at Franny's level or higher knows about it. I'd say half of Cincinnati, at a rough estimate."

"Yeah, and the other half's had their phones disconnected on account of all their money was in the hands of Home State Savings and Loan," he grumbled. "So anybody could've gone into the store, looked around to see what Franny was taking home with her, sent her off looking for something, and poisoned the grape juice."

"So that her mother, the Chemicals Queen, would drink it and kick the bucket. Doesn't sound too likely, does it?"

"What do you know about Franny's new boss?"

"Patty? What's to know about her? She came in today, left me those roses and a hundred-dollar gift certificate for merchandise."

"Uh-huh."

"A hundred-dollar certificate," I said more slowly. "Oh, god, Moses, I burned up the evidence!" I reached for the trash can, forgetting about Sidney and dumping him on the floor. After a squawk of protest, he went under the bed to look for dust bunnies.

"But wait! This doesn't make sense. Why would Patty choose a method that would ruin her business? Let's face it, one case of food poisoning can put a damper on sales. Two cases would do her in."

"Do who in?" Kevin had shown up just in time. Our speculations were growing loopier by the second.

I made him close the door before he passed around the chocolates. My stomach rebelled, but my mouth was very happy. Moses summarized the discussion so far.

"I know, Mrs. C," Kevin said.

"I knew you would," I muttered.

"Suppose she was planning to retire from the business anyway. Maybe she's the secret heir to the Sanders estate. Or maybe she's practicing some kind of insurance fraud. Anyway, she thinks you're getting too close to the truth, so she has to get rid of you. But she also has to close down the store without attracting too much attention. So she poisons you and kills two birds with one stone!"

"I like it," I said. "But who do you see in the miniseries? Roseanne Barr as Patty and, in her television debut, none other than the original Cat?"

The door swung open and a woman with a stethoscope wrapped around her neck walked in. But her hose weren't white and her soles weren't rubber.

"Ms. Caliban? I'm Dr. Goldman. I'll have to ask your friends to wait outside," she said. "All of them," she added, catching Sidney by the scruff of the neck. He purred at her happily. She gave him a smile, scratched behind his ears, and turned him over to Moses.

They left me alone with her, a dark-eyed brunette, and I read her identity card. "Goldman," it said. "P. Goldman."

CHAPTER 28

I was held hostage for four whole days. You know how hospitals are. If you're there on Friday, you're stuck until Monday, because everybody with any authority is out playing golf. I didn't think P. Goldman was out playing golf, though.

Weekends in a hospital are more fun than the early morning shift in the morgue, but not by much. Me and my neighbor Emma held wheelchair races till the nurses caught us, which was probably just as well. My lungs didn't seem to be as good as they used to be. The high point of my weekend was supposed to be blowing into that plastic contraption that tells you whether one of your lungs has collapsed. The bookmobile was heavy on romance. Their only mystery was a well-thumbed copy of *The Murder of Roger Ackroyd*. It is the only mystery besides *Murder on the Orient Express* about which I can say that I remember who committed the murder.

Mabel brought me one of those needlepoint kits of two parakeets to go with the paint-by-numbers kittens she'd already given me, but I pretended that my eyes were still going in and out of focus. Mabel was kind of looking around for Curtis, who had brought me a medal from Steel, for bravery. Bill McGann brought me a card composed and produced by

Street People United, and signed by three-fourths of its members; it began:

> *"We heard they took you to General,*
> *At least it wasn't your funeral."*

And it ended with:

> *"No, we don't like the place you're at,*
> *So get well soon and get out, Cat!"*

Actually, I'd been taken to Christ instead of University, or what most Cincinnati residents referred to as "General" six years after the name change. But I wasn't going to challenge their poetic license. And speaking of licenses, Kevin brought Diane, which I suspected was illegal and not just because we were in a hospital. Franny brought me a book on vegetarianism. Kevin brought me a book on poisons, so I could see just how close I'd come to biting the bullet. Moses brought Winnie, who left in disgrace after barking at the pigeons outside my window. Mel and Al brought me some mysteries I either hadn't read or couldn't remember, and a book of crossword puzzles from Val, who was afraid to come see me.

My daughter Sharon brought me a sexy nightgown so unlike the frumpy stuff she usually foisted off on me that I was sure Franny had gone shopping with her. My son Jason brought me Lee Iacocca's autobiography, well thumbed, and my granddaughter Melissa, who got locked in the stairwell when she went looking for a bathroom and nearly had to be taken to the E.R. to be treated for mortification.

On the night before I left, me and Emma threw a party in her room and stayed up half the night telling ghost stories to each other.

It's a wonder they hadn't dragged somebody off the golf course and thrown me out by then.

Kevin and Franny came to spring me and we hid Diane in one of my potted plants.

One thing about being in the hospital: it gives you lots of time to think. I knew that Moses was right and I should consider the possibility that the botulism contamination was no accident. But on the other hand, I couldn't reconstruct a sequence of events that seemed possible. Okay, so anybody could break into the Catatonia Arms — and frequently did. But the last two people that I knew of who had broken in had both been caught, one by Sidney and one by the barbell in the basement. Call me naive, but I just couldn't picture a steady stream of prowlers coming and going. That left Patty, who stood to ruin her business if she succeeded in killing me off.

"But Mom, maybe Steel is right — sort of," my daughter contributed. "I mean, the last two guys who broke in, they weren't, like, professionals, you know? I mean, if we're talking about the antiwar movement and the Nicaraguan Contras, there could be people involved who are, like, highly trained in breaking and entering without being detected."

"Like who?" I frowned.

"Like the same people who planted the bomb at that draft board office in 1970."

"The FBI? Alcohol, Tobacco, and Firearms?"

"Or the CIA — whoever. What I'm saying is there could be interests at stake you don't even know about."

"Well, hell, if I'm Public Enemy Number One, why don't they just fucking blow me away and be done with it?"

"Mo-om!" She got that pained expression on her face.

"Fra-an!" I matched it and raised her a couple of degrees. Me with an armful of needle tracks and bruises and her with a dark-purple forehead — we were quite a pair.

"That's not how they work, Mom. They don't want the public to know what they're up to. If they want to get rid of somebody, they have to make it seem like an accident."

"Well, this was pretty damned accidental, if you ask me. They could have killed you. They could have killed Kevin, for chrissake! He spends as much time in my refrigerator as anybody."

"They don't care about that, Mom. They'd still get you, sooner or later."

"Oh, well, that's a comfort."

"That's just the way they operate, Mom."

"How do you know how they operate?"

"I've read stuff about it. Exposés and stuff. Former agents sometimes talk to writers and journalists about things they think the public should know that they can't talk about publicly."

"I don't know, Fran. I don't even own a trenchcoat. What is it you think I know that makes me so dangerous?"

She narrowed her eyes at me and looked thoughtful.

"That's what we have to figure out."

In the background, I heard faint music.

CHAPTER 29

Mickey McCafferty, I thought, held the key if anybody did. Other people might have lied to me — probably had. But McCafferty was the only one who had seemed to be saying more than he was saying, if you catch my drift. That didn't make him guilty of anything; in fact, it made him seem available for pumping.

So on Monday morning, I called up his auto shop.

"Mickey? He's not in today."

"Oh. Is he sick?"

"Don't know. Ain't heard from him."

This struck me as a rather casual attitude to take.

"Does he miss work often without calling?"

"You his parole officer?"

"No." I thought quickly. "Just a concerned friend. I haven't seen him around."

"Well, he don't have no phone, you know. So when he's sick, he don't always call."

"Is he sick often?" I decided to press. All he could do was hang up.

"Look, lady, if you know Mickey, you know he's a moody bastard. Sometimes he just — checks out — for a few days.

We don't know if he's sick and we don't ask. He's a damned good mechanic — one of the best. We're glad when he shows up, and if he wants to wear a tutu to work, we ain't going to object. Now, I'm sorry, but I'm short-handed here and I gotta go."

Checks out? What the hell did that mean? Did he go through periods of depression? Go on binges? Take his mechanical expertise on drug runs to South America? Go to work for a rival auto mechanic? Inquiring minds want to know.

So I sat down with my map and tried to figure out where Mickey lived. The address I'd pried out of OSU was on Round Bottom Road and that was clearly marked on the map, so it didn't look like I'd have any trouble. I headed out.

Newtown is on one of the leading edges of Cincinnati's suburban expansion. Much of it is still rural, but the subdivisions are encroaching. On Round Bottom Road, addresses were still hard to come by. Houses were set back from the road and there weren't any cute Kountry signs identifying residents and their addresses. I finally settled on a battered mailbox with its bent metal flag halfway up, which, on closer inspection, still bore traces of the number I was looking for in faded black paint.

I turned up a narrow, overgrown gravel driveway.

The house at the end was a small weathered farmhouse. Its white paint was gray with dust from the fields. There was a battered Chevy pickup parked to one side. Although I could hear a train whistle from the nearby railroad tracks, the house itself unsettled me, it was so quiet and still.

I knocked on the door anyway.

I didn't expect an answer and I didn't get one. I pressed my face to the grimy front window, framing it with my hands to block out the light, but the front room was empty. Through an open door to the left I could see into a bedroom beyond.

This room was not empty.

Whereas before I had been treading heavily across the porch to announce my arrival, I now stepped lightly on my little cat feet. I circled the house, stooping below the windows, until I reached the back, and the window which I presumed to belong to the room I had glimpsed from the front.

Mickey is a moody bastard, I said to myself. If he catches you sneaking around, he is likely to blow your head off.

I took a deep breath and straightened to peer into the window. The legs I had seen through the front window were still stretched out on the bed. I followed them up to the face.

Mickey McCafferty would be moody no longer.

I don't know if you want me to tell you how I knew, but it had something to do with the flies on his nose.

Maybe I'd left the hospital too soon, I thought. My stomach was lurching around like a vaudeville drunk.

You have to go in there, Cat, I said to myself. You, Cat Caliban, Private Investigator. On the other hand, said my practical side, if you throw up all over the crime scene, Sergeant Fricke will be very annoyed.

So I threw up first and then went in.

The front door was unlocked, so I didn't even get to practice my breaking and entering skills, which was probably just as well. I was tiring easily these days, what with the lingering effects of the poisoning and the steady diet of hospital Jell-O.

I used one of Franny's hankies to turn the doorknob, then held it to my nose. It smelled of the sachet Melissa had given me for my birthday, which probably saved me from further disgrace. The window in McCafferty's room was open about two inches. I knew I had to resist the temptation to open every window in the house.

He'd presumably been sitting up in bed, and now he was slumped over sideways against the pillow. He was dressed in jeans and a plain white T-shirt or undershirt. The bedclothes were badly mussed around his legs, which made me think of convulsions. One arm was draped over the side of the bed, so I walked around to see if there was anything in it. The hand was balled tightly into a fist. When I studied it, I saw traces of something brown between his index and second fingers. The skin appeared burned slightly. I bent closer and removed the handkerchief for a smell.

McCafferty had been smoking in bed, but he hadn't been smoking cigarettes.

This was not an especially astute deduction on my part, since there were an ashtray and several reefers on the night-stand next to his bed. On the surface, he appeared to have died from bad dope. But I knew he could have died of anything — a heart attack, a brain aneurysm. Still, bad dope was a better bet than some causes — AIDS, for example, or an Act of God.

I didn't think I could get away with going through his pockets, so I settled for going through his drawers instead. I couldn't give up the handkerchief, so I borrowed a dish-towel from the kitchen. I didn't disturb anything. I just opened every drawer and took a peek inside.

The most interesting stuff I found, though, was on the small metal folding table that stood next to an armchair in the living room.

I found a page of scribbled notes I couldn't understand. But there were some dates — all from '69 and '70 — and some names I recognized. The page was headed with a number: 100-16214. Up in one corner was another set of letters and numbers that looked to me like a library call number. The last entry on the page had been underlined three times. It said: *KOS*?

I wrestled with myself, then copied down the numbers, some of the notes, and the final entry, and left it there for the cops to find. I was running out of time. The smell was making me feel faint. I headed for the kitchen, but there wasn't much there. The outside of the refrigerator did not reveal any secrets — no phone numbers, no notes, no kitschy magnets from international terrorist organizations or even from campaigning Congressman.

I yanked open the door and confronted a bottle of grape juice. It was the same brand as the one Franny had brought home from Patty's Natural Foods.

CHAPTER 30

I don't know why the cops aren't more grateful to me. I didn't have to let Fricke know about anything. You couldn't pay me enough to work for that asshole. I could have just given my report to the Newtown police without ever mentioning the possible connection to the Sanders killing. But no. Public-spirited citizen that I am, I suggested that the Newtown cops give Fricke a call.

That won me a trip down to the Investigation Bureau and another four hours in one of their butt-busting chairs.

"I'm a sick woman, Fricke." I gave Officer Eddie Landau a surreptitious wink. "You wouldn't want an old lady, just out of the hospital, to croak here in one of your spiffy interrogation rooms, now, would you?"

"I am more interested," he said slowly, trying to articulate around the wad of gum in his mouth, "in the recently deceased. I don't know what it is about you, Caliban, but every time I show up somewhere, you are the healthiest one in the vicinity."

"Good genes," I muttered. "Look, I've told you every goddamn thing I know about this business." I stuck my hand in my pocket and crossed my fingers. I always believe you should cover yourself. "Hell, you ought to know more about it than I do. You trying to tell me you never even talked to McCafferty?"

"Let me put it this way, Caliban—" His chewing speeded up and gave him a little twitch in his temple. "I know this is hard for you to understand, but down here we are dealing with the big picture. And the picture you are dealing with is a hell of a lot smaller than the one we're looking at, awright?"

"But people keep getting killed and injured in the one I'm looking at," I said with feigned puzzlement. "Don't you think maybe you should try seeing things through my eyes for a change, before somebody else drops dead?"

"Beat it," he said. This was the way all of our interviews ended. I thought Fricke could use a refresher course in public relations.

I called Val Smith at her work number.

"I need to talk to you," I said.

"Why? What's happened?" She sounded frightened. I wondered if she already knew about Mickey.

"I'll tell you when I see you."

She asked me to come by when she got off work. She looked pale and shaken when she answered the door.

"Is Penny here?" I asked.

She shook her head. "She's at work. What's happened?"

"Sit down," I said, still unsure how much she knew. "Mickey's dead."

"Mickey! Oh, no!" She stared at me in horror. "How?"

"I don't know yet. He could have smoked some poisoned dope. I wanted to ask Penny about that. It could have been something else."

"But he was murdered?"

"I don't really know, but I think he must have been. For one thing, he had a bottle of grape juice in the fridge that could have doubled for the one that put my lights out. For another, he'd been smoking dope when he died. That gives us two opportunities for murder."

She pressed a hand to her mouth and started to cry.

"Cat, what's going on? What the hell is going on?"

"I wish I knew. Listen, do you know a place called Patty's Natural Foods?" I studied her.

"What?" She looked startled, frightened.

"Patty's Natural Foods." I didn't give her any help.

"Isn't that a health food store in Clifton?"

"Yes. Ever go there?"

"No, I don't think so. Maybe once or twice — I don't know."

"Do you know the owner?"

She stared at me. "No." Just that.

"Val, did PJ Silverman really die in that explosion in Athens County?"

She caught her breath. "Cat, I can't talk about that. I *can't*. Don't ask me. It doesn't have anything to do with anything. It *can't*."

"It doesn't have anything to do with my poisoning — or Mickey's?"

"No. Oh, god, no! It really doesn't. You have to trust me."

"I don't think I can help you, Val," I said quietly.

"Cat, please!" she wailed. "You don't understand. She *loves* Mickey. She would never — hurt him."

"Or kill him?"

"Never."

"Not even to protect herself?"

"Not even then."

"Why did she run out on him, then? Why did she let him go on trial alone?"

"Cat, I don't know. I've never asked her that. That was between her and Mickey. I wasn't there. But they were satisfied, Mickey was satisfied."

We were talking about PJ in the present tense as well as the past.

"Look, let me show you something," I said. "I found a page of notes in Mickey's apartment and I copied down what I could."

I passed her my copy and she studied it with a frown. Tears ran down her cheeks and struck the page. Alarmed, I wondered if this was a new strategy for destroying evidence.

"Careful, you're smearing the ink."

"Sorry." She wiped her face with the back of her hand.

"I don't know what to say, Cat. It looks like these have something to do with AWOS, but I don't see the significance. I mean, I recognize the names, of course, and some of the content. But the dates don't ring any bells for me. It's not as if they were — oh, say, dates for the spring Moratorium or anything. At least, not that I remember."

"What about the numbers?"

"This one looks like a library call number."

"Yeah, and the other one?"

She shook her head.

"Could it be Mickey's prison ID number?"

"I don't know, Cat. It seems kind of long for that, don't you think? It's not a Social Security number and it's too long for a telephone number, too short for long distance."

"Do you know what Mickey might have been working on or thinking about recently?"

"He hasn't called since Steve was killed. I thought that was a little odd. But Linda said he was afraid the cops would go after him. And Linda was worried about it, too — thought he'd be vulnerable because of his record."

"Would you be surprised to learn that Mickey shopped at Patty's Natural Foods?"

"Cat—"

"Let me put it this way. If PJ Silverman were alive, would you have been in contact with her yourself, I wonder, or would you just have received word of her through Mickey?"

"What difference would that make?"

I had my answer.

On my way home, I stopped at the library. Twenty minutes later I was holding it in my hand: a book by Ann Mari Buitrago and Leon Andrew Immerman, called *Are You Now or Have You Ever Been in the F.B.I. Files?*

CHAPTER 31

"Do you know anybody in the FBI?" I asked Moses the next morning. He was out back, refinishing a dresser for his granddaughter. Winnie was shut up in the apartment until he finished the stripping.

"What does it cost me if I say yes?"

"I think Mickey McCafferty sent for his FBI file. I think he was murdered because of something he found in it."

"Such as?"

"I don't know. I didn't see it."

"You goin' to have to work on your search techniques, girl."

"I thought I did pretty well, considering there was a — uh, under the circumstances." My stomach was still pretty testy. "Thing is, if his notes on the file were next to his reading chair, why wasn't his file there?"

"How you know what you found was notes on his FBI file?" He had his head tilted back so that he could study an appliqué through the bottoms of his bifocals.

"Because at the top of the page there was a library call number. It turned out to be a call number for a book all about how to send for and interpret your FBI files. In the middle of the top of the page there was a number that started with 100.

According to this book, that was the classification number for domestic security — for subversives. It was the number most often given to antiwar activists."

"Okay, I'm with you. So he didn't keep his notes and his file together. You want to know where his file went. You thinking maybe the killer came back and took it." He wrapped the brush carefully, peeled off his rubber gloves, and sat down with me in the shade.

"The killer — or somebody else. I gotta tell you, Moses, these people are all keeping secrets. Some secrets are their own, some secrets are somebody else's, and they're all afraid the secrets will come out. They're all protecting each other. But I keep wondering how long that will go on now that Mickey is dead. What if somebody learns what Mickey learned? Or what if somebody thinks Mickey told somebody something?"

"Sounds kinda vague, Cat, but I think I follow you."

"Maybe the file was hidden someplace and I didn't find it. Can we trust the police to find it?"

He sighed. "Okay, I'll see what I can do about that."

"Otherwise, will have to request it from the FBI."

"That's gonna take time, Cat."

"I know. The book says it should take them ten days to respond, but it always takes longer. But if the requester had more pull than I do—"

"You don't want much, do you?"

"Well, since you asked, I'd like the files on Sanders and Silverman, too. They're both dead, as far as the Feds are concerned, so their files ought to be available."

"Cat, did you miss the part where I'm a *retired* police officer?"

"Hell, I'm a retired mother, but I got a daughter camped out on my living room couch! I'm a retired housewife, but I still gotta run the goddamn vacuum cleaner every now and then! I'd like to retire my—"

"Okay, okay! I get the picture. I'll see what I can do. But it's still going to take some time. So in the meantime, you best try to figure out what it is you think was in that McCafferty file and who you think it threatened. For example, you say this Silverman is alive."

"I think she is. Look, among the AWOS members or former members, you got family connections to a funeral home and a med school morgue. So that solves the biggest problem — where you gonna get a body to stand in for Silverman?"

"Yeah, but Cat, it can't just be any old body. Forensic pathology is pretty high-tech."

"Right. So the body has to match in height, mostly."

"Teeth?"

"You could fix that too, though, couldn't you, Moses? I mean, if you had access to a sympathetic dentist."

"You mean, one who didn't object to doing a root canal on a corpse? I don't know, Cat. An explosion would probably knock the teeth to kingdom come, but I don't think it would change their shape."

"An explosion would make it as hard as possible to identify the pieces, anyway. A fire by itself wouldn't be good enough. I've been reading about this stuff."

"Is that what you was reading in the hospital?" He eyed me with distaste.

"A fire might work if you have a big enough building and it's fast enough or far away enough from a fire department, so that the whole building collapses on top of the corpse. But an explosion would be better."

"You got a devious mind, you know that, Cat?"

"You told me before. Hell, Moses, these are desperate people. If I can think it up and research it in a few days with less motivation than they had, why couldn't they?"

"Which they you talking about?"

"Well, Silverman's the only one we know for sure. McCafferty wasn't in on it because he was in prison at the time. Any of the rest of them could have been."

"So they leave the body in this cabin in Athens County, and Silverman takes off. What happens next?"

"Plastic surgery?"

"Okay. That's possible. Cost a lot, though."

"I think a lot of these kids had access to money. They didn't live like it in college, but in those days nobody did. The question is whether it was enough to finance the disappearance *and* reappearance."

"As?"

"The owner of a natural foods store in Clifton."

"The one where your daughter's working?"

I gave him a look. "Yeah. That one."

"Don't you think we better get her out of there?"

"I don't know, Moses. I've been thinking about it. I don't think she's dangerous to anyone — except her mother, of course. The car accident was just a fluke, because I was the one who was supposed to be driving."

"And what is it they think you know?"

"That's what I can't figure out. See, there could be two things going on here."

"At least."

"Right. Patty could be out to get me because she's afraid I'll tell somebody she's still alive. But that doesn't necessarily make her the killer of Sanders and McCafferty. On the other hand, what you were saying before about the similarities between the murders — McCafferty fits the pattern. But I still think his murder was more like the attempts on me than the Sanders murder."

"You mean 'cause the killer just left something behind and split?"

"Right, and didn't hang around to witness the consequences."

"So what's the second plot involve? The McCafferty file?"

I nodded. "I keep thinking about what he said in the car that day and I've been looking over Kevin's notes. He was talking about sleight of hand and how he used to think it was 'us-versus-them.' Moses, what if he identified an FBI informant among the AWOS members?"

"Oh, I don't know, Cat. Those files get heavily censored before they're sent out. They supposed to black out anything that points to a particular source of information."

"Yeah, but let's face it: they're bureaucrats. They weren't there so how're they gonna know what might give somebody away? Don't you think it's possible that Mickey spotted something in his file that had to have come from one other person?"

"Sure, it's possible. But what difference would it make after all this time?"

"What difference would it make? Christ, Moses, one person went to prison for ten years on evidence probably planted by the FBI! Another person went underground. Two lives got ruined. Who knows what difference it could make even now? Suppose it was somebody who is active in the anti-contra movement? Suppose that person is still working for the Bureau? Suppose he's an attorney well respected by liberal types? Suppose it was a U.S. Congressman?"

"That's a lot of serious supposin', Cat. Suppose you and me have a beer while we workin' all this out?"

That was okay by me, even though my stomach might raise some objections. I went in and got us a couple. They were easy to find now that my fridge was nearly empty. Moses took a swig of his before he pulled on his rubber gloves and went back to work.

"So who's your favorite candidate?" he asked me.

"For FBI informant? I kind of like Sanders or Matthias. See, if it's Sanders, then somebody found out and killed him because of it and everything else is a cover-up for that. On the other hand, it would make more sense if McCafferty was killed because he figured out who it was. That would make Sanders a blackmailer."

"Come again?"

"Well, say Sanders figured it out and decided to try and blackmail that person. Maybe part of the blackmail had to do with finding Val and Hope. Only Sanders got offed instead. But then, McCafferty gets hold of his FBI file, or maybe he's had it. Anyway, when Sanders gets killed, he realizes something funny is going on and he looks at his file again and realizes what it is."

"So he confronts the person, who pays him off in poison grape juice, or poison reefers, one, and they drink a toast or smoke a joint together, only McCafferty drops dead."

"Okay, so there are a few thin spots! Revoke my license! You got any better theories?"

"No, no." He was scraping black gook into a coffee can. "Actually, I kinda like your theories, only, like you say, they got a few thin spots."

"Maybe McCafferty didn't figure it out. Maybe this person just worried that he would."

"Then what was all that 'sleight of hand' 'us-versus-them' talk about?"

That's what makes these discussions with Moses so damn frustrating, and at the same time, so useful: he remembers everything.

"You're right," I conceded. "He knew something."

"How does Silverman figure into this? If Silverman is Patty, your poisoned grape juice came out of her store."

"Well, either she's the killer, or she's the FBI informant, or she's protecting her identity."

"You got this case practically solved, Cat. Now, if Kevin was here, he'd be telling some wild story 'bout how the FBI was involved in Silverman's disappearance in exchange for information."

I made a face at his back.

"Well, he's not here, thank god, and I've got all the possibilities I can handle. I'm not even thinking about why Val's and Linda's daughters look so much alike. I'm assuming Sanders fathered both of them, but I'm trying to ignore that detail."

"Now, what kind of attitude is that for an aspiring investigator?"

I held the beer can to my forehead, which was beginning to throb.

"Say, Moses, ever hear of anything with the initials K, O, S?"

He didn't answer for a minute. He was concentrating on a corner. Then he looked up.

"Can't say I have."

"Well, it's not one of those FBI abbreviations like ELSUR or FISUR, is it?"

"I don't know what you talking about."

"Electronic surveillance and physical surveillance."

"I wouldn't know. I was in the Cincinnati Police, not the Bureau."

"Well, I couldn't find it anywhere in the book, but between the FBI and the whole leftist movement, I'm dealing with so damn many initials, I can't keep any of it straight. I got the SDS, the SNCC, the NL, the CAC, and the YAF, not to mention your OC's and PC's. I mean, the 'OS' part could be Ohio State, but I might have to go back to Columbus to find out. Or it could be somebody's initials. Between Sasinowski, Sanders, and Silverman, and their other names, not to mention a Stokes thrown in for good measure, half the suspects in this goddamn case have initials that end in S."

"Well, if it was me, I'd be worrying about FAC."

"What's that?"

"Your daughter, Frances Ann Caliban."

CHAPTER 32

So I headed to the place where I always go when I am lost and confused and looking for answers: the Public Library of Cincinnati and Hamilton County. I spent my afternoon sitting in a chair reading about the antiwar movement and the FBI counterintelligence campaign during the late 60s and early 70s. I thought some wag in the Bureau had named it with his tongue in his cheek; what I read about certainly ran counter to anything I recognized as intelligence.

I put it down to the physical exhaustion I was still experiencing that it took me several hours to notice what afterward seemed obvious. When it hit me, I stared at the words on the page a good five minutes. Now I knew what questions I wanted to ask.

The chances of reaching Dez Lewis on a Wednesday when Congress was in session were not great, but I put in a call to his office and left a message asking him to call me later that evening or the next evening. Dwyer was in court all afternoon, so I left a message there, too, asking him to stop by Arnold's later. I reached Linda and asked her if Tom was in town. He was, so I asked if I could come by later. She hesitated, then agreed.

By then it was late enough to catch Val Smith at home. I called and reached Hope. She said I could come over and then added, in a worried voice, "Is everything okay?"

"I think so, honey," I said. I didn't sound too convincing, I guess. Maybe that's because I wasn't convinced.

We sat out on the deck, Val and Hope and me.

I told Val that Mickey had been reading his FBI file right before he died.

"Did he ever say anything to you about it?"

"No, I didn't even know he had it," she said. "But I hadn't spoken to him that recently, remember. So maybe he'd received it since we last spoke."

"Let me ask you this. Is it possible that one of the AWOS members was an FBI informant?"

Her eyes widened in astonishment.

"I can't imagine that's true, Cat. An informant?"

I handed her another surprise. "Is it possible that the FBI informant was Steve?"

"Steve!" She looked genuinely startled. "He couldn't have been."

"Why not?"

"Well, I would have known." She paused, and then her voice dropped. "Wouldn't I?"

"Take a minute to think it over," I said.

She glanced at Hope, who gave her a funny little shrug. It said, don't worry about me, Mom. I can take it.

Val pressed fingers to her temples.

"He was on scholarship," she said quietly. "He really didn't have much money. But then where did the money come from to buy the house in Rochester? I wondered at the time. He said his mother gave it to him, but didn't want me to know about it. But I didn't think his mother had that kind of money.

"But Steve didn't have that kind of money, either. I mean, most of the time, he didn't have any more money than anybody else."

"What about your engagement ring, Mom?" Hope asked. It was odd to watch her participate in this intellectual exercise to consider allegations against her father.

Val's eyes shifted from her daughter back to me.

"He told me it wasn't as expensive as it looked. He told me he got it on sale. But when I sold it — well, I was shocked how much it was worth."

"He wouldn't have been any use to the FBI, Val, if he spent money more conspicuously."

"I suppose that's true. But he can't have been an informant from the beginning, can he? He was so committed to the movement."

"Was he?"

"Yes, at first. Well, I mean, I always thought he was. That's why I couldn't figure out why he wouldn't do more to help Mickey and PJ."

She put her fists to her mouth and all the blood drained out of her face.

"Oh, my god! He sold them out, didn't he? That bastard set them up and sold them out!" Tears sprang to her eyes.

Hope went over to sit next to her and put an arm around her shoulders.

"It *was* suspicious! It was suspicious at the time! It all happened too soon after we left. Why couldn't I trust my instincts?"

"You were pregnant, Mom, remember?" Hope said gently.

"I know, kiddo, I know." She smiled at her daughter through tears. "But whatever else it does, pregnancy doesn't drain your brain or sap your intellect."

No, I said to myself; motherhood does that.

"And that insurance job! They must have set him up in that, those bastards! And those slimy bastards who came to see him. To think I let them into my house!"

"Let me show you something." I interrupted her outrage. "Does this mean anything to you?" I handed her a slip of paper.

"K, O, S." She frowned and shook her head. "No, not to me."

She handed it back to me.

"Oh, god, Cat, do you think he was still working for them when he got killed?" Then she thought of something worse. "Oh, Jesus! Do you think they traced me for him? Do they know where I am?"

"I don't know, Val. I wish I did. But I'd wait to see what happens. They probably don't want to expose Steve's connection to the Bureau. They have a lot of information they never do anything with. I'd say sit tight a while and see what happens."

Val looked at her daughter and gave her hand a shake.

"Now, we're not going to upset Penny with this. Promise? We're not going to say anything to Penny."

"Too late." Penny, in her white nurse's uniform, stood in the doorway from the kitchen.

She walked over to Val and Hope and put her arms around both of them.

I left them there like that, the three of them, and found my own way out.

CHAPTER 33

I was sitting in the middle room at Arnold's, watching an earnest young man strum his way through "Long Time Gone."

He hadn't been born yet when the song was written, I reflected. Why didn't he stop recycling the songs of the previous generation and get busy and write his own? Maybe — I sighed — it was because the old ones were still depressingly applicable. He had some groupies up front, but their tie-dyes were the original items, like Franny's.

Lennie Dwyer dropped into the bench opposite me.

"You rang, Mrs. Caliban?"

"Two questions. First, what are the chances that one of the AWOS members was an FBI informant?"

"Boy, you don't mess around, do you? You going to ask me next if they were planning to kill LBJ?"

"I'm serious."

"Okay, Mrs. Caliban. The chances that somebody in the group was an FBI informant." He wore pin-striped suspenders today, presumably in honor of his court appearance. He pushed his glasses up on his nose and thought. "Pretty good, I'd say. FBI informants were a dime a dozen in those days."

"Were you one?"

"Me? Nah. Is that why you asked me here?"

"If not you, who, then?"

"Oh, I don't know, Mrs. Caliban. Are we sure there was one?"

I told him about McCafferty.

"Did he tell you about the file?" I asked.

"No, I didn't even know he had it."

"Did he ever ask you how to get his file?"

"Don't think so. He asked me once if I thought he could get it. He thought they might turn him down because of his prison record. I told him I didn't think they could withhold it under the terms of the Freedom of Information Act. That's all I remember, Mrs. Caliban."

"So humor me. Who would you nominate as a G-man? Or woman?"

"Well, an informant isn't exactly a G-man, Mrs. Caliban. Some of them probably don't even think they're giving away that much. Some of them probably think they're helping the cause by showing how harmless they are."

"Is that how you would have viewed it at the time?"

He grinned. "Hardly. Truthfully, Mrs. Caliban, I would at least have contemplated shooting the bastard at sunset. But Hoover was certifiable. He thought the Russians were controlling every antiwar group in the country. He thought we were being infiltrated by commie bastards. What was really going on was tame compared to Hoover's fantasies. Somebody might have thought they could reassure those guys."

"You're telling me you don't think anybody you knew in the group would have done it for money or for political reasons."

"I didn't say that. I'm just thinking out loud here."

When an attorney says he is "just thinking out loud," you'd better watch your back, in my experience. None of those bastards thinks out loud. They wouldn't last five minutes in the courtroom if that were the case.

"I like Sanders for the role," he said.

"I like him, too. Now tell me why you do."

"'Cause I didn't like him much at the time. That's as good a reason as any. And because he seemed ambitious to me, personally ambitious, you know, Mrs. Caliban? People like that will take what they can get wherever they can get it."

"What about Lewis? He was personally ambitious."

"What, you think he set up a group so he could spy on it?"

"He doesn't have to have been with the FBI from the beginning. Besides, maybe they had something on him. Maybe they cut a deal."

"If that were true, Mrs. Caliban, you would have thought he would've stuck around longer, unless you think they sent him on to greener pastures with the New Mobe because they weren't getting enough action in Columbus. But the arrests came after Sanders left."

"Sanders and Ginny."

"Well, yeah, but Ginny wasn't — I mean, I don't see her as a spy."

I didn't, either, but I thought I should keep my options open.

"Then there were the Matthiases, who got the charges against them dropped."

"I see what you mean. I'd be surprised, though, Mrs. Caliban. They always struck me as deeply committed people. Tom, in particular, was kind of an innocent idealist. Linda was more pragmatic, so they made a good team."

"So innocent idealists are never guilty? Or are they more frightened than most people of being exposed?"

"I still say Sanders is your best bet."

"What about Silverman?"

He shook his head. "She was the real thing."

"Why do you say so?"

He shrugged.

"She got out, too."

"Boy, you are cynical, aren't you, Mrs. Caliban? But why did she die in that cabin? Doesn't look like she cleared much profit."

"*If* she died in that cabin."

His eyes widened and he sat up straighter.

"You're saying she didn't? You think they put her on ice somewhere?"

I studied him, but his surprise seemed genuine.

"Nah." He flapped a hand at me. "You're putting me on now. It's good, though, Mrs. Caliban, you should write for television."

"Did McCafferty have a will?"

"Yep."

"Want to give me a teensy little hint about the contents?"

"Nope."

"Did he have anything to leave?"

"Not that I know of. His truck was probably his most valuable asset."

"If I guess something, will you tell me if I'm right?"

"Look, Mrs. Caliban, I'm supposed to—"

"Did he leave anything to somebody named Patty or Patricia?"

He hesitated just long enough before he continued. "Look, Mrs. Caliban, I'm not supposed to go revealing the contents of somebody's will."

"It'll be a matter of public record when it gets probated, right?"

He nodded. "You can see it then."

"One more thing." I handed him the same slip of paper I'd shown Val Smith.

"Koss? What's that?"

"I don't know. I was hoping you did."

"Not unless it stands for knockouts. Any prize fighters in this case?"

Fighters, I thought to myself. But not prize fighters.

CHAPTER 34

This time I was seeing Tom and Linda alone. But I had already made a few preparations. It wasn't like I left my notes in a locker in the bus terminal and mailed the key to Moses or anything. But I made sure I left records, including a folder I put on top of Kevin's VCR. I'd stopped by Moses's apartment, but he wasn't home.

I hadn't seen my client for a while, but perhaps he had forgotten that he was my client. Either he was dug into a foxhole somewhere on Race Street, or he'd gone into hiding in the woods of northern Kentucky. Either way, I wasn't too worried about him.

Right now, I was more worried about myself, to tell you the truth. Still, it looked pretty peaceful as I drove up to the farmhouse.

"Let's go in the living room," Linda said. "The girls are doing their homework on the kitchen table."

I craned my neck for a view of the blonde. She was there. How the hell did she fit in?

"I was sorry about McCafferty."

Linda's eyes teared up immediately and she looked away. Tom cleared his throat.

"Yeah. So were we."

"I guess you think I had something to do with that."

Tom and Linda exchanged looks.

"We don't know what to think," she said softly. "But maybe if you hadn't talked to him—"

"What?" I asked.

"I don't know." She closed her eyes and heaved a sigh. "I don't know."

"I have reason to believe that McCafferty was killed over something he'd found in his FBI file."

They both stared at me.

"Did you know he sent for his file?"

Tom shook his head. Linda said, "I know he talked about it once. I didn't know he'd done it."

"And you've never sent for yours, you said?"

"We've talked about it, too," Tom said. "We are — well, curious. We've just never gotten around to it."

"Why?" Linda asked. "Do you think we should? It's beginning to sound — dangerous."

"Did he ever mention an FBI informant among the members of AWOS?"

"A *what*? That's ridiculous!" Tom expostulated.

Linda had paled. "I can't believe that. I won't believe it."

"I'm betting it was Sanders."

Linda got up and went to the doorway, where she glanced into the other room.

"That's even more ridiculous!" Tom asserted. "Sanders was one of the leaders of the movement! I'm sorry, Mrs. Caliban, but you've got it all wrong."

"Do I? Why were you arrested so soon after Sanders left?"

"Coincidence. Pure coincidence."

Linda had sat down next to him again and took his hand.

"Linda?" I prompted her.

"I agree with Tom. I think you're making this up, Mrs. Caliban. Or if you're not making it up, you're just reaching the wrong conclusions."

"McCafferty was working on his file at the time of his death. I found a page of notes he took."

"It's also perfectly possible that he just got hold of some bad dope," Tom said.

"I didn't find his file."

"So you think it was stolen?" he asked.

"Maybe the FBI got it back," Linda said. "Maybe they didn't mean to let it out in the first place."

"Maybe so," I agreed. "But why?"

"There are lots of things we don't know about what the Bureau was up to in those days," Linda responded wearily. "Lots of things the public doesn't know even now. Things that would embarrass the Bureau and embarrass the late Mr. Hoover. Maybe he found the evidence he needed to prove that the FBI and ATF set him up. If he did, he could have sued them for a huge amount and given them lots of really ugly publicity."

"He would have, too." Tom smiled ruefully. "He would never have settled out of court if he thought he'd get more publicity by putting them on trial. It would have seemed poetic justice to him."

I'll admit I hadn't really considered this angle. It had certain features to recommend it. But I didn't think that's what had happened.

"So how was the Sanders murder connected?"

"Maybe it wasn't," Tom said.

I looked at him. For a survivor of the 60s, this guy had an unhealthy tolerance for coincidence. I wondered if he believed in the Tooth Fairy, too.

"Maybe they both found out something," Linda offered. "Maybe Steve sent for his file, too. Maybe that's why he came to Cincinnati — to talk to Mickey about what he found out. But the FBI got wind of it somehow."

I felt tired. Everybody wanted to blame Them. Nobody wanted to blame Us. I kept remembering what McCafferty had said about "Us" and "Them."

Suddenly, I didn't want to be having this conversation. I wanted to walk away and forget what I knew. The cops would never get evidence on Steel. They would never find Val. Everybody could live happily ever after.

Except McCafferty, I thought. Except McCafferty and the next person who figured it out. At the moment, that seemed to be me. I pressed on.

"Let's pretend there was an FBI informant," I said. "Who would it be?"

"There wasn't one," Tom said stubbornly. "That's crazy. We kept the group small so that we only dealt with the people we trusted."

"That's right." Linda nodded.

"Fine," I said, the way Franny does when she's pissed off at me.

I stood up and headed for the door.

"You know, your daughter reminds me of somebody," I said.

"Really?" Tom said, an automatic response.

Linda didn't say anything.

At the door, I turned back.

"Oh, I almost forgot."

I held out the slip of paper.

"K, O, S," Tom read. "Koss."

"Ring any bells?"

Tom shook his head.

Linda was staring at the paper. She looked up slowly, and her eyes met mine. That was all.

CHAPTER 35

It was getting late. I knew that Patty closed at nine, but I hoped she'd still be there.

I banged on the door. A startled face looked out; then she unlocked the door.

"Franny's already gone home, Ms. Caliban," she said.

"I know," I said. "It's you I want to talk to."

"Come on back to the office," she said, turning. "Watch the boxes. I'm re-stocking the shelves."

She steered me toward a small back room where a desk lamp cast a dim light on a desk covered with papers.

"It's pretty messy, but it's home. Now what can I do for you?"

She offered me a wooden kitchen chair.

"I'd offer you some tea, but you might not trust me." She smiled ruefully.

"I'm okay," I said. "I've just come from Tom and Linda's."

"Oh?" she said politely, moving back from the edge of the desk. "Tom and Linda who?"

"Matthias."

She smiled vaguely and stared off into space.

"I wonder if I know them."

"I used to wonder that myself," I said. "But not anymore. I'm pretty sure you do."

She looked taken aback by my tone.

"Only you were using a different name then."

She wound a rubber band around her fingers.

"You were going by PJ Silverman."

She let out a long breath and looked down. Then she smiled.

"You know, Ms. Caliban, you don't look anything like I pictured you in my nightmares." She had a husky voice and I found myself wondering if she'd deepened it deliberately when she had transformed herself into a new person.

"I'm not a very scary person."

"That makes two of us." She was still looking down. "It would be hard to prove what you just said."

"I'm sure it would. I'm sure you've been very thorough."

"What are you going to do?"

"Maybe nothing — about that. But I need to know about the body they found."

"I can't tell you much. She wouldn't want me to. I can only say that she died of natural causes and she knew about me and wanted to help. She was the right height and age." Her voice dropped on the last sentence.

"Does — did — she have family?"

"She'd left her family. She cut herself off from them and that was the way she wanted it."

I assumed she wouldn't tell me who else had been involved.

"It must have been hard — for you, I mean."

She looked up for the first time. Her face was impassive, but her eyes glittered. She said only, "Yes. It was hard."

"Plastic surgery?"

"I went abroad. You see, I was lucky. I had a very wealthy grandmother, whom I was very close to. Very few people have access to the kind of financial backing I had. Of course, my grandmother has been the soul of discretion. And determination. I don't think I would have made it without her."

"Do you still see her?"

She looked down quickly and shook her head.

"We talk on the phone. I've seen her twice since I became Patty Smith. I hope someday soon we'll decide it's safe enough."

"You're a Smith, too?" I asked, startled.

She smiled. "About one-third of the people who went underground took that name, Mrs. Caliban."

Well, that gave me pause, I can tell you. I made a quick mental survey of all the Smiths I knew to see if any of them might have a more interesting history than I thought.

"Your grandmother gave you the money to open the store?"

"Yes. So here I am, a thriving capitalist."

"You've had help from your friends, though, too, right?"

"Yes, I've been lucky in my friends as well. Some of them, anyway."

I waited and let the silence grow.

"Well, it's like Mickey always said: when disaster strikes, you find out who your friends are."

"And who they aren't," I said. "Like Steve and Ginny."

"I don't blame Ginny for that," she said, looking off into space again. We were sitting in a pool of pale-yellow light in a darkened room and it was more than a little creepy. "Ginny wasn't — in those days, she wasn't that strong. Or maybe she didn't think she was because that's what Steve told her. She let him make too many decisions. She called often. Lots of times, Steve didn't even come to the phone." She had let the bitterness into her voice.

"You didn't like him."

"No, I'd never liked him much, though I never disliked him as much as Mickey did — that is, until he ran out on us."

It was hard to know how to get where I wanted to go without tipping my hand too early and risking her silence.

"Why didn't Mickey like him?"

"Oh, Mickey thought he was an arrogant, ambitious sonofabitch. They didn't agree on a lot of things."

"And what did Mickey say when Sanders didn't come back?"

"He wasn't surprised. He told me from the beginning, he said, 'We'll never see that bastard again.' That was when Steve kept promising to come. But Mickey was right."

"Had Mickey said anything about Steve lately?"

"You mean, after Steve was killed? He said somebody had finally given the bastard what he deserved. He also told me he wouldn't come see me for a while. He thought it might be dangerous."

"For you or for him?"

"For both of us. But more for me. After all, the cops knew who he was."

"But he was never questioned."

"He couldn't figure that out. He knew Tom and Linda would protect him if they could. But he thought the cops would be at his door the next day."

"What about before Steve was killed? Had Mickey heard from him lately? Did he know Steve was coming to town?"

She shook her head. "Not that I know of."

"And what about you? Did you think Mickey killed Steve?"

She studied me. "No, I didn't think that."

"Why not?"

"Mickey was a very angry person," she said slowly. "He looked angry, he sounded angry. But that was just it: all his violence was verbal. He was like a cross between a pitbull and a beagle. He looked and sounded like a pitbull, but he was really harmless."

It was time for a little push.

"Then you must feel especially angry about his murder," I said.

Tears flooded her eyes, but she managed to look surprised and sad at the same time.

"Are the cops sure that he was murdered?"

"Doesn't matter. He was."

"How do you know?" Her eyes flickered over my face.

"Before he died, Mickey sent for his FBI file. Did you know that?"

"Yes."

"Did he tell you what was in it?"

She hesitated a second too long.

"Just that they had notes on various AWOS activities."

"Did he suggest to you the possibility that one of the AWOS members had been an FBI informant?"

Her voice dropped. "Yes."

"Did he suggest to you that the informant was Steve Sanders?"

A pause. "Yes."

"And you were afraid that if you told me, I'd think he killed Sanders."

"It doesn't seem to matter now, does it?"

"Oh, yes, I think it matters. It matters a great deal. Did Mickey tell you anything else about the file?"

"Just that there was something else he wanted to check out."

"He didn't say what?"

"No."

"Did he tell you where he kept the file?"

"I assume at his house. He did say—"

"Yes?"

"He said I should have it if anything happened to him. He said it would be a little souvenir of the good old days. Then he laughed."

"Was there something in there he wanted you to see?"

"I don't know."

"I found him, Patty. I searched the house. I didn't find that file." The name had never seemed to suit her and it came out awkwardly now. That was probably why she had chosen it: it conjured up a very different person from PJ Silverman.

"Are you saying somebody took it? But who?"

"I have a copy of some notes he took from the file. Could you take a look and see if you see anything?"

I fished the paper out of my purse and handed it to her. She studied it a good five minutes without speaking, then shook her head.

"Nothing jumps out at me. I mean, they look like notes on AWOS activities, or on conversations or meetings, but I don't see any reason to kill somebody over any of this stuff."

I pointed out the notation at the bottom of the page.

"K, O, S. Or is it Koss? I don't know what that means. What is it?"

"It's not the name of another Ohio State organization?"

"Oh, you mean because of the O and S? It's not one that I remember. But there were a lot of organizations during the late sixties."

I retrieved the page of notes and returned it to my purse, satisfied.

"I still don't know who'd want to steal Mickey's file."

"The same person who murdered him. And Steve. The same person who tried to kill me twice."

She stared at me. "You don't mean me? Listen, the botulism contamination was an accident! It really was! I couldn't kill anybody!"

"Does Dez Lewis know who you are?"

The abrupt change of subject took her back. "No. Why?"

"How about Lennie Dwyer?"

"No."

"So Mickey knew."

"Yes."

"And Val knows."

"She's never been here. I've seen her on the street a few times, usually from a distance. We don't talk."

"Not even on the phone?"

"It's too dangerous for both of us."

"And Tom and Linda know."

She shook her head. "Not Tom. Just Linda."

My surprise showed.

"We were afraid he might tell Steve. Even inadvertently. We decided not to risk it."

"'We' meaning you and Linda. So Linda is the one who knows about everybody?"

"She's always been the motherly type — the group caretaker."

"Linda," I said carefully, "who had a daughter by Steve."

"Linda?" She looked puzzled.

"I think her name is Gwen or Gwendolyn."

She covered her face with her hands, and at first I couldn't tell if she was laughing or crying. Then, I thought it might be a little of both, and I worried that she was having hysterics. She lowered her hands so that she could look at me, and her eyes were still wet, and very sad.

"It's Guin, short for Guinnevere. Linda didn't have a daughter by Steve, I did. That's why I ran: I didn't want to have my baby in prison."

CHAPTER 36

"I don't think I like my chosen profession, Moses. Maybe I'll get a realtor's license, like Mabel."

I had melted onto the couch when I walked in the door, too emotionally wrung to make it to the kitchen. When Moses showed up half an hour later, he didn't even ask; he took one look at me and went to fix me a gin and tonic. It tasted like a good stiff one, too.

"That be nice, too," he agreed amiably. "Be on call day and night, dressin' up in pantyhose and high heels and one of them gold jackets, crawlin' around folks' basements and inspectin' the plumbing, tryin' to talk up some broken-down house you couldn't give away to a homeless person, and the owner want eighty thousand dollars for."

"Okay. You talked me out of it. How about a beautician?" I was looking at him over the top of my head, so he was upside down.

"Why don't you finish workin' on the career you got?"

"I don't like the career I got, Moses. It's too damn messy. Plus, like I said once before, it's dangerous."

"What's messy about it?"

"Oh, you know. The people who really need to get punished never do, so the good people go bad and the bad people walk away and it's really getting me down." It was hard to drink lying down, but I thought asking for a straw would be pushing my luck.

"Last I heard, we still had a couple of murders on our hands. And I'm talking to a prospective murderee right this minute. You tellin' me that shouldn't be stopped?"

The other prospective murderee made an entrance at that point, stirring up the air and leaving a trail of tobacco smoke. I wrinkled my nose.

"You've been at Arnold's?" I asked.

"Highland Coffee House," she said, noticed my expression, and raised one arm to smell her sleeve. "I know. It's pretty bad. I wish they'd ban all smoking in restaurants."

"Dream on, kid."

"Your mother and I are in the middle of a serious discussion about her career."

"Oh." Fanny looked like she didn't know whether to believe him or not. "Well, don't mind me." She went over and turned on the stereo. "Country Girl" blared, and Sophie fell off the bookshelf again.

Franny turned the volume down to the tolerance level of the elderly and four-footed crowd and collapsed into an armchair with the indignant Sophie.

"And speaking of detection," Moses continued, when he was sure he could be heard, "Sanders didn't have an FBI file."

"I didn't think he would. At least, not a regular one, whatever that means. I guess some informants have them, though."

"Everybody else on your list has one, including Mrs. Sanders."

"Oh, hell, Moses. I know who the murderer is."

"You planning to keep it a secret?"

"No. I'm giving them the proverbial twenty-four hours. Isn't that what the boys do?"

"To get out of town?"

"To do — whatever. Get their affairs in order."

"Well, I don't know 'bout other boys, but this one always arrested killers soon as he knew they were dangerous."

"I know, but it seems so much more complicated. Look." I pulled out my page of notes and pointed to the bottom of the page. "Read that."

"K, O, S. Koss. We were talking about that yesterday. You find out what it is?"

I took a pencil and wrote underneath it: AWOS.

"Read that."

"A, W, O, S. Ay-woss."

"That's because you've heard me pronounce it. Now read this one again."

"Kay-oss," he said. "Chaos."

Franny's head bobbed up. "Chaos?"

"That's right."

"But Mom, that was, like—"

"Yes?"

"That was the code name for the CIA counterintelligence program during the antiwar movement. I did a paper on those counterintelligence operations once." God love her, after all those years in college, Franny had written papers on damn near everything.

"The CIA?" Moses frowned.

"Yeah. It wasn't just the FBI. The CIA was involved, too," Franny said excitedly. "They ran this Operation Chaos for, like, six or seven years, and reported to Hoover. It was just like the FBI's counterintelligence program — surveillance and wiretapping and paid informants and everything."

"Must've been a goddamn circus — all those undercover agents tripping over each other, trying to remember who was working for who, who was an agent and who was an informant and who wasn't. Chaos was a good name for it."

"Paid informants?" Moses shifted his gaze to me.

I nodded. "Mickey told us what to look for, but I didn't get it. He said something like, 'We thought it was Us versus Them.' Then he compared it to something. He said if you were told to watch one hand, you knew to watch the other one, but while you were watching the hands, you'd get kneed in the balls. He even said something about a third joker in the deck. I knew about the involvement of the FBI and ATF in the bombing case, but it never occurred to me to consider the fucking CIA. They were the third joker."

"The Company isn't usually involved in domestic surveillance, Cat."

"No, but they were then, like Franny says. Some book I read said it was their biggest involvement in domestic politics."

Franny snorted. "Must be an old book."

"So what you're saying is that in this little antiwar group of — what? — six or seven people, there were two paid informants," Moses said.

"That's what I'm saying."

"And Sanders was the first one."

"I think he was FBI."

"And who was the second?"

"A country girl," I said.

CHAPTER 37

The call came the next evening at 7:30. I'd just washed the kitchen floor — isn't that always how it goes? — when the phone rang. There is a lesson in this somewhere, I said to myself. Don't bother to clean; things will only get messed up again.

So I tiptoed over to the phone. It was Patty Smith.

"She's dead, Mrs. Caliban. Tom just called."

"How did it happen?"

"Carbon monoxide. Tom found her in the garage when he came home from work. All the kids were out. He found notes — two to him, one to the kids, one to me, one to you, and one to the police." There was a lot of static in the background and I had to strain to hear her.

"Why two to Tom?"

"One's official — the one he'll show them. The others don't exist. Yours doesn't exist, either."

"How are you feeling?" I asked.

"I don't know yet. It was a strange conversation. I guess Linda's note just asked him to call a Patty Smith at my number right away. He was upset and confused, of course. But — all of a sudden, he knew. I could hear it in his voice as he was working it out. I've tried to change my voice, Mrs. Caliban.

I've really worked on it. But he recognized my voice. It was a shock on top of Linda's death."

"Are you going to see him?"

"In a little while. After things have — settled down. He's mailing Linda's note. But I don't really need it. I already know what it says, or most of it, anyway. I can guess at the rest." There was a crash in the background.

"I can't hear you. What's going on there?" It sounded like a drug shipment had just arrived and was being unloaded into the warehouse.

"Sorry. I'm using a public phone. I said I know everything but the reason, and I can guess at that. Those bastards were so damn good at trapping people. Who knows how they got her? They could have threatened to jacket Tom."

"Do what?" I must not have heard her right, unless they were going to take him away in a straitjacket.

"Jacket him. That's when they start rumors that somebody is a government agent. They did that to a lot of activists — Tom Hayden, for one. They could really make your life miserable if they wanted to."

"And did," I said quietly.

"Yes," she said. "And did."

"Patty, she killed Mickey."

"I know." Her voice dropped again. "I've been thinking about that since last night. She told me we had to keep an eye on you to protect Mickey. And she was in the store that day — the day Franny took the grape juice home. I know you wanted me to realize that. And about Mickey. Damn it, I could have forgiven her anything but that! And you know what? He probably would have forgiven her. 'You gotta survive, Peej, best way you can. That's the first rule: you gotta survive.'"

"What about Guin?"

She was crying hard now, so it was even harder to make out what she was saying. "I can't take her away now. She doesn't even know about me. Besides — it's a great family she's in, even without Linda. Tom's a great guy. I didn't think about it before, but do you think he's worried I might take her back?"

"He might be, if he stops to think about it long enough."

"Will you tell him for me? Tell him I want him to keep her."

"Sure. But there's something I've been wondering about. Did Steve know you were pregnant when he left?"

"No. The only people who ever knew were Mickey, Linda, and Tom." And anybody else who might have helped you set up your disappearance, I added silently. "The thing with Steve was just stupidity. I never really even liked him. But I wanted the baby. I mean, I knew I couldn't keep it, but I wanted to have it."

"Will you ever tell Guin the truth?"

"Oh, I don't know. Maybe. Someday. Listen, there's something else you can do, too, if you would."

"Sure. What is it?"

"Will you tell Val? She needs to know. Listen, I've gotta go now. I'm — kind of a wreck. Franny's watching the store."

"Okay. Take care of yourself."

"Yeah. You, too."

* * *

Penny answered the door.

"Cat! What's wrong?"

Instead of inviting me in, she stepped out onto the porch and closed the door behind her.

"It's okay, Penny. The murderer confessed and then took her own life. But I need to tell Val. It was Linda Matthias."

"Oh, my God! Linda! But are you saying she killed Steve? Cut his throat like that?" She was keeping her voice low.

"Well, she was tall enough. And she grew up on a farm. If she'd ever slaughtered a pig, I guess she had practice."

She stood a moment, then turned abruptly.

"Come on in, Cat. Val's in the kitchen."

Val was icing brownies and the whole house smelled of chocolate. Good, I thought; they need a lot of chocolate to help them recover from my news.

Val's knife slowed as she listened to my story. Like Patty, I didn't know the whole story, but I gave them what I knew. Well, most of what I knew. I left out the part about Hope's half-sister. I thought they were getting enough surprises for one night.

Val was sitting down now. She held the knife as if she'd forgotten it.

"I can't believe it. Linda! You want me to believe that she was a CIA informant and a murderer who killed one of her best friends." She shook her head.

I was assuming she meant Mickey. Val didn't seem to think Sanders was anybody's best friend. I didn't say anything.

"It was bad enough when you told me about Steve. But now you're saying that we had two informants in the group. That's unbelievable. Don't you see what that means? All the fugitives we helped — they were all compromised! The Feds must have known every move we ever made ahead of time!"

It was hard to swallow, I admit. But not unbelievable. I gave her a little time to think it over.

"But why did she kill Mickey? Mickey, of all people!"

"I guess she thought he'd guessed. Maybe he told her he had, or maybe she just thought he was getting too close. I'll know more when I read the letter she wrote me. I think she was afraid she'd lose everything she had if it all came out — Tom, the kids, the life she loved."

"But why?"

"Tom was an idealist, wasn't he? That's what everybody kept telling me. A kind of purist. Could he have understood or forgiven her? Or — maybe that's too dramatic. The point is that things would never have been the same between them. You tell me what she would have done to protect the members of her AWOS family."

"She would have done anything," Val said softly. "She would have done anything."

CHAPTER 38

Dear Catherine Caliban: you seem to have found out so much already, this letter may not add much to what you know. But I feel I owe it to you, if only by way of apology for what I did to you and Franny.

It was a sunny spring afternoon, with the cumulus clouds playing bumper cars overhead. A nice breeze swept across the river and up to the overlook, where I was sitting on a bench, reading. The breeze was cool — not cold, but cool. Still, I shivered as I read.

I have been in love with Tom Matthias since fifth grade. You need to know that, because everything else follows from that truth. At one time, though, he became involved with someone else, and in my pain and anger I turned to a man I should never have trusted — a man who turned out to be a CIA operative. When Tom and I got back together, he threatened to tell Tom about our relationship and he told me who he was. He offered me one way out.

Now you are wondering what kind of an idiot falls for a deal like that one. You think that since Tom had an affair, it shouldn't have made any difference that I had one. In fact, you think I probably did it to make him jealous. And of course, you're right. But everything looks much clearer in hindsight. And besides, I had already compromised the security of the group by choosing this particular man, or rather, by letting him set me up. And that would have been hard to explain to Tom.

I glanced at the park behind me, where Tom was walking, head down, shoulders sagging. The explanation had been harder on him fifteen years after the fact.

It didn't seem so bad at the time, what I was doing. Of course, I felt guilty. But I was told that the CIA was only looking for communist influence on the antiwar movement, and that all the material I was gathering just went to disprove that. They weren't interested in the other things, he said — the aid to draft resisters or anything like that. They weren't the FBI. And I kept things from them. I always had to give them something, but there were things I didn't tell them. It turned out, that didn't matter.

What he didn't tell me was that the Bureau had its own agent in place. I didn't find out about Steve until we were arrested. I didn't know we were being set up. I swear I didn't. When it happened, I was in shock. Then, when I went to the interrogation room, my CIA contact was there and so was another man. He was never introduced to me, but I figured out later that he was FBI. I was told that the charges would be dropped against me. I was also told that I wasn't responsible for anything that had happened. I guess he was trying to be nice to me. What he was really telling me was that there had been somebody else, another mole in the group. He promised me that the CIA would never contact me again.

I won't tell you how hard it was to live through Mickey's trial and PJ's decision to go underground; you'll say I got what I deserved and you'd be right. Tom was more than willing to take PJ's baby, even though I was pregnant by the time Guin was born. We did what we could for them — PJ and Mickey. And later I did what I could for Ginny. Some things I didn't tell Tom because he still spoke to Steve occasionally, still considered him a friend. Tom never was a very good liar, not like me. I lived in fear that one day it would all come back to haunt me.

It did. Steve called me up one day, out of the blue, and said that he was coming to Cincinnati and that he needed to talk to me about Ginny. I tried to tell him I didn't know anything about Ginny, but he wouldn't believe that. Then he said that if I didn't talk to him, he would speak to Tom about my CIA connection.

I was stunned. Since I hadn't known about him — in fact, had never learned who the other mole was — I hadn't known that he knew about me. I don't have to tell you what I did; you already know. I know vets who say that cutting a man's throat is the fastest, quietest, surest way to kill him. So I did it. I had done it before to animals who deserved it less than he did.

I had more trouble with the people who didn't deserve it. I'm not a violent person, but I was a desperate one. I know in retrospect I wasn't even very smart about it. It was just luck that you drank the juice, just as it was luck that your daughter drove your car instead of you. I wasn't thinking clearly.

Then Mickey told me that he'd figured out Sanders had been an FBI informant. And he said he thought there had been someone else. I panicked.

I went over to Mickey's house to look at the file. He showed it to me and explained how he'd drawn his conclusions. I had made up some reefers laced with fertilizer containing cyanimide and I left them for him. I couldn't have watched him die.

I am really and truly sorry I killed him. I thought it would end with him. He was the only one who had the evidence, I told myself, and I took the evidence from his house.

I went back the next morning, but at first I thought it was too late. I saw a strange car there. I parked up the road and watched until you came out. You weren't carrying anything and I wasn't sure whether you could have fit the file inside your purse or not. I knew I had some time while you went to find a phone, so I went in and searched the house. You know what that was like. When I didn't find anything, I thought everything was over for me. Then I looked in the mailbox. He had put the file in an envelope and addressed it to Patty. So I took it.

The mailbox! I shook my head at my own stupidity. I'd even seen that the flag was up. I had a lot to learn.

But then you found those notes. And when you showed me that word, I knew that you knew it was me.

I want to thank you for giving me a chance to end things in my own way. You didn't have to do that and you had good reason to hate me. I never hated anyone but Steve. Even so, I never did anything except out of love.

She had signed it "Linda Genovese Matthias."

I gazed down at the river. That was the story she had told herself: that she had done everything out of love. But the man she loved, the man who walked desolate in the bright spring grass behind me, would have told her that personal, individual love wasn't enough — that some principles couldn't be sacrificed to love.

Me, I was the wrong person to ask.

CHAPTER 39

"Mom, Garf and I have something to tell you."

I looked at her with apprehension over my pile of laundry. Over her shoulder I could see Sadie perched on top of the refrigerator, looking as morose as I felt. But then, Sadie always expected the worst in life. Like right now, she looked like she was expecting to hear that they'd rescued a greyhound and were bringing it here to live.

"You've been elected co-chairs of the Central American Coalition and they're looking for a new meeting place."

"Mo-om!"

"You're stashing refugees in our basement."

"Mo-om! Get serious! We're moving into a house — in Clifton."

I dropped a few socks.

"Gee, Franny! What a surprise! A house in Clifton. Isn't that awfully — expensive?"

I caught myself just in time. I was going to say "close."

"No, it's kind of like a commune. We're sharing with four other people, so the rent is actually, like, pretty cheap."

"Oh," I said brightly. I hoped it had its own refrigerator.

"I mean, it's been great spending time with you and all." She said this as if we'd been on a two-week mother-daughter campout. There were people on her phone tree I'd talked to more. "But I can see it's kind of crowded here, and we both, like, need our space."

I wondered what she would do with five housemates instead of one. But, hey, far be it from me to cast aspersions on communal living. If she wanted to live with the Vienna Boys' Choir it was okay by me, as long as she took her tofu with her.

"So, when's the big day?" I said, ever cheerful.

"Tomorrow, if that's okay with you."

A few more socks hit the linoleum. They were large and must have been Garf's.

"Tomorrow?"

"If that's okay," she said anxiously. "I mean, I know you're still getting over your botulism and all. So if you want me to stick around for a few weeks, until you're feeling stronger—"

"No, no," I assured her. "I feel lots better today." A little giddy at the prospect of having my apartment all to myself again and not tripping over the damn guitar every time I went into my office, but that was all.

Garf looked relieved that I was being so reasonable. He gave me one of his most disarming smiles.

"We can't wait to have you over, Mrs. Caliban."

"That's right!" Franny enthused. "I'll cook dinner!"

"I can't wait," I mumbled into the dirty underwear.

Five minutes after they'd gone, the phone rang.

"Hi, this is Lou. I'm one of the twigs on Franny's branch of the Northside limb of—"

My doorbell was ringing.

THE END

ACKNOWLEDGMENTS

Thanks, as usual, to John Kornbluh for his thoughtful editorial advice, and to Sue Clark for hers.

An important resource for me was Charles De Benedetti's *An American Ordeal: The Antiwar Movement of the Vietnam Era.* Other sources are acknowledged in the text.

THE JOFFE BOOKS STORY

We began in 2014 when Jasper agreed to publish his mum's much-rejected romance novel and it became a bestseller.

Since then we've grown into the largest independent publisher in the UK. We're extremely proud to publish some of the very best writers in the world, including Joy Ellis, Faith Martin, Caro Ramsay, Helen Forrester, Simon Brett and Robert Goddard. Everyone at Joffe Books loves reading and we never forget that it all begins with the magic of an author telling a story.

We are proud to publish talented first-time authors, as well as established writers whose books we love introducing to a new generation of readers.

We won Trade Publisher of the Year at the Independent Publishing Awards in 2023 and Best Publisher Award in 2024 at the People's Book Prize. We have been shortlisted for Independent Publisher of the Year at the British Book Awards for the last five years, and were shortlisted for the Diversity and Inclusivity Award at the 2022 Independent Publishing Awards. In 2023 we were shortlisted for Publisher of the Year at the RNA Industry Awards, and in 2024 we were shortlisted at the CWA Daggers for the Best Crime and Mystery Publisher.

We built this company with your help, and we love to hear from you, so please email us about absolutely anything bookish at feedback@joffebooks.com.

If you want to receive free books every Friday and hear about all our new releases, join our mailing list here: www.joffebooks.com/freebooks.

And when you tell your friends about us, just remember: it's pronounced Joffe as in coffee or toffee!

Printed in Great Britain
by Amazon

61855801R00139